Caroline James always  a literary route, she f industry, which incluc country house hotel. She was also a media g representing many celebrity chefs.

When she's not writing, Caroline likes to go wild water swimming or walk with Fred, her Westie.

If you would like to find out more about Caroline's books, please visit her website:

www.carolinejamesauthor.co.uk

THE SPA BREAK

CAROLINE JAMES

One More Chapter
a division of HarperCollins*Publishers* Ltd
1 London Bridge Street
London SE1 9GF
www.harpercollins.co.uk
HarperCollins*Publishers*
1st Floor, Watermarque Building, Ringsend Road
Dublin 4, Ireland

This paperback edition 2022

First published in Great Britain in ebook format
by HarperCollins*Publishers* 2022
Copyright © Caroline James 2022
Caroline James asserts the moral right to be identified
as the author of this work

A catalogue record of this book is available from the British Library

ISBN: 978-0-00-851969-8

For my beloved sister Cathy, who is enjoying her Spa Break in heaven.

Chapter One

'What happens at Sparadise will take you to paradise.'

'Bridgette, if you drive any faster, we will be airborne!' Emily Avondale fastened her safety belt and gripped the side of her seat as the wind from an open window whipped long grey hair into her eyes. 'I hope I've packed my anxiety tablets,' she grumbled, biting down on thin lips. Her feet, encased in sturdy walking boots, pressed hard on the thickly carpeted floor.

'No time to waste,' Bridgette Haworth called out. 'Snooze and you'll lose, and with an early start, we can arrive at the spa in good time and make the most of our day.'

Known locally as 'Bossy Bridgette' and the resident owner of Flaxby Manor, the main house in the Lancashire town of Flaxby, Bridgette revved the engine of her Range Rover and sped away from Emily's driveway with purpose.

Gravel flew and Emily winced as borders of pretty

petunias and bright coloured lobelias were pebble-dashed from the spray. Rummaging about in her canvas bag, Emily pulled out a packet of Calms and flipped the top from a bottle of water. Throwing her head back, she swallowed two tablets.

'Want a handful?' Emily turned to the passenger in the back.

Serena Alleyne shook her head. 'Not for me. I love it when Bridgette drives fast.' She stared out of the window where houses and shops flashed by. 'Cornelius drives at a snail's pace and lives in fear of a stone flying up and scratching the precious paintwork on his Austin Healey.'

'I think I'd go slow if I owned a vintage sports car,' Emily said. 'It must be his pride and joy.'

Serena sighed. 'He has little interest in anything these days.' She placed a hand on Bridgette's shoulder and, with long fingers, gave a squeeze. 'Put the pedal to the metal, Bridgette.'

Encouraged by her friend, Bridgette sped ahead.

The passengers braced themselves for a bumpy ride as their driver took bends at speed, oblivious to traffic-calming measures as she drove through the outskirts of the town of Flaxby. Careering around a bend, Bridgette startled pedestrians strolling down Coronation Avenue, who stared as the vehicle screeched to a stop outside a terraced house.

Bridgette tooted the horn, and the women waited.

Either side of the smartly painted pillar box-red front door, two colourful garden gnomes stood like sentries. Their fishing rods quivered as the door slammed, and a ruddy-faced woman, handbag tucked under her arm and suitcase gripped tightly, bustled down the pathway.

'Marjory looks flustered,' Emily said as they watched their friend approach.

'No doubt she's been baking to feed the masses and stocking the fridge for days.' Serena noted Marjory's flushed appearance and high colour.

'Her kids are almost as demanding as mine,' Emily said, thinking of her two insufferable sons. Both had thrown temper tantrums when they learnt that their mother was going away.

'Except Marjory's kids have moved out and don't live at home,' Serena said, 'but they might as well do.'

'Good heavens, what *has* she done to her hair?' Bridgette gripped the steering wheel as Marjory approached.

'It looks like a bunch of forget-me-*knots*,' Serena chuckled as they stared at the mass of blue curls with wisps of white that framed Marjory's face.

'I like it,' Emily said. 'It's lovely and cheerful, just like Marjory.'

Bridgette, who was petite in height, climbed out of the car and after giving her friend a hug, helped Marjory load her case in the back. 'Jump in,' she instructed and held a door open.

Marjory tossed her handbag into Serena's outstretched hands. 'Hello, lovelies!' Her legs splayed apart and her dress rode up as her ample bottom wriggled over the seat. She gripped Serena's arm and planted a kiss on her smooth ebony cheek.

'By heck,' Marjory sighed and sank back on the

expensive leather, 'I thought I'd never get away. Reg is racing his damned pigeons today and is all in a tizzy because the weather is so hot.' She ran a hand over her perspiring brow. 'And I feel like I have been cooking for days to make sure the family are fed while I'm gone.'

'Forget about your family for now,' Serena instructed. 'Buckle up and prepare for a white-knuckle ride.' She tugged on a safety strap and adjusted it around Marjory's rotund stomach. 'Bridgette thinks she's a Formula One driver.'

'On the contrary – I simply want to get us all out of Flaxby before any husbands, partners, or sons stand in our way.' Bridgette patted her neatly cut bob and adjusted the glasses on the end of her nose. Placing a leather pump on the pedal, she accelerated hard, narrowly missing a white delivery van.

'Including Hugo,' Bridgette continued, ignoring angry gestures from the van driver. 'My husband has done everything in his power to stop me from having a weekend with my friends.' Traffic lights turned to red and, oblivious to slowing traffic, Bridgette overtook and went through. 'He even hid my bank cards, for goodness sake. It's 2018 and I have to put up with his antiquated attitude on how women should behave.'

'Aye, Reg is the same.' Marjory nodded her sky-blue perm. 'He thinks I've lost my marbles to spend good money on fancy pampering and time away with my mates.'

'Cornelius is glad to see the back of me.' Serena gripped her seat as they careered around a bend. 'He says I stand in the way of his artistic creativity.'

4

'Then Cornelius is a fool.' Bridgette glanced up at Serena's exquisite face in the rearview mirror.

'My sons are livid.' Emily knotted her wayward hair into a band at the base of her neck and frowned. Worry lines creased her pale forehead. 'They can't understand why I can have a mini-break but won't pay for them to go on holiday.'

'They probably think that four old lasses going off galivanting will lead to trouble. I can't imagine why.' Marjory giggled.

'Well, my darlings, they can simply put up with it,' Bridgette said. 'This is my birthday weekend and nothing is going to spoil my precious time celebrating with my dearest friends.'

'Hear, hear!' the women chorused.

'It's not every day you celebrate being seventy,' Serena said.

'Oh, the thought of being so old,' Bridgette said and sighed. 'I can hardly bear it. Where did the years go?'

'There's nothing to be ashamed of. We're all catching you up.' Emily patted Bridgette's knee. 'I'm sixty-three.'

'And I'm sixty-eight,' Marjory joined in. 'Unlike the baby amongst us – young Serena here.'

'Sixty-two is hardly a baby,' Serena said dismissively.

'Did you bring the book?' Emily twisted around in her seat, her eyes fixed on Marjory.

'Aye, I've got it.' Marjory reached into the depths of her voluminous bag. A tube of sweets scattered over the leather upholstery, followed by a comb, lipstick, several tissues and a pair of extra-large cotton knickers.

Serena raised an eyebrow at the knickers.

'Essentials,' Marjory muttered and, rooting deeper, grinned as her fingers found her quarry. 'Got it,' she announced and held aloft a soft-backed book.

'What happens at Sparadise stays at Sparadise!' they all chanted as Marjory began to turn the glossy pages of the publicity material for a luxurious spa retreat.

'Let's have another look.' Emily reached out. 'I want to read what it says about the yoga and meditation sessions.'

'I'm looking forward to seeing my room,' Bridgette said, her eyes focussed on the emerging countryside as the town of Flaxby began to diminish behind them.

'I intend to have every spa treatment available.' Serena closed her eyes and sank back into her seat.

'I hope that there'll be some decent grub.' Marjory unwrapped a sweet and popped it in her mouth. Folding her fingers across her belly, she gazed out of the window.

Emily began to read out loud. She began by describing the location of Sparadise in detail, stating that the retreat lay in acres of gardens surrounding a lake in the Forest of Bowland. 'There's a page with testimonials,' she said.

'Read them out,' Bridgette commanded as she sped along the road.

'This is an interesting comment.' Emily, who wore metal-framed reading glasses, squinted as she held the book closer to her face. 'One visitor says, "Sparadise is not an average spa; be prepared for an amazing transformation!"'

'I could do with one of them,' Marjory said. 'It might wake my Reg up a bit.'

'But listen to this endorsement,' Emily said, wide-eyed. '"Sparadise will change your life forever."'

'Well as long as we all get back in one piece.' Bridgette glanced at Emily. 'Does it mention the gardens and a lake?'

'Yes, and there are photos showing the grounds.'

'I wonder if we can swim in the lake,' Serena said. As a lover of wild water swimming, she took every opportunity to fulfil her passion.

'Aye, that would be a bit different to our pool. A damned sight colder, that's for sure.' Marjory unwrapped another sweet.

'I love our weekly swims,' Emily said. 'I can't wait for them to come around – it's the highlight of my week.'

'Me too,' they all chorused.

Flaxby pool hosted an over-sixties session named Women's Warm-up Wednesday where the water temperature was cranked up for maturing muscles and bones. The friends looked forward to having a gossip as they swam, four abreast, for a leisurely hour, followed by drinks in the Flaxby Arms. Over the years, the sacrosanct session had strengthened and sealed their closeness. Family upsets were discussed when they chuntered about children and partners; medical issues were raised and pondered, along with recipe sharing and general chit chat. The support they gave to each other, combined with gentle exercise, ironed out the worries of their week.

'Might I suggest a pit stop for coffee?' Bridgette asked.

'Aye, I'm gasping.' Marjory sat up and looked through the window.

'Good idea. We don't check in till two and there's plenty of time,' Serena replied.

'There's a place by the river just up ahead.'

Bridgette reduced her speed as a café came into view.

Minutes later, the friends found a table in a sunny spot overlooking the river, and Bridgette ordered. Diners sitting outside the café tucked into snacks and drinks served by friendly young staff.

'Perfect,' Emily said and made herself comfortable. She was still holding the book and, placing it on the table, began to flick through the pages.

The sun was intense under a silver-white sky and shimmered on the water. Following a recent downpour, the river reached halfway up the bank, forming a broad pool where ducks hovered, gliding across the surface, their heads cocked for any crumbs and crusts of bread that might come their way.

'This is a great place to stop,' Serena said as she looked around. She could see a dog walker on a path on the opposite side of the river, and in a lay-by, a group of bikers huddled around a mobile refreshment van. They held thick juicy burgers in beefy hands and sipped tea as they discussed the freedom and excitement of biking on an open road. Nearby, their lavish display of expensive and immaculate Harleys, Ducatis and Hondas stood in a neat line.

'I wouldn't mind getting one of those between my legs.' Serena studied the gleaming metal and chrome. 'Nothing like a warm throbbing engine to start your day.'

Bridgette cast Serena a look that could curdle milk. 'In all the years I've known you, I don't believe you've ever been anywhere near a motorbike, let alone ridden on one.'

'It wasn't the bikes I was talking about.' Serena,

attention-grabbing in a white linen shirt and ripped jeans, caught the eye of one of the bikers and waved. Bearded with long shaggy hair, he wore a leather jacket with a winged skull logo and, smiling, raised his mug.

'Well, really!' Bridgette turned away.

As soon as Bridgette had stopped the car, Marjory had gone to the ladies' room and now, as their drinks arrived, bustled back to her friends. Coffee sloshed on the table as she picked up a mug.

'Oops,' she said and plopped her plump bottom next to Emily. Glancing over her friend's shoulder, Marjory stared at the open book where an image of a yoga instructor filled the page. 'By heck, that lad is fit.' She unwrapped a chocolate biscuit and dunked it in her coffee then licked her lips with pleasure as the sweet substance melted on her tongue.

'Not only fit, but handsome too,' Serena agreed.

Emily tilted her head and, bending her neck, studied the instructor's pose. Puzzled, she asked, 'How on earth would you get yourself into that position?'

'It's called the eight-angle pose.' Serena read the caption below the image, and the women tried to work out how he balanced on two hands while holding his legs out at a right angle.

'He looks more like a light fitting than a yoga instructor,' Marjory commented and reached for another biscuit.

Bridgette turned a page. 'What a gorgeous location. Just look at the rooms – there are suites too.' Glossy photos of the retreat revealed the beautifully presented establishment with smiling, uniformed staff on hand to attend to a guest's every need.

'You can glamp by the lake,' Serena said.

'Glamp?' Bridgette stared at Serena. 'You mean camp.'

'Camping is quite different; this is glamping.'

Serena described the luxurious way of being with nature by sleeping under canvas in plush surroundings with every available amenity.

'Look,' she said, holding up a double page, 'the glamping tepees are arranged in the garden not far from the lake. For many people, it's their idea of heaven to be at one with nature.'

'Until it piddles down and your tent leaks. Then you'll wish you had a solid roof over your head.' Marjory wrinkled her nose.

Serena ran a finger over the page, her eyes bright as they fell on a king-sized bed with soft linens and a downy duvet, surrounded by twinkling lights. The Emperor Bell was spacious and comparable to the spa's suites, with the finest furnishings in abundance. 'What a shame none of us booked one of these,' she said.

'I am sure we will all be delighted with the rooms we've chosen.' Bridgette looked smug as she sipped her coffee. Having made the booking for everyone, she couldn't wait to settle into her exclusive penthouse suite. 'We'll leave camping to the other guests.'

'Well, I'm happy to be sharing with Marjory.' Emily put her arm around Marjory's shoulders. 'I am sure that our twin room will be delightful.'

'My double deluxe has a spa bath, and you can all come

and join me.' Serena smiled. 'God, it's hot. My braids are scorching.' She touched her fingers to her jet-black hair. Serena's magnificent hair was piled high on her head, the locks threaded with colourful beads. 'I'm tempted to go for a swim.'

'Don't be ridiculous,' Bridgette retorted, eyeing the river. 'You can't possibly swim here.'

'Why not? I swim in rivers, lakes, streams – wherever there is water. You should all try it. It's the most exhilarating experience.'

'But is it safe?' Emily stared at the water, her face pale and blue eyes searching for signs of a fast-flowing current.

Serena pointed to a dip in the bank. 'It is where it's pooled. We could safely swim there.'

'I've got my swimsuit somewhere.' Marjory reached into her bag and began to dig about, laying out the contents on the table.

'I forbid you to swim in those.' Bridgette was indignant. Reaching out, she grabbed Marjory's big knickers and whipped them off the table.

'Here it is,' Marjory said triumphantly. She ignored Bridgette's protests and held up a swimsuit that had seen much better days.

'I'm wearing my bikini,' Serena said, unbuttoning her blouse. 'I'm always ready for a swim in this hot weather.'

'Crikey, it will have to be my shorts and bra.' Emily, not wishing to be left out, pulled her T-shirt over her head.

'Good God, you can't be serious.' Bridgette was shocked as she watched her friends undress. She glanced around nervously, noting the attention from other diners. A mother was shielding her child's eyes with her hand, and the café staff had begun to giggle at the sight of the aged ladies removing their clothes.

'Come on, birthday girl, live a little.' Serena gave a lazy smile. 'Don't be afraid of coming out of your comfort zone. You'll love it when you do.'

Bridgette bristled at Serena's words. She had every intention of staying firmly within her comfort zone as, with horror, she saw Marjory's ample breasts and bottom fly out of her greying bra and knickers, to be manipulated into a sagging ruched swimsuit. With clothes piled high on the table, Serena led the way and, holding hands, the trio tentatively stepped over the grass, steadying themselves as they negotiated the riverbank and tiptoed across the pebbles to the water.

The bikers gathered around and, with wolf-whistles and cheers, applauded the women as the water reached their knees. Serena's Amazonian body was a sight to behold as she splashed about, her smooth dark skin a striking contrast against the white of her bikini. Subtle cosmetic surgery over the years had kept her tummy almost flat and cellulite non-existent.

Emily began to shiver and rubbed at her skinny arms and legs, threaded with blue veins, as she jumped up and down on the sandy riverbed, while Marjory, loving the attention from the onlookers, stuck out her chest and patted her perm.

'Are you ready?' Serena asked and took hold of their hands. 'One, two, three… *swim!*' She tugged hard and plunged them into the water. Submerged to their shoulders and gasping at the cold, within seconds, the women were swimming. Cheers resounded from the riverbank as the bikers whistled and clapped.

'Hang on! Wait for me!' a voice suddenly called out.

Everyone turned to see Bridgette, her short elf-like body running across the grass. With spontaneous applause, they took in the sight of her skirted swimsuit. The thin fabric of a generous sarong, knotted at her wide waist, billowed around her chubby legs. A rubber cap, red with colourful flowers, covered her hair and on her feet she wore a pair of latex bootees.

'Bridgette!' Serena yelled and, rising like a salmon leaping upstream, reached Bridgette's side. 'You made it.' She laughed and leaned down, guiding her in.

'I'm coming out of my comfort zone!' Bridgette shrieked as she dipped into the water and, with furious strokes, began to paddle towards Emily and Marjory.

'Hallelujah!' they chorused as the friends joined hands and grinned.

Ten minutes later, Serena's swimming team stood shivering by the Range Rover. Mottled flesh trembled as Bridgette handed out towels.

'That was *so* good.' Serena untied her braids and wrung the thick weaves. 'Did you enjoy it?'

'Bloody marvellous,' Marjory said. She swung her body from side to side in an attempt to dry herself, breasts and batwings flapping. Her hair was wet, and rivulets of blue dye merged with the veins on her neck.

'The heat is heaven on my skin.' Emily, with both hands on her bony hips, held her face up to the sun and closed her eyes. Her sodden shorts clung to her thin legs, and she rubbed at the goosebumps on her arms.

Bridgette peeled the cap off her head and shook out her hair. 'Very enjoyable, but I think I'll stick to the pool next time,' she said, picking a weed out from the rubber flowers.

Behind them, engines fired to life, and the women turned to see the bikers ride into a V-shaped formation. Horns tooted and visors were raised as they saluted the swimmers and roared away into the lush Lancashire countryside.

'Well, I think we were a hit with the boys and I rather enjoyed that.' Bridgette manipulated her towel to cover her modesty. 'Are we all ready?' she asked as she stepped into tailored Capri pants and buttoned her blouse.

'Born ready,' Serena replied. Sitting upright in the back of the vehicle, she was dressed in her shirt and jeans as she folded her damp bikini neatly and placed it in a plastic bag. Emily, now turned out in combat trousers and a T-shirt, helped Marjory climb into the Range Rover. Fully dressed now, Marjory's perm was a halo of indigo tangles.

'All set?' Bridgette asked, then drove out of the car park to re-join the road.

'We certainly are,' Emily said. 'Next stop, Sparadise!'

Chapter Two

'Why not join us for an unforgettable stay at Sparadise and enjoy a unique and magical journey as we nurture you back to your best.'

Emily read out loud from the opening page of their Sparadise book as Bridgette steered the Range Rover through the vast iron gates that perfectly framed the garden beyond.

Marjory's eyes were wide as she wound her window down. 'It's like Downton Abbey,' she whispered as she gazed in awe at the sight that greeted them. Acres of idyllic countryside lay before them, and cows grazed in the furthest fields where newly-shorn sheep munched on the fertile pastures.

Bridgette, for once, drove slowly. The tyres crunched on the neatly laid gravel as they made their way in stately progress to the house at the end of the driveway. The surrounding nature embraced the property, with ancient trees acting as a shield from the elements and immaculate box hedges running parallel to the perfect proportions of the honey-coloured building.

'Valet parking!' Emily exclaimed as a uniformed man appeared and guided them to the entrance.

'I'd expect nothing less at these prices.' Bridgette removed her sunglasses and clipped them into a case. 'Come along, ladies, our adventure begins.' She nodded as the valet opened the driver's door and Bridgette slid from her seat. Thrusting her shoulders back, she raised her chin and led the party forward.

'Leave everything,' Bridgette instructed as Marjory and Emily scrambled about for their bags. 'There are people to do that for you.'

Bridgette stepped through an oak-panelled door and into a vestibule where several Wellington boots stood in a line beside a collection of outdoor shoes. Rows of Barbour jackets hung on brass hooks alongside walking sticks and umbrellas stacked in a wooden frame.

Serena stood in the vast hallway and noted the highly polished parquet flooring underfoot and walls covered with expensive artwork. She studied a sparkling chandelier and was reminded of a country house hotel in Hertfordshire where she'd gone to film an episode of her now-defunct cookery show. The proprietor of the house, a woman dressed in a twinset, tweed and pearls, had greeted Serena and was quite unlike the striking young woman who greeted them now.

Over six feet tall, she appeared from a side door and moved confidently towards the new arrivals. Her white-blonde hair was cropped, and she was perfectly styled in a white tunic and trousers. Piped in red, the spa's name, Sparadise, was embroidered on a pocket of the tunic.

'Hello, and welcome,' the woman said, 'my name is Danka and I am the manager of Sparadise.'

Danka towered over tiny Bridgette as she moved her arm in a sweeping gesture, inviting them to take a seat at a huge desk that dominated the centre of the hall.

'I've never seen anything like it,' Marjory whispered as she eased into a softly cushioned chair. 'It's almost as posh as Bossy Bridgette's place.'

'Hardly,' Emily replied, her voice low to avoid Bridgette hearing. 'This is far bigger and grander than Flaxby Manor.'

'Now I will check you into our establishment.'

Bridgette studied the young woman's features and noticed that she spoke with an accent and deduced that Danka was from Eastern Europe, perhaps Polish.

One by one, they signed registration forms and listened to precise instructions about the day-to-day running of the spa and the location of the facilities.

'Thank you for booking ahead,' Danka said with a smile that spread across her smooth peachy cheeks. 'Your therapies will be energising and we hope that you have a most enjoyable weekend.'

Marjory stared at Danka and nudged Emily. 'Do you think we'll look like that by Monday?'

'Not a chance,' Emily replied.

'Okay, and now we will show you to your rooms.' Danka picked up a little brass bell and shook it gently.

Soundlessly, from a far corner of the hall, two staff

members appeared. Like Danka, they were dressed in a smart uniform of tunics and trousers.

'Alexandra oversees our pool area and all the associated facilities there,' Danka said as the first girl stepped forward and gave a slight bow. Her glossy chestnut hair, styled in a fringed pixie cut, fell across her pretty face.

Danka introduced another attractive girl, whose shoulder-length blonde hair bounced on her slim shoulders as she nodded to the new arrivals. 'Monika manages our beauty and body treatments.'

Pole-axed by youth and beauty, the four friends stared back.

'Alexandra will show Emily Avondale and Marjory Ecclestone to their twin-bedded room, which is on the first floor of the main house,' Danka continued, 'and Monika will accompany Serena Alleyne to her lake view room, which is in our new annexe. I will take Bridgette Haworth to our Emperor Bell.'

'Erm, I'm sorry.' Bridgette rose up. 'Did you say Emperor Bell?'

'It is one of our best glamping tents, and you will like.'

'T... t... tent?' Bridgette was incredulous.

'Yes, come, I will show you.'

Danka began to move away, but Marjory, Emily and Serena stood behind Bridgette and stared anxiously as they waited for her reaction.

'But I booked the penthouse suite!'

'Oh, I'm sorry, did you not get the email?' Danka asked.

'What email?' Bridgette stared up at the woman, her

brow a mesh of anxious lines, with her lips pursed and fists clenched to do battle.

'We wrote to inform you that we could not accommodate you in the penthouse and have changed your booking to one of our glamping tents.'

'B… b… but that's preposterous!' Bridgette stamped her tiny feet.

Serena winced as she watched Bridgette's nostrils flare. Emily turned, unable to witness Bridgette's bulging eyes, and Marjory held out a hand to stroke Bridgette's arm, only to have it brusquely knocked away.

'Would you like to share with me?' Serena spoke softly.

'Or Emily and I can bunk up and you can take the other bed,' Marjory suggested.

Bridgette was flummoxed. The last thing she wanted was to share a room. She hadn't shared since her days in a dormitory at boarding school. Even at home with Hugo, she insisted on separate bedrooms. The thought of a tent was almost unimaginable. She closed her eyes and took several deep breaths. Counting slowly to ten, she regained her composure. It was only for a long weekend, so indeed, she'd manage.

'I shall be perfectly all right, thank you, ladies,' Bridgette began, 'but, Danka, I want compensation for my inconvenience and expect you to pass on my complaint to the owners.'

'Don't worry.' Danka smiled again. 'All will be well, and as soon as you allow yourself to mentally and physically slip into Sparadise, you will begin to relax and leave such minor worries behind.'

Bridgette thought that her worry was hardly minor and she did not intend to slip into anything, especially a tent. Still, as she said goodbye to her friends, agreeing to meet up with them later, she reluctantly followed Danka out of the house and into the garden.

'I thought Bridgette was going to have a fit.' Emily bounced up and down on her bed. 'She turned an extraordinary colour – her face was puce.'

'Aye, I thought we might be calling for the Sparadise medical team,' Marjory said and chuckled. She stretched out on a deliciously thick counterpane, and her blue candyfloss hair covered the pillow. Her hands were folded on her tummy as her stocking-encased toes wriggled up and down. 'But she took it on the chin.'

'I almost felt sorry for her as she meekly followed Danka. I hope her tent is to her liking.'

'It's a good job she was in the Brownies. Bridgette must have gained her camping badge.'

'I'm sure she was Brown Owl. She's certainly bossy enough to have been a Brownie leader.' Emily giggled.

'I never liked the Brownies,' Marjory said. 'Too much discipline for my liking.'

'But perfect for Bridgette. I can imagine her in a uniform.' Emily stretched her arms above her head. 'Neat bob, clothes all ship-shape, shoes polished. Nothing has changed over the decades.'

'Well, let's hope she's a happy camper as this is her

special birthday weekend, and I wouldn't like anything to go wrong.' Marjory stood and began to poke about the room.

'Are you unpacking?' Emily asked.

'Aye, we're due for our medical checks in half an hour, and I want to get my things straight.' Marjory opened her case. 'Not that I've much to unpack – just a couple of swimsuits, shirt, slacks, a skirt and something smart for Bridgette's party.' She reached for a dress and placed it on a hanger.

'This room is lovely.' Emily sat up and ran her fingers over the inlaid surface on her bedside table. 'We must be in the old part. It said in the guidebook that the house dates back to the 1700s.'

Emily studied the neatness of the room and thought of the untidy chaos in her own home. Her sons, Joe and Jacob, two twenty-somethings, never stepped out of the four walls of her 1930s property and much preferred to lounge about, glued to their computer games all day. As she was parenting single-handed, Emily had her work cut out when it came to cleaning and caring for her lazy sons.

'It's certainly very posh.' Marjory nodded her head as she gazed at the antique furniture. 'I could fit my whole house in this one room.' Floor-length drapes in gold brocade framed a window, and a chaise longue stood against one wall. She moved across the room to open a door. 'And as for this bathroom,' she called out as she studied a roll-top tub and two deep mirror-backed porcelain sinks, 'just look at all the chrome to polish.'

Marjory was in awe as she picked up bottles of

expensive toiletries and ran her fingers over thick fluffy towels. She knew that Reg, her husband, who rarely ventured far, would scoff at such extravagance. 'I wish my kids could see all this.'

'This is your time now. You spend too much time running around after your family,' Emily said, 'but at least your kids are adults and stand on their own two feet.'

'Aye, but I still need to help them.'

'They have their own homes and, thanks to you, are very capable.' Emily put her arm around Marjory's shoulders.

'I like to think that they still need me.' Marjory blinked and twisted her empty, calloused hands. 'These days, Reg hardly notices me unless I'm late with his dinner.'

'What I would give for my sons to leave home.' Emily shook her head. 'And I'm sure Reg appreciates everything you do for him.'

Both women stared at their reflections in the mirror.

Emily saw a face that appeared older than its years, her long thick grey hair with a centre parting framing thin cheeks and a long neck. Her expression was weary, and Emily knew that her working life as a headteacher in a primary school had taken its toll. Almost as much as having two twenty-somethings refusing to fly the family nest. As a single mum for most of her sons' lives, she hadn't found parenting easy.

'You've got lovely eyes,' Marjory commented, her head on one side as she studied Emily.

Emily nodded. She also thought that her bright-blue

eyes were an asset, and her slim body, which hadn't gained so much as a pound since she was a teenager.

'You've got an adorable face,' Emily replied. 'You're always laughing and you radiate happiness.'

'Gawd, I don't know how you can say that.' Marjory moved her head from side to side. 'Years of sitting on the till in the Co-op has broadened my backside.' She patted her ample bottom. 'And stacking shelves has done nothing to rid me of my arm flaps.' She pinched the loose skin on her arm and frowned.

'But you always seem content with your lot, and you make the most of everything,' Emily said. 'I'm always striving to try and make my life better, but it just seems to get harder as I get older.'

'Perhaps you should give your lads a kick up the backside and get them to do more or make them move out.'

'I doubt that day will ever come. Neither seems in the least interested in standing on their own two feet, despite expensive educations and gap years that I financed as they travelled the world.'

'Aye, but we all have choices, you know.' Marjory linked her arm through Emily's. 'Age is a fact of life, but looking your age doesn't have to be. Have you ever thought of getting rid of this lot?' She asked as she touched Emily's hair.

'What and have a perm like yours?' Emily began to laugh.

'It might go a bit frizzy at times, and that dunking in the river hasn't helped it, but it's part of me and my personality – daft and a bit wayward.'

Emily hugged her friend. 'And that's exactly why we love you. Now, instead of putting the world to rights in here and feeling sorry for ourselves, why don't we get our medical checks done and dusted and go and find the others?'

'That's the ticket.' Marjory slipped her feet into a pair of slingback sandals and Emily laced her walking boots.

'Ready?' Emily asked as she opened the door and pocketed the key.

'Lead on.' Marjory followed behind and marched down the corridor. 'Keep calm and get your spa day on!'

Chapter Three

Serena was unpacking her suitcase when there was a knock at the door. She smoothed the long, multi-coloured kaftan that lay on the top of the case and looked up.

'Come in,' she called out and turned to see Monika step into the room.

The young girl held out her hand. 'I think you left your mobile phone in reception.' She'd braided her thick blonde hair in two neat plaits and as they bounced on her shoulders, she flicked them away. 'Is this yours?'

Serena recognised the diamante S on the pink casing and nodded.

'How silly of me. Thank you so much for finding it.'

'It's my pleasure, but you won't need your phone here. Sparadise is for relaxation and removing yourself from the outside world. Amazing things will happen if you let them.'

Serena watched Monika leave the room.

If only she *could* remove herself from the outside world –

she was more than prepared to let something amazing happen. Perhaps this weekend would soothe her woes and help process the frustration of no longer being a part of the workplace that Serena had known and loved for so long. That, combined with a flagging relationship, left Serena feeling deflated. She knew that there would be little time to discuss this with her friends, as they all had separate treatments over the weekend. Pushing the suitcase to one side, she sat down and flipped the cover of her phone.

No messages or calls.

Why hadn't Cornelius contacted her to see if she'd arrived safely? Their relationship was so different from the heady days when they'd first got together. Serena shook her head as she remembered the acclaimed artist who'd exhibited at a show in London. In her celebrity days, she'd often frequented such events, and not long after they met, she went to live with him in his hometown of Flaxby. When he was painting, Cornelius was an attentive partner and lover, but when his artistic brush dried up, much to her frustration, he became despondent and withdrawn. He spent his days roaming across the fells in search of inspiration with Dodger, his Labrador retriever.

Cornelius hadn't even bothered to get out of bed when she left that morning. Dodger's head had been on the pillow, tail thumping as he eyeballed his master, and Serena knew that Cornelius would now be wandering over the hills hoping that Constable would lend him his heavenly palette and inspire a scene worthy of Cornelius's brush.

Her mobile felt like an enemy in her hand. Silent yet deadly.

'Damn,' Serena mumbled to herself. 'The phone used to ring all the time.'

She looked around at her delightful annexe room. Opulently furnished, and unlike the main house, it was ultra-modern with calming pastel colours and sleek lines. Floor-to-ceiling windows allowed plenty of light to flood in, softened by pale muslin drapes. Bi-folding doors opened up to a private patio area and enclosed garden with a beautiful lake view. Serena left her unpacking and wandered out. Birds twittered from a box hedge, and swallows skimmed across the water. She sat down on a chair by a wrought-iron table and, flicking open her phone, gritted her teeth as an Instagram notification appeared on the screen.

Yvette the Chefette had clocked up another three thousand hits.

'Double damn,' Serena swore. Her dark eyes blazed as she studied a video of a beautiful young woman moving to music in her kitchen. Yvette the Chefette was skimpily dressed in nothing but a strategically placed apron, with a tall chef's hat placed jauntily on her head. In her hand, her fingers gripped a meat cleaver. French-polished nails tapped against the gleaming steel.

Serena studied the many comments that poured in as the video played.

'What lies beyond your apron?' @kissthecook.

'Let's meet and eat some meat' @platedate.

'I hope your smoke detector is working because you're HOT!' @thejumpingjalapeno.

Likes, hearts and thumbs-up emojis floated over the screen as Yvette, Serena's arch-rival in the culinary world, wriggled her shapely shoulders and blew a kiss to her followers.

'Bitch,' Serena hissed and snapped the phone closed.

Tears trickled slowly over Serena's cheeks, and she brushed them away. Closing her eyes, she tilted her head to the sun and let the warmth of the afternoon rays wash over her. In moments, she was transported back to a busy set in the studio of a morning television show, where the host told the studio audience what was on the menu that day. They applauded as he announced Serena's name.

'Now, folks, it's time for *Wake Up with Serena*! The only morning show to get your taste buds bursting and set your stomach up for the day. Here's Serena!'

For five fantastic years, Serena had been a well-liked chef. Her Monday to Friday slot on the popular daytime show received high viewing figures and had given Serena a wonderful life. Coinciding with her move to Flaxby to be with Cornelius, she had spent the week at her apartment in London, returning to the countryside at the weekend. She remembered how being signed to London's top media agency had created opportunities for guest appearances and they'd flooded in. With a new cookery book published every year, viewers had taken the fifty-something beautiful black chef to their hearts. She even had a fan club.

As Serena sat on the private patio of her room at Sparadise, she remembered the morning when her agent told her that her show was to be axed.

'I'm sorry, darling,' said Fiona McNulty of Life in the Limelight Productions, 'I'm afraid it's an age thing.' Serena could hear Fiona dragging on a forbidden cigarette. The

London traffic was a distant noise as she exhaled through an open window. 'Of course, they'll never admit that, but Rollie Johnstone, the new commissioner, is known for his love of bright young things, and I'm afraid Yvette the Chefette ticks all his boxes.'

Serena knew it wouldn't be the only thing the wretched Yvette ticked on Rollie's list, but there was little she could do about it. Her contract had run its course, and it was out with the old and in with the new. Her fall from grace had been as rapid as a sinking soufflé, and that damned Yvette was to blame. Serena was a washed-up chef with nowhere to go.

Serena suddenly stood up. 'Two can play at your game,' she shouted at her phone as her chair scraped on the patio. 'Yvette may think she's the Instagram queen of the kitchen, but I'm going to compete for the title too.'

As she stepped back into her room, she heard a knock at the door.

'Yoo-hoo!' Marjory called out. 'It's just us.'

Serena smiled as she heard the welcome sound of her friends, and, wiping away her tears and throwing the phone to one side, went to open the door.

Chapter Four

Bridgette stood by the bed in the Emperor Bell. Her eyes were closed and she wriggled her fingers while taking deep breaths, forcing herself to relax. Danka had left instructions to use the phone should Bridgette require anything more to enhance her stay. Looking around the tent, she tried to locate a phone and realised there wasn't one. She'd have to use her mobile.

Her three Louis Vuitton cases were stacked to one side, leaving very little space. With only an upright wooden coatstand to hang anything, Bridgette wouldn't be able to unpack her clothes and would be living out of the cases for the duration of her stay.

'Really!' Bridgette muttered. 'This is not what I had planned at all.'

She scrutinised the space. The bed, which occupied most of the tent, was high, and Bridgette felt that a pair of steps would have come in handy. It was fine for the likes of Danka, whose beanstalk proportions dwarfed Bridgette.

Danka would glide into the bed. But Bridgette, whose height would never reach five feet, no matter how tall she held herself, needed a trampoline to propel herself onto the mattress.

How on earth was she going to read at night before settling down to sleep? The lighting, provided by solar panels attached to the outside of the tent, illuminated strings of fairy lights on the inside. Danka had told her that it would be 'like sleeping under the stars', but Bridgette thought it was more like sleeping in the middle of a Christmas tree. The only seating that she could find were two deckchairs stacked outside beside a small wooden table. A large rug on coconut matting covered the rest of the floor space.

'I shall just have to make the best of it,' Bridgette tutted as she opened a case and pulled out a pair of cotton pyjamas. Unable to reach up and slip them under a pillow, she hurled them onto the bed. Next came her toiletries.

'Oh, hell, where's the bathroom?' Bridgette frantically searched the tent for facilities. Behind a curtain, she found a chemical toilet and a china bowl on a stand with a flask containing hot water. 'This is worse than camping with the Brownies. At least we had a shower block and fully functional toilets.'

As she thrust the curtain back into place, Bridgette pricked her ears up. Someone was calling her name.

'Yoo-hoo, birthday girl!'

'Where are you?'

'We're coming to get you.'

Marjory, Emily and Serena stood at the entrance to the

tent. Dressed in matching towelling robes over their swimsuits, Emily wore her walking boots, Marjory her slingback sandals and Serena a pair of gold trainers. Rubber-soled fabric sliders poked out of their pockets.

'Blimey, this is the business,' Marjory said as she stumbled into the tent. Having dislodged one of the guy lines securing the structure, she turned to kick it back into place. 'Poshest tent I've ever seen.'

Emily and Serena took in the surroundings and exchanged anxious glances.

'Have you settled in?' Serena asked.

'Everything is excellent, thank you.' Bridgette was terse. She was determined not to show any weakness of character nor display her disappointment.

'Well, I think it's great,' Emily said as she studied the fairy lights that studded the ceiling. 'It will be like sleeping under the stars.'

'Exactly what Danka said, although I'd prefer a sixty-watt bulb and a bathroom.' Bridgette, with her hands on her hips, tapped her foot on the rug.

Marjory climbed onto the bed. 'Yippee! This is amazing,' she said as she bounced from one side to the other.

Bridgette scowled and watched Marjory's antics.

'Have you had your medical assessment?' Serena looked at Bridgette.

'No, not yet. I wanted to unpack before I went over to the house.'

'We've had ours,' Emily said. 'Our blood pressures are bob on, and we're raring to go.'

'We're going to have a cup of tea and then go to our

sessions.' Serena studied her watch. 'Do you think we should make a move?'

'Yes, I don't want to be late for my introduction to hatha yoga,' Emily spoke up.

'I'm going to the thalassotherapy pool,' Serena said.

'And I've got a massage.' Marjory bounced hard on the bed with her bottom. 'The tea party is in our room,' she said to Bridgette as she flew past and landed with a thud on the rug. 'Are you going to join us?'

'I do hope you will, Bridgette. We may not see much of each other over the weekend, with everyone doing something different each day,' Serena said.

Bridgette reached out to pull Marjory to her feet. She smoothed her Joules jersey top. 'My birthday party on Sunday will be the highlight of our time together at Sparadise. I may join Serena at the pool. It would do me good to sit in the sauna for a while, but I don't have time for tea. I have a Radiance Renewal facial which I'm hoping will get rid of some of these lines.' She touched her face and ran a finger along the fine lines around her mouth.

'We love you just the way you are.' Marjory leaned down and hugged Bridgette, who smiled as a cloud of soft blue hair brushed against her cheek.

'Might I suggest that we regroup this evening in the lounge before dinner? The champagne will be on me,' Bridgette said.

'Whoop!'

'Go, girl!'

'Lovely jubbly.'

'See you later!' Serena, Emily and Marjory spoke in

unison as they stepped over the guy lines and waved goodbye to Bridgette.

'Yes, don't be late,' she replied as she watched her friends hurry across the lawn and head towards the Sparadise buildings.

Bridgette turned back to her accommodation. It was as hot as an oven in the tent. Her skin, normally the colour of porcelain, was blotchy and hot and she decided to dress as everyone else who wandered around the spa in swimming clothes and towelling robes. She slipped out of her top and Capri pants and unhooked her sturdy Playtex bra. Bridgette folded the soft latex fabric and, removing her high-waisted briefs, stepped into her swimsuit. The solid strapped and skirted garment suited her taste, and the pretty poppy-printed fabric was pleasing. She reached for a thick towelling robe that was laid out on the bed and slid her arms in.

Outside the Emperor Bell, Bridgette studied her surroundings.

The tent was in a field that sloped down to the lake. To one side of the water, she could see a modern annexe with rooms that appeared to have patios and neat gardens, which were more than she could say for her tent. As an award-winning garden designer, it was an affront for Bridgette to stand in such uncared-for surroundings. It was all very well to promote a back to nature environment, but undoubtedly a few flower beds and a tidy path wouldn't go amiss in the glamping area. The grass was stubbly underfoot and speckled with rabbit droppings. At Flaxby Manor, she would take Hugo's rifle and shoot the little darlings if any bunny threatened to hop into her horticultural paradise. Bridgette contemplated speaking to Danka and offering her services. She'd soon knock this area into shape, and, like her own stunning garden, they could even open to the public and utilise the setting by the lake. She could give a talk to the guests too. As a guest speaker for a cruise line, Bridgette was sure that there would be an interest in lectures that included, *Top Tips for a Top Garden* or *From Your Garden to Show Garden*. Those were two of the many topics that were popular in her portfolio.

But she was here to relax. It was no good stressing about things she couldn't change, and if she didn't get a move on, she would be late for her facial. Bridgette zipped up the canvas opening of the tent and stood back, wondering how she was going to secure her belongings. She paused with raised eyebrows and a puzzled frown to examine the zip for a locking system but could find nothing to indicate how to safeguard her items. Surely it wasn't expected to leave one's things unattended and at the mercy of all and sundry? What on earth were the owners thinking of to be so lax on matters of security?

Stamping her foot, Bridgette let out an oath.

'Damn!' she said, feeling a visible sweat break out on her skin.

'Don't worry, old girl,' a deep voice called out.

Bridgette spun around.

'Nobody will touch your gear. It's quite safe at Sparadise,' the voice continued.

Bridgette cocked her head and waited. Was there more to come? But there was only the sound of a cow mooing in the distance and a gull calling overhead. She could see another tent, not far from her own, and wondered if someone was in residence.

'I say, anyone there?'

Treading carefully, she began to creep forward. The tent ahead appeared to be occupied, with a stack of logs on one side and a long colourful windbreaker firmly staked on the other. Pretty bunting was draped around the sides.

'Hello?' Bridgette called again.

A head shot up over the windbreaker. A man with skin the colour of a conker and a long white beard stared at Bridgette.

'Greetings. You must be the Empress of the Bell.' He began to rise and held out his hand.

'W... well...' Bridgette stammered, unsure of what to say. To her horror, she could see that the man was naked from the waist up, with the windbreaker shielding his lower body. With no intention of taking his hand, Bridgette stopped and planted her feet firmly on the grass, pushing her hands into the pockets of her robe. 'I want to know how to lock my tent.'

'My name is Norman and, as you are reluctant to share your own, I will not be offended and will simply call you Empress.'

Norman gave a slight bow of his head, and Bridgette could see a ponytail.

'Really,' she whispered. 'What a ridiculous style for a man who clearly won't see sixty again.'

'The matter of security for our items is purely down to the individual, and during your time here, you will find that Sparadise is a very trustworthy place. No one will disturb your space. Should you have valuables that you consider of worth, it may settle your mind to place them in the safe in the main building.'

As he spoke, Norman used his hands to make his point. Wooden prayer beads rattled on his wrists, and for a moment, as she stared open-mouthed, Bridgette had the horrible feeling that Norman was naked behind his windbreaker. She stepped back and began to move away.

'Well, that's all jolly good. I shall speak to the manager and make sure that my valuables are locked up.' Bridgette gave him a curt nod as Norman placed his hands on his trim waist and began to sway his hips backwards and forwards. She fervently hoped that his valuables, which might at that moment be swinging in the breeze, were well and truly secured in a pair of all-encompassing boxer shorts.

'Watch out for the cow dung!' Norman called out as Bridgette hastened towards Sparadise. 'It was always a hazard when I was training with the paras.'

But it was too late.

Bridgette's leather pumps had landed smack in the middle of a crusty pile, and a sinister brown and smelly gunge oozed over the seams and onto her bare feet.

'Can this weekend get any worse?' Bridgette yelled. She stamped about, hopping from one foot to the other as she wiped her shoes on the grass. 'Blast and damn!'

Then Bridgette lost her balance.

She misplaced her foot and her feet slid from under her body. She was airborne then fell backwards. She thrust out her hands to steady herself but she fell bottom down in the cowpat. Swallowing rapidly, she tried to summon help but couldn't find the words.

Bridgette began to cry. Hot tears trickled down her face and a warm gooey substance seeped into her robe. If only she was in the penthouse, none of this would have happened. Danka had discounted the glamping tent but what did that matter? Bridgette's position in life hadn't swayed the booking in her favour and now her humiliation was complete. It was bad enough to be hitting seventy but lying flat out in a cowpat was more than Bridgette could bear.

Her self-esteem was suddenly in tatters. God knows what Hugo and his golf club cronies would say if they could see her now. This whole weekend was to celebrate her big birthday and was meant to be so special. After all, she worked so hard at the manor, creating a magnificent garden for all the world to see. Didn't she deserve a little pampering? Wiping her tears and choking back a sob, Bridgette struggled to her feet. She prayed that no one had seen her fall as she sneaked through the garden.

It was a shame-faced Bridgette who made her way to the front door and crept into the vestibule. Noting a neat line of shoes beneath the row of Barbours, she recognised Emily's walking boots, Marjory's sandals and Serena's gold trainers. Bridgette eased her feet out of her pumps and added them to the collection. Thrusting her gooey toes into a pair of fabric sliders, she grabbed one of the Barbours and flung it around her body in an attempt to cover the disgusting brown stain across her backside.

'Where *is* the manager?' Bridgette muttered to herself as she crossed the hall and picked up the bell on the desk. 'Danka, are you there?'

As if on skates, Danka appeared from a side door and glided across the hall. Angelic in a sleeveless white tunic, her long tanned limbs gleamed with youth. Bridgette, crouched in a smelly robe, huge wax jacket and muddy cowpat-covered feet, felt like a Disney witch as Danka approached.

'Now, Mrs Haworth, you're late for your medical assessment.' Danka stared at Bridgette. 'What has happened to you?'

'I fell over in your bloody cow poo. That's what's happened!'

'Ah, this happens with some of our elderly guests. Let me take your coat.'

At that moment, a door opened and a group of honed and toned Lycra-clad runners came jogging into the hall. Brimming with exhilaration from their run and full of energy and good health, they stopped in their tracks when they saw the witch-like woman huddled in the hall.

Bridgette was mortified to be caught in such a compromising position and gripped the coat around her. But it was too late and Danka's grip was firmer.

'It's okay.' Danka pulled the coat away. 'Oh dear, I see that you have fouled yourself,' she said in a matter-of-fact tone as she stared down at Bridgette's brown behind. 'Let me help you.'

Paralysed into submission and too mortified to speak, Bridgette was led away. As she passed the group, with her head bent at waist level to the towering Danka, whose hand she held, she heard one of the runners speak.

'Look at that poor old dear. I didn't realise that Sparadise had a nursing home in the grounds.'

Chapter Five

Emily sat with Marjory on their beds while Serena stood at the window and looked out at the garden. They all drank a refreshing cup of tea from china mugs, compliments of the management's welcome tray tucked tidily on a corner shelf.

'It's a shame Bridgette couldn't join us,' Serena said.

'Aye, there's not much chance of being together with all these sessions booked in.' Marjory held a timetable in her hand and stared at her personal programme for the weekend.

'I'm beginning to feel a bit nervous about my yoga lesson,' Emily said.

'Go and enjoy it,' Marjory replied and stroked the soft towelling of her oversized robe.

Serena turned from the view. 'It will do you a power of good to stretch out your tired muscles.'

'I suppose so.' Emily stood and was about to go to the bathroom to rinse her mug, but Marjory held up her hand.

'Leave that. I'll tidy up in here,' Marjory said. She unwrapped a shortbread and, dunking it in her tea, munched happily.

'Very well,' Emily replied, placing the mug on the tray. 'Here goes. Let's hope I can do this. See you both later.'

'Have fun,' Serena called out.

Closing the bedroom door, Emily slipped into the corridor and made her way to the main stairs. Now that it was about to begin, she wasn't at all sure about a yoga class and wished she'd chosen to join Serena in the pool. Did she really want to learn something new at her time of life? But having made the booking for an introduction to hatha yoga, she knew that she would have to pay for the missed session if she didn't attend. At these prices, it would be foolish to waste money.

Emily had always been thrifty and knew that her frugalness stemmed from her childhood. Her father's dark periods, when he suffered from depression, had limited his ability to work. The doctors said his depression was a result of his time as a soldier, incarcerated in a Japanese prisoner of war camp during WWII. Her mother, a nurse, had been the breadwinner, but she'd developed early dementia. As an only child, Emily had to combine her teaching career and her own demanding family life with physical and financial support for her parents. When they died, Emily and her husband, Stephen, a Spanish language teacher, had moved into her parents' home with their young sons.

Now, as she hurried along to the yoga class, Emily thought of the difficulties she'd faced as she scrimped to get by after Stephen had shockingly announced his love for a

Spanish student twenty years his junior. He'd upped and left, leaving behind his job and his family, to live in Alicante.

Emily had never got over the scandal and, alone with two small children and little support from their father, she didn't treat herself to the luxuries that her friends seemed to enjoy. She rarely took a holiday or bought any new clothes. Fell walking was her only salvation and it cost nothing to put one foot in front of the other and head off into the hills where no one could criticise how she looked or laugh at her for losing her husband to a younger woman.

Emily felt self-conscious in her old leggings and baggy T-shirt as she descended the sweeping staircase. The Sparadise brochure said to wear something comfortable for classes and, despite hand-stitched repairs to the crotch, her leggings were as comfortable as they got.

'Ah, Mrs Avondale,' Danka said as Emily stepped into the reception hall. 'I see you are off to yoga with Yannis.' Danka sat at the desk and studied a computer screen. She looked as cool as a cucumber with her immaculate hair, ice-white tunic and neatly crossed long, lean legs free of veins or dimples.

Emily wiped the sweat from her forehead and tugged her T-shirt over her tummy. 'Er, yes, but I'm not sure which way to go?' Rapidly blinking behind her glasses, Emily stared at the stylish young woman and felt every one of her sixty-three years.

'Come, I will show you.' Danka led Emily through the hallway and into the newer addition to the house. As they progressed, she pointed out the facilities. 'Here is where you come for the beauty and body treatments,' she said as they passed a reception area. 'Monika is in charge and will look after you.'

Monika, sitting behind a desk and filing her nails, looked up and waved. A heavily pregnant woman wrapped in a gaping robe sat nearby in a comfortable armchair.

'We do baby-on-board treatments too,' Danka said and smiled at the expectant mother. 'But not for mature ladies like you.'

Emily gritted her teeth. She was about to tell Danka that she'd not needed such treatments when, as a hard-working mother in her thirties, she'd pushed out two bonny bouncing babies. But the thought was lost as she suddenly found herself in a spacious room where at least a dozen guests sat cross-legged on mats on the floor.

Emily winced. Floor-to-ceiling mirrors on all the walls displayed multiple images of a grey-haired, bespectacled older woman staring back.

'Yannis will take care of you,' Danka said and left the room.

Heads turned and eyes ran up and down Emily's body as the designer-clad participants studied the newcomer. Emily felt her face flush. Her palms were sticky and she wondered what the hell she was supposed to do. Turning to the door, she began to move towards it but stopped when a young man stood before her.

'Namaste,' he said and pressed his palms together then bowed from the waist. 'You must be Emily?'

Before Emily had time to change her mind and leave, he reached out and took her hand.

'My name is Yannis, and I am your class instructor.'

Emily recognised his face from their Sparadise book. Here was the eight-angled pose in glorious technicolour, and he was even more handsome in the flesh.

Yannis led her to a mat. 'Come, sit down. Don't be nervous. There is water in the fountain and, if you become too warm, just tell me and I will alter the room temperature.'

Emily, still flushed and hot as hell in her thick leggings, melted into her mat as Yannis guided her down then walked to the front of the class.

With everyone's full attention on him, Yannis began.

He told them that he was born and grew up on the island of Bessaloniki, a jewel in the Ionian Sea. After he left school, he had practised yoga in Athens. It had been the most significant influence on his life, and now he wanted to share all his knowledge and help others achieve their dreams through yoga.

When he spoke, his face lit up with a smile that immobilised his audience. Smooth olive skin crinkled softly around the brightest blue eyes, and his dark hair, sun-streaked with lighter shades, curled softly on broad shoulders. His calm gaze studied each of them as he described his hatha yoga class.

'Hatha is derived from the Sanskrit words *Ha*, representing the sun, and *Tha*, the moon, which means that the moon restores the mind and mental energy, and the sun replenishes one's life force, which in turn awakens your higher consciousness.'

Everyone's higher consciousness appeared to be fully

awake as students craned their necks to stare at Yannis's toned body. Muscles rippled, his bulging biceps showing beneath a taut white vest, and matching yoga pants hugged his derriere.

'Great buns,' someone whispered.

'Shush, you'll get us into trouble.' Emily, suddenly the schoolteacher again, looked around anxiously, expecting Bossy Bridgette to appear and finger wag, but everyone was mesmerised by their tutor.

For the next ten minutes, Yannis chatted about meditation and yoga and talked about the retreat. 'Sparadise is paradise,' he said, his voice stilted yet smooth and soft as chocolate. He looked around the room, his eyes lingering on the most receptive faces. 'At our spa, your health will improve, engaging your spirit and emotions. You will learn to lead a happy and healthier life, and hatha yoga will prepare you for the higher practice of meditation.'

Emily decided that she would happily settle for the lower practice if Yannis were the teacher. Sod the higher – anything this man taught over the next three days would be a bonus.

'And now, I would like you to prepare yourselves for some simple beginner's exercises.'

Following Yannis's warm-ups, Emily soon found herself in the reverse-corpse pose, face down on her mat with her arms and legs outstretched. In considerable discomfort, she raised her head to peep at the others. Everyone was relaxed and at one with their world. Emily wished that she'd had the sense to invest in more comfortable clothing. She was the odd one out, not only because she was a beginner, but her attire was so shabby. She felt miserable as she studied the colourful array of harem pants, crop tops, wide-legged joggers and open-backed tops that covered lean bodies that moved with ease.

'Inappropriate clothing can hinder your limb movement and hamper your practice.' As if reading Emily's mind, Yannis spoke as he walked around the room, reaching out to touch an arm or move a leg into the correct position. 'And now, I will demonstrate the downward facing dog.'

'Christ!' Emily whispered as she struggled into a standing position.

'Come.' Yannis held out his hand, and to her horror, Emily realised that he wanted her to step to the front of the class. 'I will demonstrate with you,' he said and, standing behind, gently lowered Emily forward until her hands touched the floor and her backside stuck out at an angle.

Emily was grateful that she couldn't see the mass of faces staring at her contorted body. Her glasses had steamed up, and as she gripped her buttocks tightly, terrified that she was about to break wind, she heard a ripping noise. Mortified, she sank to her knees and clamped her legs together.

'Very good, Emily, you are an excellent student.' Yannis reached down and stroked her shoulder, and for a moment, Emily forgot that the red cotton she'd used to sew up the crotch on her leggings had sprung away from the fabric, leaving a gaping hole.

A cool-down period followed, and Yannis ended the session.

'Namaste,' he said and asked the class to turn and look

each other in the eye, bow and repeat the salutation, 'The light in me sees and honours the light in you. Namaste.'

Emily turned and came eye-to-eye with a thirty-something. She'd forgotten the words and mumbled as she stared at the unlined face and wrinkle-free skin.

'Namaste,' she concluded, then waited for the class to disperse before leaving the studio. The seams on her leggings had split even further, and she was desperate that no one else should witness her acute embarrassment. Emily felt ancient as she kept her back to the wall and edged out of the room.

'Emily,' Yannis called out and ran over. 'Did you enjoy it?' His handsome face was endearing, and with his eyes the colour of tropical pools, Emily was mesmerised. She felt the urge to dive in.

'Er, yeah… yes, it… it was great,' she stuttered.

'You'll come again?'

Emily felt that she might come on the spot if Yannis got any closer. She battled to stop her knees from buckling and stammered, 'Yes, of course.'

'I can do one-to-one if it helps you. I can increase your flow of energy so that you become at one with the cosmic world.' He touched her arm and stroked it gently.

Convinced that she had already landed in the cosmic world, Emily felt a white-hot poker of desire pierce through her skin from his touch, connecting her pounding heart directly to her groin. She found herself agreeing to a series of personal sessions beginning the following day.

As she slipped from the room, she let out a long sigh

and wondered what the hell had just happened. She hadn't even discussed the price!

'Bugger the cost,' she said as she jogged through a lounge area where yoga participants sat in comfortable chairs, sipping juices and shakes, replacing their celestial energy. They looked up at the bespectacled, archaic woman, bedraggled in gaping clothing.

'Namaste,' Emily called out as she hurried by. 'When in doubt, yoga it out!'

Chapter Six

Serena left Marjory to finish her tea and now, in the comfort of her annexe room, she applied fresh makeup and re-arranged her hair. Satisfied with her appearance, she picked up her sports bag and made her way to the pool area.

Alexandra, head down with her gaze firmly fixed on painting her nails, sat at the reception desk.

'Hello Alexandra,' Serena said as she approached and watched the young girl blow on her nails and flap her fingers. A smile brightened her cherubic face as she pushed a bottle of pearly pink varnish to one side.

'Great outfit.' Alexandra's eyes roved over Serena's tall and toned body. 'You look amazing.'

'Thank you.' Serena wore an animal-print swimsuit beneath a matching kimono-style robe.

Alexandra handed Serena a pen and asked her to sign the register.

Serena shook her head when offered a towelling robe and slippers. 'No, thank you, I have my own.'

'Will you be using our mud chamber or hydro pool today?'

'Not for me.'

'You might like to try the snow room. It will invigorate your immune system.'

'I'll let you know.'

Serena didn't feel in the least inclined to plunge into a freezing cold room and douse herself with ice crystals to pep herself up. There was no need. A decision that she'd made earlier had energised her into action, and now, remembering her agent's hurtful words, it was time to make a start. Fiona had made it quite clear that Rollie Johnson, who'd commissioned Serena's TV show, preferred younger chefs. Serena had meekly accepted the dismissal and done nothing to remedy her career. It was as if Fiona had flicked an off switch and Serena had become invisible.

Now she felt determined to fight back and resurrect it. There was nothing Serena liked more than to demonstrate her own unique and popular recipes and teach people how to cook. But her media livelihood had been abruptly cut short by a younger chef. Yvette the Chefette was an Instagram influencer who exploited her attractive appearance to increase her followers and Serena decided that if the way to regain notoriety was to copy Yvette and use her looks to create attention, she was determined to give it a go.

Serena strolled into the changing rooms and placed her

bag on a wooden bench. It reminded her of the one in the cramped kitchen of her childhood home in Brixton. That was where her mother had magically produced delicious colourful concoctions for Serena and her siblings.

Reaching into a locker, Serena thought about the pleasure she'd felt when cooking with her mother. When food had been the glue that bound her family together. Jamaican dishes were an integral part of the gatherings that had been crammed into the tiny terraced house where Serena had grown up. Her parents, immigrants who'd come to Britain post-war, had endured many hardships, but meals around their table represented harmony and created a warm and loving environment.

Serena's mother had patiently taught her everything she knew about the heady and eclectic diet of spicy, nutritious Jamaican dishes. It was this foundation that had built Serena's cookery career, and she'd made a good life for herself with a successful business and celebrity status. But both had slipped away after Serena's sudden dismissal, and now, as she slid the kimono from her shoulders, she was determined to get them back.

Reaching into her bag, she smoothed moisturiser generously over her skin. Chanel Rouge Allure gave vibrant colour to her lips, and the final touch was to slip her feet into a pair of gold designer sliders. Satisfied with her appearance, she stared at herself in a full-length mirror and smiled.

@SaucySerena was born and ready to do battle!

Grabbing her phone, she took a deep breath and strolled

out to the spa, where, for the next hour, she postured in various locations. With a change of outfit, she pouted and posed and slowly but surely, created images to use on Instagram.

'Loving my life at Sparadise.' Serena added hashtags and straplines and saved them to a file.

Guests using the facilities became fascinated by the mature woman using the spa as a one-woman studio. They peered over magazines as another outfit was modelled and a cleavage shot snapped. Serena's pouting lips were caught on camera as she licked the rim of a mocktail and grazed on fresh fruit.

The jacuzzi had filled with a group of sales representatives from Lancashire Automotives, a local car dealership whose employees had come to Sparadise for a company bonding weekend. Tucking in tummies and pumping sagging muscles, they swept their hair over various bald patches as Serena sat on the side of the hot tub and fluttered her eyelashes at the eager team.

'One for this year's company calendar, boys?' she asked as she draped herself over the tiles before eight ruddy, wet faces and joined them in a photo.

'You can start my engine anytime,' a pimple-faced rep tittered.

'She'd eat you alive,' his rotund middle-aged boss replied.

Serena called out as she moved away, 'Don't forget to use my Instagram handle when you look for the photos.'

'@SaucySerena!' they chanted as the jacuzzi, like a raging cauldron, bubbled over.

In a quiet corner, two men relaxed on loungers. They watched with interest as Serena came and went. Both held plastic beakers and took an occasional drink.

'I wonder what she'll be wearing this time,' Robin Haines, the older of the pair, said. His tanned and athletic body was lean. He wore a pair of minuscule Speedos and raised his head to peer over tortoiseshell-framed glasses.

'Here she comes,' Stevie, his partner, replied.

They both sat up as Serena appeared in an emerald-green bathing suit and sarong embellished with tiny coloured jewels. Little silver spoons hung from Serena's ears, matching the necklace that sat in the curve of her neck.

'Oh,' Stevie exclaimed. 'She's like a Christmas bauble.'

Robin ran his fingers through closely cropped, thick dark hair with a streak of grey that added distinction to his handsome face. 'Do you think I could sneak a photo?' He reached for his phone.

'Why not ask her over? She's heading our way.' Stevie sat up. He tightened the belt of his robe over a bulging waistline and swung pale, plump legs to the tiled floor.

Serena moved towards them, selfie stick thrust out as she posed for the camera.

'You look gorgeous,' Robin called out. 'I love your outfit.'

Serena stopped and smiled. 'Thank you. I hope I'm not disturbing you.'

'God, no. We're finding it very entertaining and wonder why you're photographing yourself.' Robin shuffled on his lounger.

'You'd be bored if I told you,' Serena said.

'On the contrary, we'd be intrigued.'

Stevie ran a hand over his head, conscious of his receding hairline. He surreptitiously arranged a handful of highlighted locks then patted the seat beside him. 'Come and join us,' he said. 'We've got some bubbles if you'd like a tipple.'

He dug into a sports bag under the table and produced a plastic beaker and an open bottle of champagne. Looking over his shoulder to check on the absence of staff, Stevie poured. 'There are no CCTV cameras in this area, and my hubby and I always sit here,' he explained and handed Serena the beaker. 'They don't like guests drinking alcohol by the pool.'

'Thank you,' Serena said as she took the drink and sat down. 'I'm delighted to make your acquaintance. I'm Serena.'

'What a lovely name. I'm Stevie and this is Robin. Our friends call us "Fatman and Robin", which explains why I spend quite a lot of time at Sparadise and Robin comes along for the ride.' He patted his bulbous belly.

The two men looked lovingly at each other.

Robin held up his beaker. 'Cheers to whatever lies beyond your lens. Now tell us what you're up to.'

'Well, if you're sure you want to know?'

'We're intrigued,' Robin said.

Serena crossed her legs and took a sip of the champagne. 'I used to own a delicatessen in Brixton in south London, and I worked for years to build it up from a little shop serving West Indian vegetables and spices to a well-stocked deli with produce from all over the world. There was a thriving café too.'

Stevie and Robin sat forward.

'A few years ago, I entered a competition called Britain's Best Deli. It was televised over several weeks with a panel of food critics judging the regional entries, which culminated in a grand finale.'

'How exciting,' Stevie breathed.

'To my absolute shock and surprise, I won.'

'You clever girl,' Robin said.

'Following the show's success, I was approached by an agent convinced that I was an ideal candidate to host a mainstream cookery show. A few weeks later, she secured a deal for a television series.'

'*Wake Up with Serena!*' Robin smiled.

'Yes, that's right. Did you watch it?'

Robin turned to his partner. 'Stevie, you're far too young to know, but this lady was one of the best cooks ever to grace our screens. I always started my day to *Wake Up with Serena!* and rarely missed an episode.'

'How thrilling!' Stevie clapped his hands.

'I have all of your cookery books in our library at home, but what happened? Why don't we see you on TV anymore?'

'I was dropped like a stone when a younger chef came along.'

'No!' the men exclaimed.

'Yes, the commissioner of the television station has a penchant for young female presenters, and in a flash, I was history.'

'But they can't do that.' Stevie turned to Robin. 'Can they?'

'I'd like to think that it wouldn't happen now, but as Serena knows, a lot of things happened in the media then that wouldn't happen today. Everything from ageism and unequal pay.'

Serena nodded her head.

'There are many popular and influential movements that were born because of these injustices, and quite rightly so.'

'What's the name of the younger chef who replaced you?' Stevie asked as he reached for the bottle and topped up their beakers.

'Her name is Yvette.'

'Yvette the Chefette. Yes, I've seen her. She can't boil an egg if truth be told, but by posturing all over Instagram, she seems to get away with it.'

Stevie's face lit up. 'She has squillions of followers and posts all the time.'

'Several times a day.' Serena scowled.

'Are we to understand that you want to build up your own following?' Robin asked.

'I care passionately about teaching people to cook and enjoy good food and lead a healthy lifestyle. I sold the deli when the show was popular. I'm a talented chef and still have a lot to give, but the media has dismissed me and put me out to seed in a culinary graveyard.'

'So, you're about to launch your own Instagram account?'

'Yes. If Yvette can gain popularity this way, why can't I?'

'Indeed, why not?'

'I'm staying here with my close friends to celebrate a birthday on Sunday and we've all booked different things during our stay. I thought I might take advantage of the solitude and use Sparadise as a background for my first posts.'

'Perfect,' Robin said. 'We will help you. If you'll allow us.'

'I'd love to have your support.'

'I think this is cause for celebration.' Stevie reached into the bag and began to twist the wire from another bottle of champagne.

At that moment, the Lancashire Automotives team piled out of the jacuzzi. They filed past, penguin-like, along the wet surface on their way to the hydro pool. Stevie, his face contorted as he grappled with the bottle, suddenly fell back as the cork shot out at lightning speed as if fired from a gun. It struck the sales manager right across his forehead, then darted into the jacuzzi.

'He's been shot!' the pimply-faced rep exclaimed as the manager collapsed on the tiled ground. Fearing a terrorist attack, the salesmen abandoned their boss and ran like the wind to the changing rooms with their hands above their heads.

A young woman who'd been swimming in the pool scaled the steps and crouched by the man. 'I'm a nurse,' she explained.

'Time to retire to our rooms,' Robin urged once he was satisfied that the man was benefitting from the nurse's competent administrations.

Stevie gathered their belongings and stuffed everything

into his bag. He took Serena's arm and guided her past the dazed body.

'Hashtag emergency evacuation,' Serena said as she took a selfie and Stevie led her away.

Chapter Seven

After Emily and Serena had gone, Marjory lingered in their bedroom. There was time to spare before she needed to make her way to the spa. She was looking forward to her first ever massage. As she sat upright on the pillows on her bed, she studied a pamphlet explaining that each massage was tailored to the guest's needs and provided the utmost in relaxation and rejuvenation. Marjory remembered Bridgette's words as she read.

'You mustn't risk an inexperienced massage therapist doing untold damage,' Bridgette had said. 'If they don't know what they're doing, they can do you more harm than good.'

Marjory had booked her session with the spa's most senior therapist. The fifty-minute massage promised to increase her blood and lymphatic flow. Marjory hadn't a clue what her lymphatic flow was, and, as she filled in a health questionnaire, she wondered if it was the reason for her varicose veins. The spa didn't recommend the treatment for anyone suffering from a fungal infection, epilepsy or pregnancy. Confidently, Marjory put a cross through all the boxes.

After checking the time on her watch, Marjory climbed off the bed. Bridgette had informed her that she need only wear her undies, robe and slippers. Comfort was the name of the game. Standing in front of the dressing table mirror, she patted her hair into place. She'd spent ten minutes with a gadget that had tamed the indigo tease. Emily's GHDs were another new experience and a long way from Marjory's sponge rollers, but the heated hair irons had done the job, and now her hair was tidy.

'Come on, girl,' she said as she fastened the belt of her robe around her tummy. 'Let the battle commence.' Pocketing her room key, Marjory made her way to the treatment rooms. Having rehearsed the route to ensure that she wouldn't be late, she soon reached the reception desk.

'Hello, lovely,' Marjory said to the receptionist.

Monika was assisting a heavily pregnant woman into a comfortable chair. The flush-faced mother-to-be, who was panting, looked as though her child's birth was imminent.

'Be with you in a moment,' Monika said as she eased the woman down and handed her a glass of iced water. Returning to her desk, she whispered to Marjory, 'She's had a baby-on-board session with our maternal massage therapist.'

Marjory hoped she wasn't about to witness the birth, which looked sure to commence at any moment and thought that the woman's session would have been more beneficial if a midwife and obstetrician were in attendance. 'I've come for my five o'clock massage.'

'Let me check the booking.' Monika studied a screen on the computer. 'Ah, yes, you're with our senior massage therapist, Lars.'

'Lars?' Marjory frowned.

'Yes, Lars. He excels in unique Swedish techniques.'

'A man?'

'Our most experienced massage therapist – you are very fortunate.'

Marjory felt her heart pound as Monika led her along a softly carpeted corridor. *A man?* Was she going to be mauled by a man? Whatever would Reg say? Marjory knew her husband would be appalled, and her stomach had a sinking feeling. Staid old Reg would be livid at her brazen behaviour. He was so set in his ways and had been against the entire weekend away with her girlfriends.

An illuminated exit sign lit the end of the corridor, and Marjory was tempted to bolt. But Monika had taken her arm and ushered Marjory into a dim scented room. In the middle, covered by a cotton sheet and draped with a large towel, stood an adjustable padded bed.

'Please remove your clothes and place them on the chair, then lie face down on the bed. You can use the towel to cover yourself.' Monika handed her client a bandana. 'Place this over your hair.'

Marjory took the bandana and tucked her curls under the firm elastic.

'I will leave you now, and Lars will attend when you are ready.'

Monika slipped out of the room.

As Marjory she removed her robe, she said to herself, 'Oh, well, in for a penny, in for a pound.'

Despite the relaxing music playing in the background, Marjory struggled to manoeuvre herself into a restful position. It took forever to arrange the towel to cover her body. There was a hole at the top of the bed, and Marjory raised her neck to get a better look. Should she place her head there? Her breasts felt heavy, as did her tummy as soft folds of unfettered flesh spread out.

'What the devil do I do with my arms?' she mumbled as her limbs hung. She wriggled about to secure them under her body then scrunched her face into the hole. Her feet fell to one side, and Marjory was tense as she awaited her fate.

What on earth would Reg think if he could see her now? He'd have a fit at the very thought of his wife alone, stark naked, in a room with another man, let alone a man who was about to massage every inch. Not that Reg would know much about that. The only thing Reg knew how to massage was the plump breast of Polly, his favourite pigeon, when he was preparing her for a race.

Marjory sighed. Other than their grown-up children, she had little in common with Reg these days. She hadn't a clue what still glued them together. It wasn't as though she couldn't support herself. She had her job and savings hidden for a rainy day, but Marjory felt trapped in her marriage. In a small town like Flaxby, she wasn't sure that she could live with the scandal of being divorced.

She imagined the gossip. Folks would relish her humiliation and what would the kids have to say? They thought their mam and dad were the perfect couple when everyone sat down each week for Marjory's lavish Sunday roast dinner. But love was a thing of the past in their marriage. Unlike many men, sex had been an obligation for Reg instead of the obsession she heard about when listening to housewife tales from her seat at the Co-op till.

'I've been at it all night!' Jean, who also lived on Coronation Avenue, would chunter as she piled tins of beans and loaves of sliced bread off the conveyor belt and into her shopping trolley. 'Two pints of beer and he thinks he's a sex machine.' Bleached-blonde Jean, who would never see a size sixteen again and favoured leggings that made her thighs look like crumpets, was a goddess in the eyes of her old man.

Marjory felt sure that there was more to sex than the brief grunts and groans she'd experienced with Reg. The pages of her Mills & Boon books suggested many delights and she longed to know what 'feeling the earth move' really meant. But she'd given up trying to entice Reg, an ex-soldier who became a bus driver. His days of doing his duty for Queen and country were long gone, as was sex with his wife. The only passion Marjory ever heard Reg utter was when he was cooing sweet nothings to Polly and her pigeon family.

The door opened and Marjory stiffened. Someone had come into the room. With her face scrunched through the face cradle, her eyes searched the floor for signs of life other than her own. When a soft voice spoke, she jerked up and almost fell off the bed.

'Hello, Marjory. My name is Lars,' the voice said.

'Hel… lo,' Marjory mumbled.

'Let me make you more comfortable.'

Marjory felt the bed rise. The mattress began to warm and adjusted to her shape. A hand manipulated her head until the noose-like hold from the cradle became supportive and soft.

All her senses were heightened as she waited.

'Your therapy today will include a full-body massage,' Lars began.

Marjory could hear lotion being squeezed from a bottle. She felt cool air on her skin as the towel was lifted and folded across her bottom, and she blushed as she visualised her rotund cheeks wobbling in all their glory.

'Massage therapy will clear your thoughts and allow your body to accept that the environment it exists in is safe and nurturing.' Lars' voice was like velvet.

Marjory struggled with the notion that a busy Saturday in the Co-op was a safe and nurturing environment, especially if Flaxby FC were playing at home.

Two giant hands held her shoulder blades and fingers began to pummel her skin. The scent of jasmine filled her nostrils. 'I will heal your body and spread feel-good chemistry by dialling down your cortisol,' Lars said, and Marjory wondered if he was about to make a phone call.

'Think of your hormones as nature's built-in alarm system.' Lars placed his fingers on Marjory's shoulders and manipulated her muscles. 'They control your every mood.'

Marjory hadn't a clue what he was talking about, and with pain shooting through her spine, she braced her body and gripped the bed.

'Relax. Take deep breaths and slowly release. I cannot help you if your body is tense.'

Focussing hard, Marjory obeyed. Her eyes were open as she breathed in, but to her alarm, she realised that Lars now stood at the head of the bed, and as she breathed out, all she could see were his size ten feet, in leather sandals, on the floor beneath her.

Marjory had never studied a man's foot before. Reg had the ugliest feet she'd ever seen and always wore a pair of white socks under his sandals, even in summer. But these digits were something else. Smooth and long, with perfect half-moon nails the colour of opals, they looked like pink lollipops, and she had the sudden urge to suck one.

'Good, you are beginning to unwind.'

The music had changed, and a brook gently babbled through the room. Birds had flown in; their gentle cries distant. Marjory hoped that she wasn't going to wet herself as she listened to the sound of water alerting her weak bladder, but as strong hands moved and manipulated, she felt her lids droop and her mouth fall open as the massage therapist's fingers worked their magic and lulled her into a warm cocoon.

Marjory drifted into a deep and soothing sleep. She dreamt that she was lying in bed with Lars. His arms had encircled her body, and her legs were entwined around his naked, muscled back. As he stroked and caressed, her body felt as though it was on fire, and as his enquiring fingers crept deep into places no fingers had crept before, a wave of emotion hit her like a freight train. The earth seemed to move beneath her, and with exquisite pleasure, she cried out.

'Aagghhh…' Marjory moaned.

From somewhere in the distance, a man's voice was faint. 'Good, you are waking up. I'll leave. When you are ready, you can dress.'

Marjory opened her eyes to discover that she was lying face up. She wriggled her fingers, began to move her toes, and, raising her torso, turned from side to side. Lars had gone. Flopping back down on the bed, Marjory felt pole-axed. Her groin tingled with an exquisite sensation and her legs trembled like jelly.

What the hell just happened?

Struggling into a sitting position, Marjory looked up. She stared with astonishment at her reflection in a mirror on the opposite wall. In the warm glimmer of candlelight, she saw a woman far younger than herself. With flushed skin that seemed flawless, a golden glow lit up her face.

'Bloody hell…' she whispered and pinched the skin on her arms to make sure she wasn't still dreaming. In all the years that she'd been married, she'd never felt like this.

Sliding off the bed, she reached for her gown and, slipping it on, stuffed her undies into the pockets. Undergarments might subdue the thrill that still nibbled at her nerve endings and was rippling through her body.

Marjory peered into the corridor. Monika was sitting at her desk and looked up when she saw Marjory.

'This way,' she called out.

Marjory put one foot in front of the other and, confident that she could walk without collapsing, floated blissfully towards the reception area. Taking a glass of ice-cold water from Monika's outstretched hand, she sank into a comfortable chair and smiled as she heard the girl ask a question.

'Would you like more massages? I can book you in with Lars again.'

Marjory's face was radiant and her body relaxed as she nodded beatifically in reply.

Chapter Eight

D inner at Sparadise was served in the restaurant. The chef and his team had designed a menu of the finest seasonal produce and endeavoured to make the dining experience memorable for the guests. On the first night of their stay, neither Bridgette, Serena, Emily or Marjory knew quite how memorable the evening was to be.

The dress code was smart attire, and Emily and Marjory had chosen comfortable tops and trousers. Serena, out to impress, wore a silky silver jumpsuit, which flattered her skin tone and dazzled as she walked through the bar.

'Over here!' Bridgette, perched on a chair in the bar area and dressed in a silky wrap dress, called out to her friends. 'Champers is on the way.'

As Serena sat down, she saw Stevie and Robin nearby on a cosy banquette. They called out, 'Good evening,' and raised their glasses.

'Hello, boys,' Serena returned the greeting.

'Who are they?' Bridgette asked. She tilted her head to peer around Marjory's shoulder.

'A couple of guys I met by the pool,' Serena said.

'Where are they staying?' Bridgette's tone was inquiring as she studied the two men. She noted their expensive outfits, cashmere sweaters, and silk shirts teamed with well-tailored trousers and hand-crafted leather shoes. Bridgette smelt money and, fixing her most engaging smile, raised her hand in greeting.

'They're staying in the main hotel,' Serena replied.

'Twin room? Same floor as Marjory and Emily?'

'Not exactly.'

'Oh, I didn't realise there were other rooms on that floor.'

'They're on the second floor.'

'But there's only the penthouse up there.'

'Yes.'

Bridgette's eyes bulged as she stared into the eyes of the enemy.

These guests had claimed her booking and reduced her to a tent pitched on a piece of scrubland! She had endured a mortifying afternoon and felt ridiculed and embarrassed. Even now, she was dreading the small hours ahead. God only knew what would happen when darkness fell and she had to grope her way back to the Emperor Bell to try and settle under the stars for the night. It had taken all the strength she could muster to put on a brave face and carry on as though nothing had happened and tidy herself up to turn out tonight. Yet here, large as life and brazenly flaunting their wealth, was the reason her weekend was ruined before it had begun.

'Would you like me to introduce you?' Serena asked. She prayed that the drinks would arrive soon. Bridgette looked as though she had swallowed a thistle and was fit to burst, but a couple of glasses might calm her down.

'No, that won't be necessary.'

The glance Bridgette shot at the men would send an army into retreat.

'They're regular guests at Sparadise,' Serena explained. 'They always book the penthouse but were only able to give short notice for this weekend, and the management didn't want to turn them away.'

Bridgette's mouth dropped open, and she was about to protest at the injustice, but a waiter had appeared with a bottle of champagne. Bridgette read the label. 'I ordered the *house* champagne. Please change it.' She dismissed the young man.

But the waiter remained. He pointed to the banquette. 'This is with the compliments of the gentlemen sitting over there.'

'Dom Pérignon! I've never tasted such an expensive drink,' Emily exclaimed.

'Very fancy.' Marjory sat forward to see who'd been so generous.

A moment passed as Bridgette contemplated the label. 'Very well,' she said, her tone softened. 'You can pour.'

The finest champagne soon worked its magic and Bridgette began to relax. She crossed her legs, pointed her dainty kitten-heeled feet and sank back into her chair.

'My facial was fabulous. I feel at least ten years younger; my skin is so smooth.' Holding her chin high, Bridgette ran her fingers over her dimpled neck. 'Does it look radiant?'

'It's glowing.' Emily peered through her glasses and studied Bridgette's apple-shaped face. 'Your cheeks are rosy too.' Emily thought Bridgette looked like one of the ripe English Russets that hung on a tree in her orchard at home.

Bridgette patted her cheeks. 'A flushed complexion is a sign of good health. I had the electrolysis radiance facial. The high frequency helps tone and tighten the muscles and prevents signs of ageing.'

Emily leaned in to study Bridgette's fine lines and wrinkles. Convinced her friend had been ripped off, she sat back and told herself that she wouldn't be investing in a similar treatment.

Marjory had never tasted champagne before and knocked her drink back in one. 'It's like a lovely lemonade,' she declared as the bubbles hit her empty tummy. 'Much nicer than half a cider at the Flaxby Arms.'

She held out her glass for a top-up. A long slate had been placed on the table before them displaying a selection of canapés. 'It's like a painting,' Marjory said and bit into a blini topped with slivers of smoked salmon and dressed with fronds of fresh dill. Licking her lips, she drained her glass again and picked up a tiny cheese tart decorated with edible flowers. As she picked a nasturtium stalk from her teeth, she began to feel light-headed.

'How was your massage, Marjory?' Bridgette asked. She held the stem of her champagne flute and circled it as she spoke.

Pastry flakes fluttered from Marjory's mouth, and with her drink refreshed, she took a gulp and peered over the rim. She wondered if there had been any gossip about her experience with Lars, and her eyes nervously checked her friends' enquiring expressions.

'Well, did you enjoy it?' Bridgette asked.

'Aye, it was very relaxing – so much so that I fell asleep.' She looked sheepish as she waited for their reaction.

'Your massage therapist must be good. I struggle to let go during a massage,' Bridgette said.

Marjory gripped her empty glass and lowered her eyes. She'd had no trouble letting go. The experience had left her feeling elated, and, like a drug, she was anxious for more.

'It's down to my rigorous gardening,' Bridgette continued. 'My muscles are always taut; they're impossible to loosen after a long session.'

'Bridgette, the only muscles you use are in your tongue.' Emily was indignant. 'You have a team of gardeners who bend under your instructions at Chez Haworth. Flaxby Manor's estate could never open to the public if it was left solely to you. You merely prune the roses. The only thing you plant are your size three feet on any gardening backside that doesn't follow your precise instructions.'

A vein began to pulse in Bridgette's forehead. 'Well, really! You have no idea how much hard work I put in. If it weren't for me, the manor would never have open days for the public to enjoy.'

'We know how hard you work,' Serena butted in. 'The garden is a credit to you, Bridgette.' She smiled at the waiter, who'd returned with another bottle of champagne.

She nodded when he asked if he should pour and decided to change the subject. 'I had a lovely relaxing day by the pool and I've decided to start an Instagram account which I will launch here at Sparadise.'

'Insta what?' Marjory asked. Her glass had been replenished and she ran her tongue around the edge, funnelling her lips, and then sucked.

'Serena, I don't understand why you need to do that,' Emily said, thinking of Joe and Jacob, who constantly used social media.

'Isn't it rather vain?' Bridgette frowned.

Serena sighed. Her friends knew how disappointed she'd been when her show was axed and how difficult the time that followed had been. But as they tried to digest the logic behind Serena's news, they struggled to follow her intentions.

'So, let me get this clear,' Emily said and stared at Serena, 'You parade about in the skimpiest of outfits, then take a selfie and post it online? What on earth has that got to do with your cookery career?'

Serena explained her plan. 'When I was on TV, fans rarely used the internet, but now you *have* to engage with social media. If I can create an online presence by posting on Instagram, I can guide my followers to my genuine passion for cooking.'

Marjory was struggling to keep up. She wasn't sure who Serena was posting her pictures to and wondered if she had a good supply of stamps. The champagne had made her feel light-headed. She wasn't used to alcohol other than the swift half pint she had with the girls after swimming.

Surprisingly, Bridgette was entirely in tune with Serena's reasoning and, with her head tilted to one side, considered the possibilities. 'I can see why you would do it. If you can't get back on TV because your profile has fallen through the floor, gaining followers and notoriety on social media will give you visibility again.'

'Yes, exactly!' Serena sat forward, suddenly enthusiastic.

'Perhaps you could make the photos of yourself more food-focussed?' Bridgette asked.

Emily scoffed and shook her head. 'Like a naked Nigella?'

'Why not?' Bridgette asked. 'Sexual suggestion whilst demonstrating recipes hasn't done Nigella any harm.'

'You're absolutely right.' Serena beamed at Bridgette.

Bridgette took a sip of her drink. 'We never looked back once we got an Instagram account for the manor. When the gift shop opened, I had the team take photos of everything and the account went crazy. It's your window to the world and the perfect place to sell yourself.'

'I don't like the idea of "selling" yourself,' Emily said. 'Why on earth would you want to compete with this young chef, Yvette? Especially if it means taking your clothes off all the time.'

'It's the only way I can think of to get back in the media.' Serena sighed.

'But you are beautiful just the way you are,' Emily insisted. 'Surely that's enough?'

'Not when the world I know is passing me by and denying me the chance to work.'

'If I looked like you, I would be so grateful. You should

try a day in my shoes and see how the world passes me by.' Emily shrugged. She couldn't reason with Serena.

'Serena, you don't need to compete with anyone. You are perfect as you are, and you have a lovely home and happy life,' Marjory declared.

Serena resisted the urge to scream. Her lovely home felt like a prison, and the happy life that Marjory mentioned sent Serena climbing up the walls as she tiptoed around Cornelius's deflated ego. Why couldn't they understand that she longed to cook again and share her extensive skills? To be in the limelight with the buzz of a studio, being a celebrity with nerves on edge and adrenaline throbbing as the cameras filmed her on live TV? It had been a white-knuckle ride in her heyday, and Serena wanted her seat back on the media roller coaster.

The waiter returned and told them that their table was ready. Everyone stood as he took their glasses and placed them on a tray. But Marjory, who was giggling, had fallen back onto the sofa. 'Whoops!' she said as she attempted to get to her feet.

Serena hooked her arm under Marjory's shoulder and soon had her upright. 'Come on, let's get some grub into that tum of yours.'

They were led into the restaurant and Bridgette's eyes lit up when she saw the table with crisp white linen, cut-glass goblets and gleaming cutlery. 'This is perfect,' she said and reached for the wine list. 'Drinks are on me. Wine all round?'

Emily unfolded her napkin and, shaking it out, placed it on her lap. A group from the yoga class sat at the adjacent table. As she glanced at their elegant loungewear and smelt their designer perfume, she felt sure that they were giggling at her expense. Running her fingers over the creases in her cotton slacks, Emily heard the words, "Red cotton crotch." She winced, wishing that she was anywhere but in the presence of these yoga vipers who made her feel so inadequate. *Damn!* she thought as she reached for her wine. She'd come to Sparadise to relax but felt so wound up.

'Everything alright, Emily dear?' Bridgette asked.

'Yes, I'm just a little bit tense.'

'Have you heard from your boys?'

Emily rolled her eyes. 'Constantly. I've had an endless stream of missed calls and messages.'

'Joe and Jacob must be missing you.' Bridgette leaned across the table and patted Emily's hand.

'They're missing having me wait on them hand and foot.' Emily sighed. 'They can't cook for themselves and have ignored the stash of meals that I prepared and placed in the freezer. Now, they're adamant that I deposit money into their accounts to cover their takeaways for the weekend.'

'I see.' Bridgette frowned as Emily continued.

'Their Skybox has stopped working, and fearing that life as they know it has come to an end, they're demanding that I sort it all out.'

'But will you?' Serena asked.

'God, no. It was me who suspended the subscription and the internet.' Emily grinned and looked at the concerned faces of her trusted friends, their expressions wide-eyed with surprise. She sipped her wine, and as it aligned forces with the champagne she'd consumed, Emily felt her shoulders loosen and her anger subside. 'I don't know why I'm getting so worked up. I set out to teach Joe and Jacob a lesson and it's only for the weekend.'

'It might do them good,' Bridgette agreed.

'And make them realise how much you do,' Serena said and nodded.

'Enough of me.' Emily sighed and picked up a menu. 'What are we going to eat?'

As they discussed their choices and placed their orders, Emily's thoughts drifted to her earlier experience with Yannis. She would be a fool to let outside forces spoil what had been a superb session. As she'd listened and learnt about yoga and thought about the instructor, Emily realised that she'd forgotten what it felt like to be attracted to someone.

Until now.

Yannis had touched a nerve. With a few kind words, a touch of his hand and a smile, he'd awoken an emotional state that she'd never expected to acknowledge again. Now, as she stared at the plate of food placed before her, Emily knew it was ridiculous to feel this way. Yannis was hardly older than Jo and Jacob and at least half her age. She knew it was wrong to have feelings about the young man that could never be reciprocated. But as she picked up her knife and fork and placed finely minced chicken into her mouth, she made up her mind to change. Emily wasn't quite sure what the change would be, but as she turned to glance at the yoga students, she vowed that they would never laugh at her again.

'Penny for your thoughts?' Marjory leaned over the table and touched Emily's hand. 'You're miles away.'

'Er, sorry… I was thinking about my yoga class today.'

'Yezz, yoga! Did you enjoy it?' Two-thirds of the way down a bottle of wine, Marjory had begun to slur her words.

'I did and I've booked some one-on-one sessions with the instructor.'

'With Yannis?' Serena and Bridgette chimed in.

'Yes, why not?'

'Coz, he's gorgeeeeous.' Marjory swayed in her seat.

'He's very young.' Bridgette looked puzzled.

'Yannis is an excellent instructor, and I think he will fast track my learning. I know it's expensive, but to hell with the cost.'

'Good for you,' Serena said. She was pleased that another member of their group was using the weekend to enhance their life. Raising her hand, she high-fived Emily.

'I've booked more mazzages,' Marjory announced. She closed one eye in an attempt to focus on their faces.

'Good grief, Marjory, you're squiffy.' Emily's cutlery clattered as she dropped her knife and fork on her plate.

'Yez, and it's as good as a mazzage.' Marjory grinned.

Serena placed her elbows on the table and cupped her chin in her hands. 'Why don't you tell us all about it?'

Marjory wobbled to her feet and shouted, 'It woz bloody marvellous. I had one of them organisms!'

The room suddenly became silent as heads turned to stare at Marjory.

'You know when folks talk about sex and th'earth

moving?' she continued, 'Well a bloody big bulldozzzer came ploughing throoo the room and shifted 'alf a ton from under me.' Marjory raised her arms then blew kisses towards the ceiling. Her blue curls bounced as her head swayed. 'I've never felt owt like it,' she exclaimed and thumped the table with both hands. 'Lars should be bottled and wrapped and sent to everyone for Christmas.'

Serena began to giggle as Robin and Stevie called out, 'Another bottle of bubbles for the ladies on table four.'

The pimply-faced rep from Lancashire Automotives got to his feet and pointed towards Marjory and said, 'I'll have what she's having!'

His sales manager, who had a lump on his forehead the size of an egg and the makings of a black eye, grabbed the edge of the youth's jacket and tugged him back into his seat.

Bridgette saw the group of runners who'd witnessed her humiliation earlier. They were seated at a circular table nearby and now, with knowing glances, recognised Bridgette.

Marjory, who rocked at an angle, began to move. 'S'cuse me,' she said and lurched forward. 'I need the ladies room – I feel a little strange...'

Serena grabbed Marjory's arm in an attempt to steady her friend, and Emily took Marjory's shoulder. Bridgette attempted a smile as the runners frowned and shook their heads.

'Sorry,' she said, 'it's been a long day, and her treatment must have taken it out of her.'

But it was too late.

Marjory, her skin the colour of custard, began to retch.

Despite Serena and Emily's superhuman effort to hoist her into the air and shove her swiftly through the restaurant, there was no stopping the copious amount of champagne and wine that was swilling about in Marjory's stomach, and it was determined to find its way out.

Sensing an imminent disaster, Stevie grabbed an ice bucket in a flash and threw himself in front of Marjory. As iced water flew through the air, soaking the Lancashire Automotives team, Marjory began to projectile vomit. It shot into the container at speed, splashing several runners.

'Oh really!' one of the runners exclaimed. 'This is too much.' He dabbed at a stain on his shirt with a napkin. 'First, the old woman over there shits herself in public, and now her blue-rinsed friend is throwing up! These people should be locked away. We must speak to the management.'

'Zorry...' Marjory's apologies were faint as she was carried from the room.

Shell-shocked by the runner's cruel words and Marjory's behaviour, Bridgette was rigid as she watched her friends disappear. Stevie still held the slopping bucket and ran alongside. She hardly noticed that a hand reached out to take her elbow and guide her from the room.

'Would you like a brandy?' Robin asked and led Bridgette to a quiet corner in the bar.

'Yes, I think I would.' Bridgette's voice was faint. She appeared traumatised as she collapsed on a sofa. When the drink arrived, she held it to her trembling lips and sipped. 'Everything is going wrong. This was supposed to be such a happy weekend.'

Robin patted her arm and his warm fingers were comforting. 'Whatever has happened is irrelevant.'

'But what must everyone think of us?' Bridgette gulped back a sob.

'Does it matter?' Robin made steady eye contact as he continued, 'I'm sure the staff have seen far worse, and as you don't know any of the guests, why worry? Put it behind you; don't carry it forward into tomorrow.'

Bridgette finished her brandy. The alcohol had a therapeutic effect, and she placed her glass on the table. She'd come to her senses and now stared at the man who had been the start of all her problems. It was all very well for him to be so flippant, but he was sleeping in luxury in the penthouse suite while she had to endure a wretched tent in the garden.

'Thank you for the drink.' Bridgette was curt as she got to her feet. 'I hope you sleep well and that Sparadise has provided you with every possible comfort in the penthouse for its exclusive guests.' She ignored Robin as he rose to accompany her. 'I don't need any help. I am quite capable of making my way back to my tent in the garden, but thank you and goodnight.'

With her head held high and nose in the air, Bossy Bridgette made herself as tall as possible and marched away. As she left the main house and headed to the garden, she told herself that tomorrow, come what may, was another day.

Chapter Nine

Tomorrow, come what may, came far too soon for Bridgette. As dawn broke and a cockerel began to crow, she lay exhausted on her bed. Sunlight, determined to make an entrance, flooded into the Emperor Bell, creating a canopy of gold above Bridgette's head. Over her eyes, Bridgette wore a softly moulded eye mask, but despite the thickness of the fabric, beams of brightness pierced through.

The night had seemed endless, and remembering her shame from the hurtful comments the night before, Bridgette found herself tossing and turning as childhood memories haunted her dreams. She shook her head to clear the teasing cries of the boarding school bullies who'd relentlessly taunted their fellow pupil about her lack of height. 'Here comes Bridgette the midget!' they would chant whenever she braved the group of young girls who were intent on making Bridgette's school life a misery.

She sat up and, with a sigh, pulled off her eye mask. Her university days had hardly been any better. For four long years, she studied hard to gain her horticulture degree, and it had been hell. Students studying alongside joked and joshed when Bridgette climbed onto seating in the lecture rooms or perched on her bicycle to travel around campus, her little legs struggling to reach the ground.

'Fight back!' Bridgette's mother had instructed whenever she found her daughter sobbing at the start of a new term. 'Stand up for yourself.' She held little kindness for her daughter's despair.

'I could have done,' Bridgette grumbled, smarting even now at her mother's inappropriate words, 'if only you'd blessed me with taller genes.'

Over the years, she did toughen up. It was Bridgette's survival instinct not to give in to anyone who put her down. When she married Hugo, with status at her fingertips, staff at the manor had named her Bossy Bridgette. She had ignored the nickname and determined that she would never be ridiculed again. But now she flushed as she remembered how humiliated she'd felt last night when the group of runners had hurled their insults.

'Can things get any worse?' she wailed and pinched the top of her nose.

Rubbing her weary eyes, Bridgette could scarcely believe that Marjory had made such a damn fool of herself. It wasn't as though she was a slip of a girl. The woman was sixty-eight, for heaven's sake. To announce to a packed house that she'd had an orgasm during a massage was distasteful and, to top it all, she had been as drunk as a skunk. Thank goodness Serena and Emily had dragged her out before she could do any more damage.

Bridgette swung her legs over the side of the bed. But she suddenly stopped when she remembered a more disturbing event that had occurred when she returned to her tent.

At the edge of the garden, with no additional lighting to guide her, darkness had fallen like a thick, muggy blanket. Bridgette opened a gate that led to the glamping area and fumbled about for her mobile. She retrieved her glasses from her bag and squinted at the screen to find the torch on the phone. A narrow beam of light was sufficient to illuminate the route. Bridgette cursed as she stepped over clumps of grass and negotiated piles of crusty cow poo. Two bunnies hopped ahead and froze in surprise, their eyes glinting in the torchlight as Bridgette approached.

'Bugger off bunnies!' she had shouted.

A little way off, the shape of the Emperor Bell came into view. The silhouetted structure looked sinister in the dark, and Bridgette glanced nervously from side to side. Going back to nature was all very well, but an electricity cable wouldn't have gone amiss with a few lamps to light the way. To her surprise, as she tentatively made her way around the side of the tent, she saw flames flickering from a campfire, sending sparks high into the sky.

Puzzled, Bridgette stopped in her tracks. Who on earth had lit a fire on such a hot and humid night? Flames crackled and waves of smoky heat wafted over her, and just when she thought she'd seen it all that night, a naked man appeared from the other side of the campfire.

'Oh, my goodness!' Bridgette exclaimed and jumped

back. Her mouth fell open and she clutched a hand to her racing heart.

'Good evening, Empress,' Norman said. 'I thought you might head a little off course on your return in the dark, so I lit a fire to guide you in.' Norman stepped towards her, his long, knobbly feet as naked as the rest of his body. 'Fires were a lifeline when I was lost in the desert. If you take my hand, I can escort you to your abode.'

'N… no.' Bridgette thrust her hands into the pockets of her skirt. She turned her body away to shield her eyes from this flagrant flaunting of naked flesh. She couldn't remember the last time she'd seen Hugo's genitals, and she had no desire to be reminded of what swung between an elderly gentleman's legs.

Norman stood before Bridgette. 'I can see that you're unused to naturism, but don't be afraid. It is a lifestyle of non-sexual social nudity and a joy to embrace, especially as one matures.'

'I'm p… p… perfectly happy with my clothes on, thank you very much,' Bridgette spluttered.

'When you peel off your outer layers, you remove your worries and stresses. You look to me as though you have the weight of the world on your clothed shoulders.'

'If you could please point me in the direction of my tent, I'll be happy to be on my way and let you get back to…' Bridgette flapped her hand in the direction of the fire.

'I'll do better than that. I'll escort you.'

Norman reached down and took Bridgette's shoulder and gently guided her away from the fire and over the guy lines to the stretch of grass that led to the Emperor Bell.

Bridgette was horrified.

She silently prayed that no one could see into the garden from the house. Imagine what people would think if they saw her being led by a naked man to her tent! But, in truth, she was grateful. The route had been dark and bumpy, and as they reached their destination, she'd almost fallen as she clumsily banged into a deckchair.

'Ouch!' Bridgette cursed as her shin hit the hardwood.

'My fault. I should have been more attentive. I dealt with darkness when I was a sniper in the Foreign Legion.' Norman bent to examine the injury.

Bridgette stared at his naked back as his fingers rubbed at the area where she felt pain. She thought he was in pretty good shape for his age as she flashed her torch over his firm skin. Norman stood up and his thick chest hair, the colour of snow, brushed softly against the flesh on her arm. Bridgette, with a flinch, pulled sharply away.

'Take these,' he said and removed a bracelet of wooden beads. 'They will keep you safe.' He took her arm and placed them on her wrist. 'The great Dalai Lama gave them to me when I was at a prayer retreat in Nepal.'

Powerless to resist, Bridgette felt the smooth wood against her skin.

'If you'll allow me to find the mechanism to allow entry,' he said and, bending at the waist, reached for the zip on the tent.

It was a sight that Bridgette thought of from her bed as she looked at the bracelet of wooden beads wrapped around her wrist. If Hugo had been there, he would have remarked that Norman's exposed behind was the perfect place to park a bike.

Bridgette shook her head to get rid of the memory of the previous night. It was simply unacceptable! How much more would she be asked to endure?

She tentatively lowered her toes until they encountered the top of her Louis Vuitton cases, having piled them up the night before to enable her to climb into bed. Easing her body down, she vowed that she would complain to the management. But, as her weight landed on the top case, it slid away and with a cry of despair, Bridgette stumbled, ending up face down on the rough coconut matting. With a shudder, and feeling useless, Bridgette thought she might sob.

In the distance, she heard the gentle tinkling of the wind chimes that hung outside Norman's tent, and the cockerel continued to crow his morning chorus to the wakening world. Bridgette thought of her luxurious home in Flaxby and Hugo, who would laugh his head off if he could see his wife now. The bullies' taunts from her earlier life whispered in her ears.

In less than twenty-four hours, she would be seventy years old, and at that very moment, she felt twice her age. But as Bridgette heaved herself to her feet and straightened her pyjamas, a surge of adrenalin began to course through her veins.

What on earth was she doing? She was Bridgette Haworth, owner of a beautiful manor house and president of Flaxby Women's Institute. She might be reaching her final years, but she was an award-winning garden designer and guest speaker on cruise ships worldwide.

'Pull yourself together,' she told herself, 'and sod being seventy!'

Perhaps it really *was* time to come out of her comfort zone, Bridgette thought as she reached for her robe. She was determined to find Danka to insist that more suitable accommodation be made available. Tucking slippers into her pocket and slipping her feet into her leather pumps, Bridgette set off.

The grass was damp with dew underfoot, and she trod carefully. Above, a misty blue sky was tinged with puffs of brilliant white clouds and birds, as though dancing, swooped and spun on warm thermals. For a moment, Bridgette began to relax. She paused and held her face up to embrace the sun which, as it rose, held the promise of another scorching day ahead. Her shoulders loosened and she took a deep breath, then closed her eyes, breathing in the scents and rhythms of the countryside. Cows mooing in an adjacent field sounded like music, and even the cockerel was no longer annoying. Slowly, a smile spread across Bridgette's face.

'Empress! Let your skin feel nature. Cast off your clothes and be at one with the earth.'

The smile disappeared as fast as it had arrived.

Bridgette scowled as she spun around to see Norman, silhouetted in the sunshine and standing as straight as an arrow with his hands resting on the windbreaker by his tent.

Bridgette's feeling of well-being dissolved. Her nostrils flared as she glared at the man. Did he never sleep?

'Be brave! Now is a time of light and life. Align yourself with the splendour of nature.'

Bridgette felt the urge to reach up and align her fist into Norman's face and end his insistence that she remove her kit and join him in naturism. She would not be bullied again! Unable to think of a suitable reply, she turned on her heel and stomped off.

Leaving her pumps by the door in the hallway of the main house, Bridgette stood by the desk and, reaching for the bell, shook it for several seconds.

'Where is that wretched girl?' she mumbled.

Bridgette was surprised to see Emily, dressed in leggings and a vest, race barefoot down the stairs as she looked around.

Emily stopped when she saw Bridgette. 'What on earth are you doing up at this time? I thought you'd be flat out breathing in the scents of the countryside and enjoying all that fresh air.'

'You have no idea, Emily dear,' Bridgette sighed. 'My weekend is turning into a nightmare.'

'I know Marjory overdid things a bit last night, but there's no need to be so dramatic; she's probably overexcited about being here.'

Bridgette decided not to argue. Reasoning with Emily when she had her headmistress's hat on was pointless. Marjory's behaviour was inexcusable, but Emily would give her the benefit of the doubt.

'I want to find Danka,' Bridgette said. 'I need to speak to her urgently about my neighbour.'

'Well, I'd like to help,' Emily glanced at her watch, 'but I've managed to book a very early appointment, and I don't want to be late.'

Bridgette watched Emily hurry from the hall and into the corridor that led to the beauty treatment rooms. Was that red cotton dangling from an uneven seam across her bottom? Bridgette wondered how her friend allowed herself to be seen in such shabby attire. What was Emily up to?

A door opened and Danka appeared 'Hello Mrs Haworth. Are you looking for me?'

Danka was wearing the shortest skirt Bridgette had seen since the sixties. White leather clogs highlighted her long legs, and a tunic top emphasised the golden tan on her youthful face and arms. A false ponytail swished from side to side as she moved, reminding Bridgette of a pony she'd owned as a girl.

'I like your beads,' Danka said, staring at the wooden bracelet on Bridgette's wrist.

Bridgette looked up as Danka towered over her. 'I need to speak to you about the gentleman residing in the tent next to mine.'

'You mean Norman, our naturist.'

'Yes, that's him. I find his parading about in the all-together quite unacceptable.'

'Mrs Haworth,' Danka began and reached down to pat Bridgette's shoulder. 'Norman is a gentle soul who spends all his holidays at Sparadise. Guests who come to stay in our glamping area are charmed by him. They join in with his way of life, embracing the freedom in the safe environment that we provide.'

With a sinking feeling, Bridgette began to feel as though she was pushing water uphill.

'In fact, we have many repeat bookings for the Emperor Bell for that reason, and you were fortunate that we were able to accommodate you there.'

'B... b... but,' Bridgette began to splutter, 'I reserved the penthouse, and you put me in a tent. It's the last place I want to be.'

'Don't upset yourself.' Danka smiled an angelic smile. 'We don't want a repeat of yesterday's little accident, do we?'

'It wasn't my fault that I fell into cow poo...' Bridgette bristled, suddenly sensing that she was being manipulated, but Danka took her arm and led her to the restaurant.

'Please be calm. To benefit from your stay at Sparadise, it is important that you rid yourself of any stress. After all, it is your big party tomorrow night.'

Bridgette hardly heard Danka's words as she struggled to keep up with the woman's sizeable strides.

'Why don't you relax and start the day with a delicious, invigorating smoothie?' Danka pulled out a chair and Bridgette sat down. 'I'll be back in a moment.'

Feeling grumpy and cross that she hadn't got her way, Bridgette looked around. It was still early, and she was the only guest up for breakfast. A shadow fell across the room as a group of runners in matching caps, T-shirts and shorts, jogged past the long windows that ran down one side of the building. Ducking her head, Bridgette hoped they hadn't seen her.

Danka reappeared with a tray and placed it on the table. She handed Bridgette a cloudy green mixture in a tall glass. 'Here you are. Drink this lovely pick-me-up – it is full of beneficial herbs and all your cares will vanish away.'

Bridgette took the glass and sniffed at the contents. Taking a sip, which left a frothy moustache on her upper lip, she sighed deeply then put her head back and drank.

The smoothie was delicious and Bridgette felt herself relax. As she sat enjoying the peace and quiet, she ran a finger around the rim of the glass and licked every last drop. Eventually, she looked up to catch sight of a waiter. Perhaps it *was* time for her to let some of her cares vanish away, Bridgette thought, and with a smile, she ordered another drink.

Chapter Ten

E mily felt furtive as she hurried along the corridor and hoped she didn't meet anyone else. Bossy Bridgette had wanted to question her about her activities, but Emily had no intention of sharing anything until she'd completed her task. Finding a stylist to open the hair salon so early on a Saturday had been difficult. Now she was financially twenty quid lighter before she'd even had her consultation.

Marjory had been sound asleep when Emily crept out. The woman's snores vibrated off every surface – the tremors must surely register on the Richter scale. Marjory's sleeping cacophony had reached a crescendo of deafening proportions and Emily just hoped the residents in the penthouse above hadn't been disturbed.

She'd reached the salon and, glancing eagerly through the window, saw a lean and muscular man jingling a bunch of keys as he came towards her.

'Hang on. Phillipe is coming and the gateway to loveliness is about to be unlocked.'

The door opened and Emily nervously stepped in.

The man took one look at Emily's hair and shook his head. 'I can see why you need an emergency appointment,' he said. Clipping the keys to a loop on his perfectly pressed Versace jeans, he took her hand. 'Come this way. Step forward and let me lead you to another life.'

Emily was guided to a chair and settled into the soft, squishy leather. With a flick of his wrist, the stylist engulfed Emily in a massive cloak-like gown. She saw a flash of gold from a bracelet that sat amongst layers of leather and beads, twisting around his heavily tattooed arm.

'Do you like the sleeve?' he asked and rolled his shirt up to reveal the full extent of the tattoos on his arms. 'Have you ever thought of having body art?'

Emily had never considered putting her flesh under an inky needle. The very thought made her feel queasy. 'No, I haven't, but yours looks great.'

'So, tell me, what are we going to do with this lot?' His fingers pulled at a section of Emily's long grey hair. 'It looks dreadful and the condition is appalling.'

Tugging at chunks and moving her head from one position to another, he stared at their reflection in the mirror. 'You look like an old witch, if you want me to be brutally honest.'

Emily hadn't wanted him to be quite so realistic about her appearance, but the words hit home like a sharp slap. Gritting her teeth, her bright-blue eyes locked with his steely grey gaze.

'Chop it off!'

'Atta girl!'

'I want colour too. Brighten me up and make me noticeable.' Emily was caught up in the spirit of the makeover. 'Channel the energy of a late-blooming flower into my hair.'

'You betcha.' He began to smile and his pearly-white veneers shone like a dental advert.

'I want people to sit up and notice me. Make my days of disappearing into the wallpaper a thing of the past.'

'Challenges like this are as rare as rocking-horse droppings, but it is a challenge that I accept.' He beamed at Emily and, tossing back the chocolate-brown tinted curls that lay on his shoulders, asked, 'Are you ready?'

Emily nodded.

Ten minutes later, she sat with her hair washed and combed.

'Now, I want you to put your complete trust in me.' He raised knife-like scissors and a long-tailed comb.

Emily thought Phillipe looked like he was about to conduct an orchestra, not redesign her appearance. She sipped at a delicious green smoothie that he'd kindly ordered, describing it as a 'pick-me-up'. The chilled drink slid easily down her throat and she licked her lips. 'Cut away, maestro.'

She wished Stephen could see her now. For years her errant husband had nagged Emily to cut her hair, but she'd always refused. Before grey had taken over, Emily's locks had been caramel in colour, and she'd worn various Alice bands to scoop the tresses back – a style that Stephen claimed aged his wife.

As Phillipe chopped, Emily's hair fell to the floor. The

years fell away too. She realised Stephen had been right. No wonder he'd left her for a student twenty years younger who had short and spiky hair. Who'd want to wake up next to a woman who looked twice her age?

Emily finished her drink and soon began to relax. The snip of Phillipe's scissors was almost melodic, and Emily yawned. Was Stephen happy, she wondered? She hadn't seen him since the day they'd mutually agreed to divorce, with Emily retaining the house and Stephen sending periodic payments to support the boys. Over the years, she'd learnt that he'd become a father again and was surprised that this knowledge was painful.

Emily had cried in anguish when Stephen remarried and cried even more when his daughter was born. Unable to endure the heartbreak, she'd vowed that she'd never have another romantic involvement. Her teaching career became her priority, along with raising her sons. But as Emily gazed at her reflection and Phillipe continued to style her hair, she began to think of Yannis.

There was no harm in looking, she told herself.

'I'll have another one of these, please,' Emily said and, holding out her glass, she looked in the mirror. She was surprised to see that a confident smile now lit up her face.

Marjory was asleep on her bed with her back flat on the mattress. Around her head and shoulders, Emily had thoughtfully positioned two pillows to stop Marjory from lolling to one side. Her hands were folded across her body, the fingers intertwined, and her plump legs, heavy and horizontal, resembled logs on a forest floor. At the same time, her feet, like the branches of a tree, stuck out at right angles.

An almighty snore that began in her tummy and roared through her chest woke Marjory. As her eyes popped open, she felt a red-hot poker of pain in her head and, not daring to move an inch, closed her eyes as quickly as she'd opened them.

Marjory wondered if she was dead.

Every joint ached, her mouth was as dry as a desert, and her head pounded liked it was being drilled. Daring to move her fingers, she connected with a cotton sheet. Had she been laid out and embalmed? Was this how hell felt? The temperature in the room had reached furnace levels, and she could almost see the shape of the devil, a goatlike creature dancing before her, horns sharp and pointed.

'I promise I will never drink alcohol again,' Marjory whispered through dry and cracked lips as the devil's red trident thrust out. '*Please*, just let me live a little bit longer.'

There was a banging noise, and she wondered if someone was beating on a drum. Marjory tried to move but felt dizzy, and the room began to blur and sway.

'Don't get up.' A woman spoke and a key turned in the lock. Danka came in carrying a silver tray. 'I thought you might be feeling a little under the weather this morning and I've brought you something to restore the electrolytes in your dehydrated body. It is a healthy pick-me-up, full of vitamins and herbs.'

Marjory opened one eye and tried to focus on the angel that stood before her.

'Let me make you more comfortable.' Danka eased Marjory's limp body forward, then plumped up her pillows and, placing both hands under her shoulders, tugged her into a sitting position. 'Drink this,' she said and held out the glass. 'It will help.'

'You're so kind,' Marjory mumbled as a glass connected with her parched lips, and she sipped the cold liquid.

'You have a massage today,' Danka said and moved to open the window wide. 'It will be difficult to re-schedule and there has been a flood of enquiries. Everyone wants to book in with Lars.' Danka tweaked and straightened the sheet on Marjory's bed.

'I w... won't miss it.' Marjory drained her glass. 'Thank you, Danka.'

Danka took the glass. 'All part of the Sparadise service. It's a beautiful morning, and I hope you have a wonderful day.' She opened the door and disappeared.

Marjory lay still, and as minutes ticked by, she began to feel better. Miraculously, the pain had started to disappear, and the aching in her skull was fading. Her mouth no longer felt like the bottom of Reg's pigeon coop, and the lurching and gurgling in her stomach had subsided. She reached out to see if the bed was still rocking, but that too had calmed, and her body, now restful, suggested that the devil wasn't cursing her wicked ways. As she felt her muscles relax, she wondered what Danka had given her in that drink. She said it was full of vitamins. Marjory thought the ingredients should be patented and bottled as a hangover cure. She visualised filling the chiller cabinet at the Co-op with the wonder drink. It would sell out in seconds on a Sunday morning when half the male population of Flaxby came in for a newspaper, instantly undoing the effects of Saturday night in the working men's club next door.

With the pillows supporting her back, she raised her head and noticed a nightshirt folded neatly on the counterpane of Emily's bed. Emily must have chosen an early breakfast too. Craning her neck to look out the window, she saw a figure in the garden below.

'Eh, fancy. What's Bossy Bridgette doing up so early?'

Bridgette was heading away from the main building, and Marjory wondered if her friend had risen to take advantage of an early breakfast. The little woman had a spring in her step, and it was with surprise that Marjory watched her take hold of the wooden strut on a gazebo, lean to one side and begin to dance around it. Cocking her ear, Marjory felt sure she could hear Bridgette singing.

'I am sixteen, going on seventeen...'

Marjory swung her bare feet to the carpet. She hurried to the window to stare out at Bridgette, now sitting on a garden swing, feet airborne and swaying from side to side.

'Fellows I meet may tell me I'm sweet and willingly I'll believe.'

'Gawd,' Marjory said. 'We just need Julie Andrews and Captain Von Trapp, and Sparadise will have its very own musical.'

But Bridgette had swung too hard and was suddenly

flying through the air, having reached an enthusiastic chorus. Time stood still as Marjory waited for the fallout.

Bridgette landed with a thud, on her hands and knees, in a rose bed.

'Crikey!' Marjory winced, her face screwed up as she waited for the explosion that was sure to come.

'I am sixteen, going on seventeen, innocent as a rose...' Bridgette's head appeared from a tangle of old-fashioned Blossomtimes. Pink petals clung to her unruly bob as she pulled herself to her feet and brushed peaty black soil from her face and hands. She skipped away from the border and disappeared down the path.

'Well, I never!' Marjory said and plonked her bottom back on the bed. 'Bridgette must have had an excellent night's sleep to be so perky.'

Marjory looked at her watch. Her hangover had lifted and as she lay back and adjusted the pillows, she thought she might as well have another five minutes in bed, luxuriating in the peace.

As she relaxed, Marjory let out a satisfied sigh. It was lovely to have time to herself and not worry about getting the house clean and Reg sorted. But she felt anxious when she thought about her family. How was Reg coping without her? Were the kids managing? Saturday mornings were always spent picking up washing, dropping off ironing, and arranging to babysit for the evening. She'd been worried, too, about cancelling her Saturday morning cleaning job at Flaxby Civic Centre. Still, Willie, the centre's caretaker, had assured her that he would step in and take of her duties. He told her not to worry and to go and enjoy herself.

With her fingers laced, Marjory rotated her thumbs and, closing her eyes, found herself thinking of Willie. She'd known the widower since they were kids at Flaxby Juniors and, when they'd moved up to secondary school, had enjoyed a bit of a fling. Fumbles behind the bike shed at Flaxby Comprehensive had soon come to a stop when Reg Ecclestone came on the scene and announced that he wanted Marjory as his girl. He'd been about to join the army and she'd felt duty-bound to promise to wait for Reg. But as soon as he got his discharge, she found herself pregnant with their eldest, and they were married before her dad could take his shotgun and blow Reg to smithereens. Willie, she knew, had been heartbroken when his first love was marched, military-style, down the aisle.

'Aye,' Marjory sighed to herself. 'Marry in haste, repent at leisure.'

Over the years, Willie had never given up hope. Despite his marriage, which had ended when Willie's wife went off with the secretary of Flaxby WI, they'd got into the habit of texting each other. At first, it had been to arrange Marjory's cleaning shifts at the centre, but as time wore on, Willie had often asked Marjory to go for a walk with him and Fred, his Westie. Marjory always turned him down – not that she didn't like walking, or dogs for that matter, but it wouldn't be right to be seen out with a widower when she was married herself.

Willie would joke that he still fancied Marjory and was sure that she'd enjoy an illicit weekend away with him. He tempted her with a trip in his vintage motorhome, which, he assured, was always on standby. She had only to name the day.

As she lay on the bed, studying the ceiling, she wondered what might have been if, as a young girl, she'd carried on seeing Willie and they'd married. Would he have been a loving husband, considerate and kind? Reg had none of those qualities, and yet they stayed together.

The story of Marjory's married life began on the day she fell pregnant. It hadn't read well, and while she knew it was hardly a blockbuster romance, despite her frustration, she'd stuck with it.

Marjory sat up. Tears pricked at her eyes, and it was with surprise that she choked back a sob. Why was she so emotional? Was her experience on the massage table the day before the wake-up call that she needed? It had felt like an epiphany and had deeply shocked her. For the first time in her life, Marjory had understood that sexual feelings could be gratifying, pleasurable and not a chore. She shook her head and sighed again. She'd never drunk more than a couple halves of cider in the past, yet last night, feeling elated, she'd necked heaven knows how much champagne and wine. Something strange was happening to her at Sparadise, and she didn't understand what it was.

The phone by the bed suddenly rang, making Marjory jump and shaking her out of her daydream. She ran her fingers through her tangled hair then reached out, wondering who on earth could be calling. 'H... hello?' Marjory's voice was hesitant.

'Hello, Mrs Ecclestone, it's Danka here.'

'Oh, hello Danka.'

'I am calling to tell you that your massage with Lars is in fifteen minutes. Are you feeling better and able to attend?'

'Yes, of course. I'll come straight down.' Marjory sat up.

'Very good. We have a long waiting list, so don't be late.'

Danka hung up, and Marjory eased off the bed and hurried to the bathroom. 'Fancy,' she said to her reflection in the mirror. 'I've got another session with Lars.'

Naked and grinning like the Cheshire cat, Marjory ran to the shower to prepare.

Chapter Eleven

Serena had also risen early and stood on the balcony of the penthouse with Stevie. Thunderous snores vibrating from the room below had driven them out of the lounge, and Serena was under no illusion that Marjory was the cause.

'After her exploits last night, I'm sure Marjory will have a monumental hangover,' Serena said as she took a seat and tapped her fingernails on the glass surface of an outdoor table.

'Don't worry, Danka will have a pick-me-up prepared for your friend, and she will be as right as rain in no time.' Stevie fiddled with the camera on his phone. 'The people at Sparadise are experts at providing the feel-good factor when it comes to blending their smoothies. They have a recipe for every ailment imaginable.'

'Do they have something for washed-up chefs who yearn to capture the limelight again?'

'I am sure they have.' Stevie pushed a plate across the

table. 'Now look sexy and get your laughing gear around this fruit.'

Serena moved her body into position and leaned back into soft squidgy pillows, then crossed her long legs to display acres of buffed and polished flesh. A breakfast buffet was laid out on the table, delivered earlier by room service, with yoghurts, fruit, croissants, and coffee. She picked up a dainty fork and speared a ripe strawberry. Opening her mouth to show a gleam of white teeth, she bit into the fruit. Her eyes twinkled as juice oozed over her chin.

'Perfect.' Stevie zoomed in. 'So sexy.'

Serena wore a high-waisted animal-print bikini and matching wrap. Gold jewellery clinked on her wrists and dangled from her ears, and wedge-heeled sandals added inches to her height as she stood.

'Let me see?' she said.

Robin, who'd wandered out into the sunshine from the French windows that fronted the bedroom, found the pair on the spacious patio. He reached out to pour a coffee and saw that they were scrolling through scores of images as they decided which to post to Serena's Instagram account. 'Do you think we should have a look at the pictures you uploaded yesterday and see how many hits you've had?'

'I hardly dare,' Serena replied.

At their invitation, she'd joined the couple for breakfast.

'I know who you are,' Serena had announced with satisfaction as she'd entered their suite. 'You're the world-famous Haines Hats.'

'You've discovered our secret,' Stevie said and smiled.

'I can't believe it took me so long, but I've been out of the limelight while you have both been basking in it.'

'Hardly, but we do have some famous clients,' Robin said.

'I googled you last night; you're the darlings of the millinery world and I'm so thrilled to have met you.'

'Not as thrilled as we are to make your acquaintance, and we want to help you.'

As the owners of Haines Hats, Robin and Stevie were only too aware that social media could make or break a company. Both remembered how hard their early days had been when they were eager to get hats on heads. They knew that the internet was a powerful tool and had substantially built their followers. Stars of stage and screen regularly posted photos of their well-groomed heads ensconced with a Haines hat at society events.

Robin also knew that Serena would look fabulous in one of his creations. He intended to have her model something suitable during the weekend.

'Be brave, darling,' Stevie said. He fiddled with his phone and opened Instagram, and soon found Serena's account. Scrolling through the half a dozen images of Serena in the spa, sipping a drink or nibbling on an apple, he noted that she'd included the hashtag "#Sparadise" throughout.

'Am I an internet sensation?' Serena bit on her lips as she waited for Stevie to reply.

'Er, not exactly. You have a few likes on each post – some more than others.'

'How many likes?' Serena asked. She gripped her phone in her hand, unable to open it and check for herself.

'Umm, well, there are six likes on the photo of you by the jacuzzi.'

'Six?' Robin and Serena both exclaimed.

'Surely you mean sixty at least?' Serena pleaded.

'I'm afraid not, but it is very early days. Your account has only been activated for a few hours.'

'But Yvette the Chefette gets thousands of likes within minutes of posting.'

'Yvette has been posting pictures for some time,' Robin said.

'And she's also decades younger than me.' Serena's face fell as she found her Instagram account and scrolled through the names. 'The only likes I've had are from the men at Lancashire Automotives. @LocoLad should be blocked – his comment is most distasteful.'

Serena searched for @YvettetheChefette, and her misery was complete when she saw an Instagram video of Yvette wearing a teeny bikini. A chef's bandana was placed jauntily on her pretty head, a serving cloth over her arm. As her dainty mouth bit into a fat spongy scone, the chef fluttered her eyelashes and said, 'Bartley's strawberry jam is my favourite.' She licked thick jam from her pouting lips. 'And I just love Chappells clotted cream.'

Suggestively, Yvette sucked her sticky cream-covered fingers as the hashtags "#Bartleys" and "#Chappells" flashed across the screen. 'Happiness is when everyone likes my cooking,' she continued, pushing her body in front of the camera.

The post had received four thousand likes since it appeared an hour ago, and the comments were still pouring in.

'Bake me happy,' wrote @TumTumTommy.

'You take the cake!' @drooloveryou.

Serena tossed her phone to one side. 'What do I have to do?'

'Be patient. I have an idea.'

'Brace yourself,' Stevie said. 'When Robin has an idea, we all pay attention.'

'You need to continue posting. Keep your theme on food and cooking, which is your passion. Clothes too because everyone loves to see designer items. I have a little trick up my sleeve that may assist your popularity.' Robin looked directly at Stevie, and his smile lit his handsome face. 'I've sent for The Plumed Chapeau.'

Stevie gasped and held his hands to his face. 'Oh, my…'

'The hat will be here by courier this afternoon, and I feel that with one or two adaptions, we will have @SaucySerena making quite a splash.'

'A hat?' Serena asked and leaned forward, tilting her head to catch Robin's words.

'Hats are on trend in the Instagram world,' Robin said. 'The hat is a means of expression and bespoke to the wearer.'

'We normally need at least four weeks' notice to make a bespoke hat,' Stevie added, 'but the hat Robin is referring to would be perfect for you.'

'It will need a few alterations.' Robin sat down opposite Serena and, taking a knife, sliced into a kiwi fruit.

'We made the hat for Deeta von Please. Do you know her?'

'Er, no…'

'She had nipples that you could hang your coat on.' Stevie gave a slight shudder. 'The hat was for the last night of her famous burlesque show in Berlin, but she caught a nipple tassel on her pole the night before the hat was due to be shipped, and you probably know the rest.'

'I have no idea. What happened?' Serena's eyes were wide.

'She was famed for twirling the longest tassels in the business; it was her signature act.' Stevie closed his eyes. 'That night, when the tassels unfortunately wrapped around her pole, they caught her neck too.' He placed his hands on his throat and shuddered. 'In seconds, paralysed in a vice-like grip, upside down and doing the splits, she was strangled.'

'Everyone thought it was part of the act.' Robin gazed into the distance where a line of cows, returning from being milked, wandered into a meadow, tails swishing in a hazy heat.

'By the time anyone realised that she was being throttled, it was too late. She fell like a stone and never danced burlesque again.' Stevie shook his head.

Serena looked from one to the other. 'Oh dear. Was she wearing the hat at the time?'

'Lord, no.' Stevie laughed. 'Wait till you see it, then you'll know why.'

'I couldn't wear anything that's cursed.'

'She never wore it, and anyway, this hat is blessed and it

will be perfect for you.' Stevie patted Serena's arm. 'Now let's tuck into our breakfast, and then we can decide which photos to post today.'

As they ate, Robin and Stevie discussed ways of raising Serena's profile. She poured coffee and, holding the delicate china cup and saucer in her hands, stared out to study the grounds at Sparadise. There was a fantastic view from the penthouse, and she could see as far as the lake.

On such a beautiful day, the water looked enticing, and Serena contemplated a swim. In a field alongside, the glamping tents were grouped in twos, some distance apart. Serena's eyes followed a female figure who was dancing along the garden pathway. Wearing a robe, she appeared to be enjoying herself. She watched the person stop and unlatch a gate, then pirouette into a field and skip towards the first pair of tents. The sun was dazzling, and Serena couldn't make out who it was. She only hoped that they didn't disturb Bridgette, who was probably still asleep.

The coffee was delicious, and as she sipped, Serena's attention was caught by an object moving haphazardly through the maze directly in front of the hair and beauty salon. A bright ball in shades of red, lilac and orange bounced between the manicured hedges. As it bounced toward a path that led to the yoga studios, she realised that the ball was the head of a body clad in the brightest and tightest Lycra Serena had ever seen.

'My goodness, someone's going to light up an exercise class today. They will put Emily in her scruffy old leggings to shame.'

'What did you say?' Stevie looked up and licked flakes of pastry from his lips.

'Nothing important,' she replied.

Stevie reached for a croissant and slathered it with butter. He rolled his eyes as he caught Robin shaking his head. 'I know I shouldn't, but these are so hard to resist.'

'We'll be here for at least another week if you keep filling your lovely face.' Robin leaned in and moved the plate out of Stevie's reach. 'Haven't you got a session with a trainer in the gym this morning?'

'Don't remind me of the torture. I need this to keep my energy levels up.' In two bites, Stevie had eaten the croissant.

'I think I'd better catch up with my friends. Should we meet up later?' Serena placed her empty cup on the table.

'Of course. Leave your Instagram account to me,' Robin said. 'I have your login details.'

Serena picked up her robe and placed it over her shoulders. 'Thank you both,' she said and gave each a peck on the cheek.

'Have a restful morning,' Stevie called out as Serena crossed the patio and stepped into the suite. 'Don't twizzle any tassels!'

Serena took the stairs to the floor below and knocked on the door to Marjory and Emily's room. There was no reply. She wondered if they'd left a message in their WhatsApp group and, digging into her pocket, found her phone.

A text message appeared.

'Dodger sends doggie love.' An emoji of paw marks followed a heart. Cornelius had sent a message from his dog but no news to Serena from himself. She deleted the message, not bothering to reply. Dodger was a delightful animal and she always had a treat for the lovely old Labrador in her pocket. The poor thing was probably plodding across miles of deserted fells behind Cornelius with not a soul to be seen nor a rabbit to chase.

She scrolled through her phone until she found the WhatsApp group chat. Marjory had left a message to say that she was having a massage but asked if they could all catch up for coffee at elevenses?

Emily had been cryptic and said, 'There's a new me at Sparadise. Meet for coffee and you will see.'

Bridgette hadn't replied.

'Hmm,' Serena sighed. 'Bossy Bridgette is still in bed. I'd better go and wake her up before she misses the morning's activities.'

Placing her phone in a pocket, Serena set off for the glamping area.

The Emperor Bell appeared larger to Bridgette as she returned from her meeting with Danka and bounded across the grass. She waved to a family of bunnies munching on their morning meal, and as she approached the tent, Bridgette saw that the top seemed to rise high into the sunny sky. Supporting guy lines were staked to the ground and reminded her of string that she had often wound around her little fingers at Brownies when playing the cat's cradle game. As she came around the side of the tent, not looking where she was going, she tripped over a line and reached out to steady herself. Grabbing hold of a deckchair, Bridgette teetered. But the chair put up a fight and collapsed into itself in true deckchair fashion, taking Bridgette with it.

'La di dah,' Bridgette sang as her bottom landed on the damp grass, her unkempt head protruding through the striped canvas.

'Oh! Mrs Haworth, you made me jump.' A housekeeper appeared, work bucket in hand. She stared at Bridgette, then nodded her head knowingly. 'You've had one of Danka's vitamin smoothies for your breakfast. You need to be careful at your age – Danka grows some of the ingredients in a greenhouse and they can be very addictive.'

Placing her bucket beside the chair, she leaned down to assist. She pulled Bridgette out of the canvas, but the wooden frame was not giving up so quickly and clicked, concertina-like, almost severing Bridgette's head.

'Whoops-a-daisy,' Bridgette said as her head fell back, only to be pushed forward again as the housekeeper grappled with the chair and released her.

'There you go,' she said as she hoisted Bridgette to her feet. 'And your tent is all nice and tidy too.'

Bridgette's fingers had left a layer of soil on the woman's hands, and with a frown, she reached into her overall pocket, pulled out a cloth and wiped her fingers. 'I'll be off. I've got Norman to see to now,' she said as she stepped carefully over the guy lines. 'There's a message from your husband by your bed – and go easy on those smoothies.'

Bridgette ignored the housekeeper and went into the

tent.

'Oh, goody,' she said when she saw a note on a table beside the bed. Picking it up, she studied the words.

Message received at 8:30, Saturday morning, 20th June.
To: Bridgette Haworth
From: Hugo Haworth

Message: *Answer your damn phone! You've had your fun and been away overnight. I insist, as your husband, that you return home immediately. Hugo.*

Bridgette blew a raspberry and played with the beads on her wrist. Waving a middle finger at the note, she began to rip it into tiny pieces, which she scattered over the floor.

'Bog off, Hugo,' she sang. 'Bridgette's having the time of her life.'

'Hello? Anyone home?' a voice called out and Serena, stooping low, peered into the tent. 'Is that you, Bridgette?'

'My friend Serena,' Bridgette replied, 'come into my gorgeous glamping tent.'

Serena stepped in and almost stepped right back out again. Was that Bridgette in the soil-stained robe, with rose petals in her unkempt hair, hands and knees blackened and face the colour of soot?

'Good grief, what on earth has happened to you?' Serena asked.

'I had a little drinkie and now I feel sleepy.'

'What on earth have you been drinking at this time of

day?'

'Danka's vitamin pick-me-up.' Bridgette climbed onto the bedside table and leapt onto the bed. 'It's a smooothie...' Her head hit the pillow, and in seconds, she was snoring.

Serena moved forward and, taking a blanket, gently covered her friend. Underfoot, she realised that she had stepped on tiny scraps of discarded paper, and she leaned down to pick them up. Reading the words 'return' and 'home,' Serena wondered who had been in contact. Probably Hugo, she thought, knowing that he was vehemently opposed to Bridgette being away.

She tossed the scraps into a bin. Bridgette appeared comfortable and, deciding to let her sleep, Serena crossed the tent and made her way outside.

'Good morning!' A man passing by on a bicycle touched his hand to his forehead to acknowledge Serena. 'How's the Empress?' he asked as he came to a halt and swung an agile leg over the crossbar.

Serena's jaw dropped. She tried hard to stifle a giggle as she stared at the naked man.

'Norman by name, naturist by nature,' he said as he came forward and saluted Serena. 'Pleased to meet such a glorious goddess on this blessed sunshine day.'

'Hello, Norman,' Serena replied. 'My name is Serena Alleyne, and I'm a friend of Bridgette – I mean, the Empress.'

'Any friend of the Empress is a friend of mine.' Norman gave a bow. 'She's a fine feisty woman who will soon settle at Sparadise.'

'I'm sure she will.' Serena smiled and thought of the body out cold on the bed inside the tent. 'She's asleep at the moment – Danka gave her a vitamin drink.'

'Ah, Danka and her magic potions. Marvellous stuff. We mixed a similar recipe when I was stationed in Algeria.' Norman had a twinkle in his eye. He leaned forward and, in a conspiratorial whisper, said, 'I have the stuff bottled every day and keep it in a fridge in my tent.' He looked up from beneath bushy white eyebrows. 'Would you care to join me for a livener?'

'I'll take a rain check on that, thank you,' Serena replied and tightened the belt on her gown.

Norman stood back. 'Very well. Don't worry about the Empress – I'll keep an eye on her.' He touched a finger to his nose and gave a knowing wink.

'Thank you.' She watched him turn, pick up his bicycle and, with the sagging flesh on his bare buttocks swaying in time with his strides, set off to his tent.

Serena began to laugh. The glamping area was most enlightening. Bridgette had confided to them all at their swimming class that she was tiring of the life that she knew. Reaching seventy was a wake-up call that she hadn't wanted. With the years advancing and no sign of any change in her life, Bossy Bridgette appeared transformed. Serena couldn't help but wonder what on earth her friend had been drinking.

She couldn't wait to meet up with Marjory and Emily and tell what she'd seen. Endeavouring to keep her trainers neat and clean, she sidestepped cow pats and rabbit droppings and hurried back to the spa.

Chapter Twelve

The yoga studio was humming with excited chatter as students in Yannis's class waited for their instructor. For many, these sessions were the highlight of their stay and combined physical practice with mental and emotional well-being. For others, the sight of Yannis was the predominant factor when deciding which classes to take, for the young man had the kind of face that stopped his students in their tracks.

From the depths of his mesmerising blue eyes, Yannis had a natural expression that wore his beauty well. His lean, mean and muscular body meant business, and his students were spellbound when they watched him move gracefully from one position to another. When Yannis glanced at them through long, luscious lashes, he made them fall for him all the more.

Mid-morning sunshine flooded the studio. With the promise of yet another scorching hot day, Yannis stood by the air-conditioning unit, moving the controls until he selected the ideal temperature for his class. With a packed session ahead, he was anxious to have a perfect ambience in which to enjoy it.

'Namaste,' Yannis said and, with palms pressed together, gave a bow. 'Please repeat our salutation.'

Scrambling to their feet, the students turned to one another. 'The light in me sees and honours the light in you. Namaste.'

'Thank you. We are waiting for one more person to join us.' He checked the names on a clipboard and scanned the room. 'However, perhaps, instead of waiting, we should make a start. Please sit comfortably.'

Yannis began with some simple breathing exercises and, in a soft and calming voice, issued instructions. But as the class closed their eyes and inhaled, moving their heads slowly in a circular motion, the door was suddenly flung open. Heads jerked up, and eyes popped wide as a vibrant female vision appeared in the room.

'Namaste, sorry I'm late. I've been up since dawn, but as I was finding my way here, I got lost in the maze.' Emily heard whispers as she moved to the front of the room, and as she unrolled a mat and placed it on the floor within inches of Yannis's feet, several students gasped.

'Emily?' Yannis asked.

'Yes, so sorry, I didn't mean to disrupt the class. Have I missed anything?'

'No, we have only just begun.'

A smile broke across Yannis's face as his gaze travelled

over Emily's appearance, taking in every inch. Her flame-red hair was streaked with lilac and orange and styled in a short cut that flowed with soft, flattering curls around her face. Lavender shades of Lycra moulded to her slim body, lifting and rejuvenating both bottom and bust. Her finger and toenails sparkled with glittery polish, and her skin glowed with tinted moisturiser, highlighting her immaculately made-up face.

'Namaste, Emily,' Yannis said. He gave a bow and smiled at the transformation before him. Then, holding his hands up to quieten the class gossips, Yannis took control.

'We begin again,' he said, 'and today, during our practice, we will discover our doshas.' Yannis spoke with authority and confidence as he slid to the floor in a fluid movement.

Emily had no idea what her dosha might be, but with Yannis guiding the way, she was ready to find out and, folding her legs beneath her body, sat down. She watched Yannis as a shaft of sunlight burst into the studio, and diamonds seemed to dance in a sparkling halo around his head. Dreamlike, she was sure she could hear birdsong, sweet and musical, as a chorus of winged wonders soared on thermals beyond the windows.

As the class lay on their stomachs and performed a backward bend, Yannis's eyes met with Emily's, and, like heat from a fire, his look was warm and reassuring. Secretly, he winked at the new woman who had metamorphosed before him.

Emily broke into a coy smile on her peach-coloured lips

and her pale skin flushed. *He's far too young!* her conscience implored. But Emily thought of Stephen and his young Spanish lover and, biting down on her lip, it was a determined Emily who returned Yannis's intimate look.

Marjory had showered, moisturised, and with freshly styled hair, moved confidently through the corridor leading to the body and beauty treatment rooms. Familiar now with the route, she beamed when she saw Monika in the reception area.

The girl, handing a jar of cream to a pimply-faced young man, waved when she saw Marjory. 'I'll be with you in a moment.'

The youth, known as Loco Lad to his workmates, stood by the desk, dressed in swimwear and slippers. He nodded as Monika assured him that the Sparadise preparation of tea tree oil, lavender and an exclusive herbal ingredient would soon clear his acne.

'Use it twice a day,' Monika said as she watched him apply a coating to his oval-shaped face. 'It will get rid of excess oils and stimulate the circulation.'

Marjory stared as a thick coating of a greenish emulsion covered the lesions and eruptions. She hoped the poor lad was made of stern stuff, for he appeared to be turning into an avocado as the cream adhered itself.

'Good luck,' she whispered as he hung his head and skittered away.

'Hello, Mrs Ecclestone,' Monika said. 'How are you?'

'I wish I felt as good as you look. You must know the secret of Sparadise to look so pretty and healthy,' Marjory replied.

'I've worked here for almost a year, and I take advantage of all the facilities.' Monika held out a towel. 'You have a double treatment today.'

'Have I?' Marjory looked puzzled.

'Yes, Lars has insisted on it. He calls it the Clearing Cleanse; you are most fortunate.'

'But I've just had a shower...'

'Not that sort of cleanse.' Monika touched Marjory's hand. 'It will make you feel fabulous.'

'Oh, very well, if Lars thinks it's necessary.'

Marjory took the towel and, for the umpteenth time, wondered what Reg would think. She knew her husband would shake his head, a frown knitting his brow if he could see his wife following Monika along the corridor and into a treatment room. He'd never embrace anything new unless it had something to do with his pigeons.

As before, she took a towel to cover her body and lay down on the massage table. Gentle music played in the background: waves lapping against a seashore and dolphins whistling. Marjory drifted into a light sleep and had a vision of Flipper and his friends in a Disney movie that she'd taken her grandchildren to see.

Suddenly, she was jolted awake and felt two large hands spread wide across the skin on her back, the fingers gently kneading.

'Today,' Lars whispered, 'we will restore your balance.'

Marjory knew that her balance must be terribly out of sync as she felt the bed sway beneath her and strained to hear what he was saying.

'To begin, we will cleanse the colon to remove waste and gases.'

As Lars explained the procedure, Marjory became tense. *Colon? Gases?* She put a leg out and began to squirm away from the bed. Lars was planning to go where no man had been before, and Marjory, like a horse, was about to bolt. But firm hands grabbed her thigh and manipulated her back into position.

'I will perform a lymph system massage too, which will open the body and draw out toxins using cups.'

Hearing the word 'cup', Marjory relaxed, relieved that they would be having a nice cup of tea with all that was going on.

'After the cupping method, you will have a full-body exfoliation using sea salt and Kama oil, followed by your favourite massage. Soon, you will reach your nirvana.' He spoke softly.

Marjory wondered where nirvana was and if it was a particular treatment room located somewhere on the complex. But as the lights dimmed and Lars began his preparations, she crossed her fingers and gave in to whatever lay ahead.

Bridgette had slept and now, sitting up in her bed, tried to piece together the events of the morning. She knew she'd been to see Danka but couldn't recall why and had a feeling that she'd complained about something, but the reason had escaped her. She remembered sitting on a swing in the garden and, as she soared high, was reminded of happy days in the garden of her childhood home. There had been a message from Hugo, too, insisting that she go home.

The cheek of the man!

Hardly twenty-four hours had passed, and already he was losing his grip, fearful that his wife might be enjoying herself. Thank goodness she'd kept hold of her bank cards and moved money about to ensure that her party tomorrow would be memorable. Celebrating her seventieth birthday with her friends would be no cut-price affair.

Bridgette stretched out. She felt remarkably calm, and tension had eased from her body, leaving her with an unfamiliar feeling of well-being as she looked around her tent. Strangely, it all seemed quite cosy this morning. Why had she kicked up such a fuss when told that the penthouse suite wasn't free? Yawning and rolling her shoulders, Bridgette realised that the aches she felt in her back and associated with old age seemed to have disappeared. She'd dreaded being seventy and couldn't leave the manor fast enough the day before. Hugo and their day-to-day routine had suddenly become stifling but already, Sparadise seemed to be living up to the testimonials they'd all read on arrival.

As she caressed the smooth wooden beads on her wrist, her tummy made a rumbling noise, and she tried to remember if she'd had any breakfast. The delicious smoothie that Danka had given her had been an excellent start to the day. The combination of vitamins must pack a healthy punch, she thought. Whatever it was, to her surprise, Bridgette was beginning to relax and enjoy Sparadise.

She decided that she must catch up with her friends and carefully edged across the bed, gripping the sides, to ease herself down to the floor. That had been easy! Why on earth had she made such a fuss about the height of the bed?

Bridgette pulled back a curtain and, finding a clean robe on the coat stand, she slipped it over her pretty poppy-patterned swimming outfit. Reaching for her phone, she read the messages in the WhatsApp group. Everyone was meeting for coffee, and if she hurried, she might be in time to join them.

Stepping out into the sunshine, Bridgette found her sunglasses in her pocket, then zipped the tent and sidestepped a dismantled deckchair.

'Empress!' Norman called from behind his windbreaker. 'Will you join me for a livener?'

'Oh, really,' Bridgette mumbled, her irritation levels returning. 'Does he never give up?'

Ice clinked against the glass as Norman held out a drink.

But Bridgette decided that it would be rude to ignore his kind gesture. After all, the temperature was cracking the flags, and not only was her tummy still rumbling, but her mouth was parched too.

Stepping forward and keeping her distance, she took the drink at arm's length. 'Thank you,' she said and sipped the delicious, cold liquid. 'I think I had something similar this morning.'

Norman, too, had a drink and pale green froth circled his mouth and beard. 'It's a Sparadise special, and I keep plenty of supplies here in my fridge.'

'Very nice.' Bridgette took another sip.

'Where are you going?' Norman, for once, kept his distance with his lower region screened.

'I'm catching up with my friends. It's my birthday tomorrow and we're having a party. I also need to talk to Danka to plan the food and drinks and decorations.'

'A birthday party!' Norman held his arms out wide as if he was hugging the world.

Two-thirds of the way through her drink, Bridgette began to feel very relaxed as she observed her neighbour's demeanour. 'Well, I'm glad someone is happy, unlike that miserable old git I'm married to, who doesn't know the meaning of the word.'

Bridgette thought of Hugo's constant rants about life and anything that he disagreed with, including Bridgette's busy schedule in her garden and attending her various achingly boring committees. Throughout their marriage, she'd felt that she had to stand up to Hugo to stop him from dominating her completely.

'His misguidance is my gain.' Norman gave a bow and, when he looked up, smiled. The old boy placed his fingers to his lips and blew Bridgette a kiss.

Suddenly, Serena's words telling Bridgette to come out of her comfort zone rang in her ears and, before she could stop herself, Bossy Bridgette Haworth had invited Norman the Naturist to her seventieth birthday party.

'It would be my honour to attend. I remember the grand parties at Raffles when I was out in Singapore,' he said and blew another kiss. 'Shall we celebrate my invitation with a swim?' With a broad sweep of his arm, Norman indicated in the direction of the lake. 'It's a beautiful day and the water will be warm.'

Bridgette looked at the lake, which reflected puffy white clouds and a clear blue sky in water that looked calm and inviting.

'It's quite safe,' Norman said, 'and I will look after you.'

'I'm not a very good swimmer.' Bridgette was hesitant. She felt safe in Flaxby pool with her friends, where a lifeguard patrolled the perimeter, but a lake was a different matter.

'I have inflatables that we can use.'

Bridgette remembered the tall, agile girls from the swimming team at school who had laughed and mocked her tiny hesitant strokes. They'd never included Bridgette in their gang. But again, Serena's words repeated themselves and, without stopping to change her mind, Bridgette knocked back the rest of her drink and handed her glass to Norman.

'Sod it. You only live once.'

Tearing at the belt on her robe, she shrugged the garment off and began to run towards the lake. The poppies on the skirt of Bridgette's swimsuit swayed as her pale arms flung out and her plump legs padded across the grass with Norman in hot pursuit.

'Last one in is a cissy!' she called out and her laugh echoed throughout the grounds at Sparadise. When she reached the jetty, Bridgette stopped and, almost losing her balance, stepped out of her swimsuit, casting it to one side. As naked as the day she was born, she ran along the boards.

'Geronimo!' Bridgette yelled and, holding her nose with two fingers, jumped into the lake.

Chapter Thirteen

Serena had been for a dip in the pool. The weather was getting hotter. As much as she longed to go down to the lake and plunge into the cooling water and wild swim for an hour or two, there wasn't time if she was to meet up with her friends for coffee. She felt relieved that she wasn't focussing on taking endless photos and videos that day. Robin had kindly said he would upload a selection, and she was happy to leave things in his capable hands.

As she showered and towelled herself dry in the changing room, she thought about the wretched Yvette, who seemed to constantly churn out content for social media as though she was a product on a production line. Now considered one of the most important influencers in the culinary world, Yvette was making a fortune endorsing merchandise on top of her TV earnings. Suppliers queued up to knock on her agent's door, offering deals that would keep Yvette financially stable for the rest of her honey-coated life.

Serena felt grateful that for now, she didn't have to worry about money. She'd built up a nest egg while working and her flat in London gave an excellent Airbnb rental return. It was just as well, for Cornelius contributed little these days and other than owning the roof over their heads, had no income, with no art on display and nothing on his easel that he considered worthy enough to sell.

It wasn't that she minded. In his heyday, Cornelius had been generous, and they'd enjoyed many extravagant holidays in exotic locations. 'What's mine is yours,' he'd told her after a trip to Jamaica to retrace Serena's family connections. Despite never officially tying the knot, they didn't quarrel about money. Neither had they minded that their relationship was childless; their careers had been their babies. But now, she thought with sadness, the career babies were unable to grow up and mature. It was as though time had stood still, with Cornelius unable to paint and Serena incapable of reviving the job that she adored.

How she longed to demonstrate in a cookery school again, with a sea of faces eager to learn every tip and skill that she could impart; to receive copious amounts of correspondence from would-be cooks anxious for her advice. Serena had thrived on imparting her culinary knowledge. She missed the satisfaction of seeing students cook for themselves instead of relying on takeaways, or young mums preparing healthy, cost-effective meals and pensioners inspired by her delicious, spicey one-pot wonders.

Things had to change.

Serena scooped her braids into a top-knot and, throwing her bag over one shoulder, went to meet her friends.

It was busy in the Lakeside spa café, which served lighter bites and drinks throughout the day, and had an unspoiled view of the garden and lake. A group of runners occupied most of the lower section seating area, and the team from Lancashire Automotives sat alongside a cluster of yoga students in a balconied section. Serena wandered through the café until she reached a terrace. There was no respite from the heat for those sitting out of the shade, but Serena noted an empty table under a large umbrella and made her way over.

Sitting down and making herself comfortable, she glanced at her watch and wondered where her friends were. Marjory's elevenses could be anytime, but Emily and Bridgette were always punctual. A waiter took her order for iced water and peppermint tea, and as she waited, Serena, unable to help herself, flicked open her phone.

There was another text from Cornelius. It was a photo of Dodger standing on the edge of a tarn, with miles of fells in the background. "Wish you were here, woof!" read the caption. As Serena stared at the daft old dog with his mournful brown eyes and soft, silky ears, she wished she was there too. The water in the tarn looked cool and tempting, and had she been at home, she would have plunged in beside Dodger and taken him for a swim. Damn Cornelius, why does he have to communicate via the dog? A personal message would have been far more meaningful. Wrapped up in himself and his inabilities, she knew he would never think of sending something that suggested love and affection.

Feeling angry with her partner, Serena opened her Instagram account.

There were two new images: one of Serena in the animal-print bikini, suggestively eating a strawberry, and another of her standing on the penthouse balcony, looking out at the countryside.

Moments ticked by as she stared at her image. The camera work was excellent, and the boys had captured her perfectly and edited well. These were magazine quality, and, feeling a flicker of excitement, she scrolled down to see how many likes the images had attracted.

In disbelief as she stared at the screen, Serena felt her heart sink. There was a sad total of twenty-two likes and one comment.

'Pathetic old has-been,' @Love2Run.

She gasped, her breaths rapid as she read the hurtful words. How could anyone be so cruel? With fumbling hands, she shut her phone and put it in her bag, then closed her eyes and slumped into her chair.

'Yoo-hoo!' A voice came from the other side of the terrace. 'You look like you've lost a pound and found a penny.' Marjory, hot, flushed and sweating heavily, pulled out a chair.

Serena looked up. 'Hello. You look rather warm.'

'Aye, I'm like a bitch on heat, boiled to a frazzle in this.' Marjory shrugged off her gown to reveal her sagging old swimsuit.

'Have you seen Emily or Bridgette?' Serena asked.

'Nope, I haven't seen Emily since she went to yoga and the last time I saw Bridgette, she was dancing the fandango in the garden.'

'Are you serious?' Serena sat forward. 'Bridgette *was* acting very strangely when I went to visit her in her tent, but before I had time to ask her what she'd been doing, she'd fallen asleep.'

Serena's drinks had arrived, and Marjory, taking the iced water, almost downed it in one. 'Three more glasses and a couple of gallons of this, please,' she said to the waiter. 'Oh, that's better.' She wiped the perspiration from her forehead with a napkin.

Serena and Marjory were deep in conversation as they discussed the whereabouts of their friends and didn't notice that a woman had come into the café. As she moved through the diners, she was causing quite a stir. Heads turned and voices whispered.

'Hello,' the woman said as she reached Serena and Marjory's table.

'Oh,' Marjory began, 'I'm afraid these seats are taken.'

Serena, who was pouring peppermint tea, paused and stared as the woman sat down. 'I'm sorry, but our friends will be here in a moment.'

'I *am* your friend, you silly buggers!' Emily beamed as she looked from Serena to Marjory.

'*What?*' Serena's eyes were like saucers. Her cup overflowed, and tea flooded the table as she stared at Emily's flame-red hair and Lycra outfit.

'Eh?' Marjory spluttered on her water.

'No… it can't be you…'

'By heck, I think I'm dreaming.' Marjory's mouth hung open.

'What... when... how?' Serena was gobsmacked, the teapot motionless in her hand as she stared at Emily.

'Put your eyeballs back in their sockets.' Emily laughed and placed her hands on the arms of her chair. 'Last night, I had an epiphany and I vowed that my life was going to change.'

'Blimey, there's quite a lot of them epiphany thingamy jigs going round at the moment.' Marjory thought of her massages and blushed.

'You've got to tell us what made you do this.' Serena mopped the spilt tea then sat back as she waited for Emily to explain.

'It's because of Yannis.'

'*Yannis?*' Marjory and Serena frowned.

'Yes, Yannis, the yoga instructor.'

'Yes, yes, we know who he is, but what on earth has he got to do with you making a *Stars in Their Eyes* appearance at Sparadise?' Serena asked. 'You've transformed yourself in record time.'

'It took a few hours. I had to pay a fortune to get Phillipe, the hair and makeup stylist, to give me an appointment so early in the day.'

'The colours in your hair look amazing. Much better than my boring old blue.' Marjory wound a curl around her finger, then ran a hand over Emily's bony elastane-covered knees. 'Nice Lycra.'

'He chose that too. There's a sports and swimwear boutique in the beauty salon.'

'But why?' Serena was intrigued.

Emily poured water into her glass and took a sip. First, she looked at Marjory and studied her halo of hair. Then, lingering longer on Serena's immaculate appearance, Emily took a breath and began.

'Serena, you are naturally beautiful and will always attract attention, and Marjory, your personality shines out and people adore you. But do either of you have any idea what it is like to be a drop in an ocean? An invisible fly on the wall?' Her eyes searched their puzzled faces. 'I've never been good-looking or one to turn heads. I don't even warrant a glance.' Emily sighed. 'The only man I've ever loved never gave me a compliment and said I hadn't a clue how to style myself or make the best of what few assets I have.'

'Stephen wasn't a very nice husband. So, why now?' Marjory's voice was gentle as she took Emily's hand.

'Coming here with you all, I felt like I was wearing an old slipper. Being with my friends is safe and comforting because none of you criticise or judge how I look or what I wear. At home, I was invisible to Stephen, which is why he left me and now, I am invisible to my sons. I'm just a silly old woman who hasn't a clue how to communicate with young people anymore. My day-to-day life feels like a treadmill: the same old routine and the same old arguments with Joe and Jacob, pleading and cajoling with them.'

'What changed, Emily? This is such a massive turnaround for you. Tell us – why?' Serena asked.

'I was indifferent when I went to the yoga class. I didn't think it would matter that I wore old clothes. I thought that, like any other day, no one would notice me.' Emily's lashes flickered. A lump had formed in her throat. 'But I… was… so… humiliated.'

'Humiliated?'

'Yes.' Emily paused. 'The others in the class giggled behind my back and sneered and made sarcastic comments when I sat beside them at dinner last night. I was so thrilled by Marjory's outburst – you may have been tipsy, but you dared to announce that your life had changed and to hell with keeping it secret.'

'It was only one of those organisms…' Marjory said.

'An orgasm is life-changing,' Emily said and smiled.

'Aye, well, you have a point, I suppose.'

'So, during the night, while you were sleeping, I made up my mind that I was going to change dramatically, starting with my appearance.'

'Wow…'

'It wasn't hard to get hold of the main stylist at Sparadise. I gave the night manager a very generous tip, and by doing the same with Phillipe, the stylist, I explained that I was only here for the weekend, that time was of the essence, and I found myself sitting in his chair not long after the sun came up.'

Marjory tugged on the sagging elastic of her suit and pursed her lips. 'I wonder if he can do the same with me?' she asked hopefully.

'It's cost a fortune.'

'But it's worth every penny! You look magnificent,' Serena exclaimed.

'Where are your glasses? How can you see?' Marjory asked as she looked around for the plain metal frames.

'I've had contact lenses for ages but never bothered to wear them until now.'

'They seem to make your eyes bigger and bluer.' Marjory examined Emily's eyes.

'I love your makeup. You look years younger,' Serena said as she studied Emily's face.

'Thank you. I appreciate that. I can't tell you how different I feel. It's so exciting, and I feel reborn.'

'Reborn because you've changed your appearance?' Serena looked puzzled. 'Feelings like that usually come from something deeper inside.'

'Well, there is something else.' A flush crept across Emily's cheeks, and she began to shuffle her feet.

'Tell us then.' Marjory edged closer.

'It's Yannis.' Emily looked down, unable to meet their eyes.

'He must be a good instructor to make you feel—'

'Shush! Let her finish,' Serena said.

Moments ticked by as the women waited for Emily to reply.

'I've fallen in love.'

'*In love?*'

'I have fallen in love with Yannis.'

'Bloody hell...' Marjory slumped back in her chair, her arms and legs spread wide as she stared in disbelief. 'You've only just met him!'

'But Emily, Yannis is years younger than you.'

'Yes, I know, but I can tell that he feels the same way.'

'Well, you might find it beneficial to chat through this with all of us.' Serena was thinking rapidly, wondering how she could slow down the pace of Emily's racing emotions.

'By heck, I'd like to see Bridgette's face when she hears this news.' Marjory chuckled.

'Bridgette will go ballistic.' Emily dabbed at her eyes and began to smile. 'But if my bloody husband can hook up with a younger model and get away with it, why can't I?'

'You have a point,' Serena said.

'Aye, you certainly have,' Marjory said and grinned, 'but Mrs Prissy Knickers will blow a fuse when she hears you've got a toy boy.'

'Bridgette can be set in her ways... perhaps we shouldn't tell her just yet?'

Serena suddenly stood up. She'd noticed a crowd, including the runners and yoga students, had gathered on the terrace. They were all looking out across the garden towards the lake. 'I think you might want to see this,' she said as she followed their gaze.

'What is it?' Marjory stood on tiptoe to see what all the fuss was about.

Cries of laughter drifted across the garden from the lake, where two people were flapping about in the water. A woman, astride a giant pink pelican inflatable, clung to the plastic bird with one hand while trailing her free hand to splash her playmate. The playmate, riding a rubber hippo, was not to be outdone. With a rallying cry and galloping legs, he skimmed the surface and upturned the pelican, causing its passenger to fly through the air.

'Good grief. It's Bridgette!' Emily exclaimed.

'Blimey.' Marjory took a step back, her eyes bulging. 'It *is* Bridgette! There's a man with her and unless my eyes are playing tricks, they are both completely naked.'

Serena tucked her hands in the pockets of her robe. She began to laugh as she watched the antics in the lake.

'I think, my lovelies,' she said, 'that Emily's news might not shock Bridgette quite as much as you think.'

'Come on, let's go down to the lake and see what Bridgette is up to. I think the man with her is her neighbour from the next tent.' Serena steered Emily and Marjory away, but as she turned, they heard one of the runners talking to his friends.

'It's hideous. That incontinent old woman is at it again, polluting the lake, disturbing the peace with her obscene antics. We really should address this with the management.' The runner, legs planted wide, was dressed in the tiniest of shorts and a cut-away vest. He removed his cap to reveal a bald head and his nostrils flared as he spoke.

'Oy, Usain Bolt, take a chill pill.' Marjory called out. 'You should be grateful we're not charging you for ringside seats at this show.'

'Well, really...' The runner stared at Marjory's sagging swimsuit and bright-blue hair. 'I hardly think that you and your "organisms" can tell me what to do.'

Emily and Serena closed ranks on either side of Marjory.

'And as for your friends, the ludicrous vision in lavender and the pathetic old TV has-been...' His words trailed off as he stared defiantly.

In a flash, Marjory swung out, her fist narrowly missing the runner's face. Serena and Emily pulled her back and tried to lead her away.

'We've seen your crappy Instagram account!' he called out to Serena. 'You should be banned from posting.'

In an instant, Serena recognised her Instagram troll. Gritting her teeth and tensing her body, it was all she could do not to join Marjory and swing a sharp right hook into @Love2Run's pompous jaw. Marjory, face as red as Emily's hair, fists balled and feet scrambling, tried desperately to reach the runner, but between them, Emily and Serena had her in their grasp and walked her out of the café.

'Vile man,' Serena muttered.

'Pig,' Emily said, loosening her grip.

'If I had a face like his, I'd sue my parents.' Marjory shrugged away from her friends.

'Ignore him and his cronies. More importantly, let's check on Bridgette before you go to your next appointments.' Serena picked up her pace as they headed towards the garden.

'Yes, I mustn't be late.' Emily almost ran to keep up with Serena's long strides. 'I discovered doshas this morning during Yannis's hatha yoga teachings, and we're going to be working on them this afternoon.'

'Dosh?' Marjory pulled a face. 'Are you spending money?'

'No, no, a dosha is your dominant element. It influences your behaviour and physical and emotional health. Knowing your dosha can help you lead a healthier and more balanced life.'

'Eh?' Marjory stopped. 'Slow down a minute, I can't get my breath.' Bending over, she placed her hands on her knees. 'Now, explain this dosh business to me.'

'Yes, do tell us, Emily.'

'Yannis says that doshas are the energies that define everyone's makeup. There are three types of dosha and mine is called Vata, which is someone who tends to be thin and wispy and all over the place.'

'Aye, I can see that.' Marjory stared at Emily and nodded her head. 'What I am then?'

'You would be Kapha and are kind and have your feet firmly planted on the ground.' Emily didn't mention that Yannis had explained to the class that Kaphas were also prone to weight gain and sluggishness.

'Do I have a dosha?' Serena asked.

'Oh yes.' Emily's vibrant hair shone as she nodded. 'You would be Pitta, intense and intelligent and very goal-oriented.'

'I thought pitta was something you ate with a dip?' Marjory asked.

'No, that's *pita* – like bread.' Emily's schoolmistress tone dismissed her puzzled friend. 'Understanding your dosha can help you to find your balance in life.'

'Well, whatever it is,' Marjory said, 'your dosha has worked like a glass of tonic wine on you. I've never seen anyone's behaviour buck up so quickly.' She straightened up and began to jog ahead. 'Come on, Vata and Pitta, let's find Bossy Bridgette and see if her dosha is working too.'

Some distance away, deep in the heart of the glamping site, Bridgette sat on a deckchair, obscured by a windbreaker, cradling a half-deflated plastic pelican. Norman sat forward and slowly but painstakingly rolled a joint on his naked thigh in a deckchair alongside her. Leaning back, he lit up and took several deep drags.

'Care for a puff, Empress? From the finest growers on the sunny slopes of Antigua. I've spent many a month with the locals harvesting their gold.'

Bridgette stared curiously at Norman and wondered if the local Antiguans were also naked when they gathered in their crops. At that moment, she felt as though she was having an out-of-body experience, sitting starkers, wearing nothing but Norman's gift of a bracelet of wooden beads. All her flesh was on show with a man she didn't know. Bridgette hadn't seen Hugo without his clothes for as long as she could remember, yet here she was, bold and brazen, letting it all hang out.

Strangely, she didn't seem to mind.

Was she beginning to let go of the pent-up anger from all the years she was bullied? Bridgette felt an exhilarating sense of freedom, as though she were sticking two fingers up to her bullies and saying, 'Just look at me now!'

Or perhaps it was Danka's replenishing vitamin drinks.

Whatever it was, Bridgette felt entirely at ease. Instead of worrying about tidying her hair, being immaculately groomed and staying in a luxurious suite, nature could take its course. Bridgette would allow her mind and body, as Norman had told her, 'To be bold and beautiful.'

'Don't mind if I do,' Bridgette replied and leaned forward to take the joint from his fingers.

'Easy does it, old bean,' Norman said and watched Bridgette through half-closed eyes. 'Go slowly.'

Bridgette took a tentative puff and, pulling a face, held the smoke in her lungs, then slowly breathed out. She hadn't smoked since her university days. The bitter, acrid taste wasn't pleasant – not that she'd ever enjoyed smoking. She had only ever indulged when trying to make friends and be sociable. Taking another drag and squinting against the sunshine, she handed the smouldering object to Norman.

Sitting in her chair, gently stroking the pelican, Bridgette felt her body relax. Time seemed to stand still as she looked out at the lake and the world beyond. Studying the grass leading down to the water, Bridgette was engrossed by each blade. Why hadn't she realised that the soft, damp carpet wasn't a uniform colour but a riot of many shades of green? She would look at the lawn at Flaxby Manor quite differently in the future.

If she ever went home.

Home felt a million miles away on this magical day, and even the birds sang as though they'd never seen a morning so beautiful. Hugo and her day-to-day routine of supervising the gardens, entertaining his cronies and running her life around his every need and her many committees felt very distant and alien. Sparadise, in its simple form, had become Bridgette's promised land, her place of peace and harmony, as she absorbed the wonders all around. It was the change that she'd been longing for. Her tent no longer annoyed her, and she felt calm as she thought about the basic furnishings and open-air living.

'Are you cold, Empress?' Norman asked. He stood before her, a blanket in his hand.

'No, not at all,' Bridgette replied. 'I feel deliciously snug.' With the pelican's head draped over her shoulder, its soft, deflated body was a warm pillow across her tummy.

'I'll light the fire.'

'No need – the sun is getting hotter.'

Bridgette smiled as she stared up at Norman. She was no longer in the least offended by his nudity. It seemed acceptable to be without clothes. In fact, she was beginning to love every inch of her tiny frame and realised that she was embracing being vertically challenged for the first time in her life. Bugger the bullies – she was in the minority, and it felt terrific! Why would she burden her beautiful little body with the socially imposed barriers that go with the textile world? There was nothing shameful or unwholesome about celebrating the human form. Bridgette felt immensely grateful to Norman for freeing her so quickly of the hang-ups she'd endured all her life.

'Danka normally drops off a light lunch at this time of day, and we can share it if you like. You must be hungry after your swim?'

'I'm ravenous,' Bridgette exclaimed. She thrust the pelican to one side and bounced out of her chair. 'I'll call reception and ask them to bring a light lunch for me too.'

'I'll set the table,' Norman said.

'Back in a jiffy,' Bridgette replied as she stepped over guy lines and strode confidently to her tent. With her chest thrust out, arms swinging by her sides, her plump little legs marched forward. Her breasts swayed as she walked, and the feeling of unfettered bosoms bobbing about in the breeze felt quite incredible. She decided that she would burn all her Playtex bras on Norman's campfire.

In the tent, she rummaged about in her bag for her phone. Flicking it on, she could see that Hugo had called repeatedly and left several angry messages.

'I must put him out of his misery,' she told herself and, switching the phone to FaceTime, waited for Hugo to pick up.

'About time too!' Hugo yelled within seconds of connecting to the call.

Bridgette stared at her husband. His face was the colour of a tomato with his whiskered moustache twitching, brows knotted together, the crease deep.

'Calm down, Hugo,' she soothed. 'You'll bring on one of your angina attacks.'

Hugo had been slim when, as a healthy young man in his late twenties, he left the army and married Bridgette. But the world of finance, years of high cholesterol lunches at the bank, golf club events and the finest wines had done little for Hugo's weight and blood pressure.

'*Calm down?* My wife buggers off without so much as a

"would you like to join me?" and goes gallivanting with her oddball friends. You've had your fun and a night away, and now it is time for you to come home.'

Staring intently into the phone, Hugo eyeballed Bridgette as he waited for her reply. When there was no response, he changed tack and, in his most persuasive voice, continued. 'Come on, poppet, I've arranged a surprise party for your birthday tomorrow. I wasn't going to tell you.' He gave a clenched half-smile. 'I've got all the crowd from the golf club coming to the manor to celebrate, and I've hired caterers. You don't need to do a thing.'

Bridgette groaned.

The old fogies from the golf club and their equally decrepit wives were like a bus trip from an old folks' home. She had no intention of spending an interminable Sunday afternoon listening to their tales of missed shots and holes-in-one from days gone by while sipping sherry.

Holding the phone at arm's length, Bridgette studied her husband. 'Hugo, I am not coming home today or tomorrow. I shall be celebrating my big birthday here, with my friends.'

Hugo's brow funnelled deeper as he stared at his wife in disbelief. Her nakedness was apparent, and shocked, he began to spew. 'Good God, woman, get some clothes on! You can't wander around your room like that. What if a housekeeper comes in?'

'My room, Hugo?' Bridgette asked and, turning her phone, panned around the Emperor Bell to give Hugo a circular tour. When the lens returned to face Bridgette, she held it further away and gave Hugo a full frontal.

'Welcome to my tent,' she said. 'This is where I am staying: in a tent. In the countryside. Yards from a lake. Where I have been swimming naked.' Bridgette gave a silly, lopsided grin.

'The hell you are!' Hugo exploded. 'Have you been drinking?'

'I'm drinking in life.' Bridgette fluttered her eyelashes and pouted.

'If you're as pissed as a fart and prancing around the place without your pants, then I'm coming to get you.'

'Then I shall inform the management to ban you from Sparadise. You'd be surprised how accommodating the staff are here.'

'B... b... but—' Hugo was spitting mad. 'I am warning you, Bridgette!'

'Warning me to do what? I am embracing naturism and loving it. It's giving me a freedom I've never felt before. I actually like my *"little"* self and I like this change of circumstances from the stuffy life I lead. If you don't like it, you'll find life very lonely at the manor in the months to come.'

'Naturism?' Hugo's eyes appeared to be popping out of the sockets. 'You're a nudist?'

'A naturist, dear,' Bridgette corrected her husband, remembering Norman's words. 'Nudists take their clothes off, but naturists are at one with their surroundings and the beauty of the environment.'

'B... but... that's illegal!'

'Wrong. I am suitably informed that the 2003 Sexual

Offences Act excludes naturism on the proviso that the naked person doesn't cause alarm or distress.'

'Well, you're damn well distressing me! Get dressed immediately!'

Bridgette watched Hugo pound his fist against a wall. Deciding that further conversation would only induce a stroke, she smiled sweetly, gave a little wave, then disconnected the call.

Dialling reception, she waited for someone to pick up and ordered a light lunch.

Bridgette found a hat, drew back the canvas, and stepped out. Placing the wide brim at a jaunty angle on her tousled and unkempt hair, she called out to Norman, 'On my way!'

———

Serena, Marjory and Emily stood by the front door and removed their slippers, then slipped their feet into their outdoor shoes. Serena led the way through the porch and around the side of the house. Still bristling with anger from the runner's comments, it was an animated trio that trooped through the garden at Sparadise on their way to Bridgette's glamping site. As they opened the gate to the field, they made a mutual decision not to mention his vindictiveness to Bridgette. It wouldn't be the first time that they'd protected her.

'Do you remember the time the outgoing president of Flaxby WI told Bridgette that she'd lose if she stood for election for the post?' Emily asked.

'Aye, we rallied the troops and the members voted a landslide victory for our girl,' Marjory said.

'The president was jealous. She'd always longed to be on Bridgette's Christmas card list,' Serena said.

'And she craved an invitation for the monthly dinner party at the manor,' Emily added.

The three linked arms as they thought about their solid friendship alliance, which had grown over the years as they supported each other through life's ups and downs.

'We mustn't let anything spoil her party,' Serena said. 'This is Bridgette's special weekend and we have to ensure that everything runs smoothly.'

'Yep, let's make it memorable,' Marjory agreed.

'I think it's already memorable,' Serena said, 'and I can't wait for Bridgette's reaction to the new Emily.'

'Hmm, I think she may be a bit shocked.' Marjory skirted around a cowpat, treading carefully in her sandals.

'Not as shocked as I was when I saw Bridgette cavorting in the lake.' Emily laughed.

'Quack! Quack!'

'What on earth…' Serena, startled by the noise, stopped and, together with Emily, turned to see Marjory dig into the pocket of her robe.

'Sorry, girls, it's my ring tone,' Marjory said, silencing the quacking and fumbling about for her phone. 'The grandkids downloaded Donald Duck when I wasn't looking.' She flipped the cover of her old Nokia and held it to her ear.

'Hello, who's calling?' she asked and, recognising the

voice, placed her hand over the phone. 'I need to take this. You two go ahead and I'll catch up.'

Marjory turned back to the house and began to speak. 'What's going on, Willie? I thought I'd told you I was at a spa for the weekend to celebrate Bossy Bridgette's big birthday.'

'Aye, lass, I remember,' the community centre caretaker replied.

'Then why are you calling me?'

'After getting up early and cleaning the centre, I fancied a Flaxby-free day and have had a ride out to the countryside with Fred. We've been for a walk.'

His voice was deep and familiar and Marjory felt a flutter in her tummy. 'Well, I hope you're both enjoying yourselves. No doubt you're parked up in the motorhome now with the kettle on the boil.'

'As a matter of fact,' Willie said, sounding excited, 'we're not far from you.'

'Eh? What do you mean?' Marjory's eyes darted across the garden, searching the bushes for signs of Willie, his Westie, and his vintage wheels.

'I'm in the main car park at Sparadise.'

'Bloody hell, Willie. You can't stop there with a dog.' Marjory was flustered. 'The management will move you off. It's private property.'

'I want to see you.'

There was a note of urgency in Willie's tone, and Marjory pulled her robe tightly around her body. With only her swimsuit underneath, she suddenly felt vulnerable. 'Well, you can't. I'm on holiday.'

'Exactly. This is a chance for you and me to have a bit of time together in the motorhome, far away from wagging tongues in Flaxby.'

'But...' Marjory couldn't think clearly and knew from the way he spoke that Willie meant business. After all their teasing on text messages, he was earnest in his desire to meet up.

'Come on, Marge, come and have a cuppa and let me show you my engine.'

Marjory began to chew on a fingernail as she considered her options. She knew that if she put one slingbacked foot into Willie's wagon, she was likely to see far more than his engine. Years of flirting were suddenly a reality and away from the constraints of home and the possibility of someone seeing her chatting intimately with Willie, she found herself in a difficult situation. Taking a deep breath and patting her hair into place, she knew she had to knock this nonsense on the head.

'Be off, you old fool. I'm in between treatments and can't be late. This has cost a lot of money and I'm not going to waste it.'

'But Marge...'

'No buts about anything. You'll get done for loitering if you stay any longer.' Marjory was adamant 'Be on your way and take that daft dog with you too. We'll chat again when I get back.'

Reluctantly, Marjory ended the call. But as she thought about Willie, she still felt a tingle in her body and a flush of warmth that spread from her groin. After the most intimate cleansing procedure with Lars, followed by his special massage where he assured her that she would soon reach her nirvana, the sound of Willie's deep and throaty voice almost made her combust with lust. As comprehension dawned, she half expected to see a signpost for nirvana on the very spot where she stood.

'Oh, heck,' she whispered and looked around anxiously. 'What *is* happening to me?'

If only she had the courage to cast off her inhibitions and be free of Reg once and for all. Knowing that Willie's cosy motorhome was just a short stroll away, it was hard not to give in to temptation and hot-foot it over to the car park. To hell with a cup of tea and a chat, she longed to climb the steps to her first love's passion wagon and rip off his chequered shirt and moleskin trousers and discover what lay beneath. Her libido had finally burst out of hibernation after all these years of Reg falling into bed, unconscious, after a session in the pub, his snores keeping her awake for most of the night.

'Gawd!' Marjory exclaimed and hopped from one frustrated foot to the other. Should she put Willie out of his misery and satisfy herself at the same time? She closed her eyes and shook her head to pull herself together.

She must not give in. Her friends were waiting for her. The weekend was supposed to be a time for female bonding and plenty of pampering, but as she turned away from the main house and made her way to Bridgette's tent, all she could think about was Willie, his willing body and the privacy of his motorhome.

Her phone quacked and Marjory flipped it open.

A text message from Willie. *You're so near and yet so far away! But I'll be back.* A row of heart emojis followed.

'Phew,' Marjory sighed. She flapped the lapels of her robe to try and get some cool air to her body, and with the weight of Willie's ardour lifted and an affair in his passion wagon temporarily postponed, she set off to find her friends.

Chapter Fifteen

E mily crossed the driveway at the same time as an old split-windscreen motorhome started its engine. Curtains fluttered from open windows and a little white dog, sitting on the passenger seat, began to bark. Clouds of blue smoke billowed from the exhaust as the vintage vehicle chugged into life and slowly moved away from the house.

She left her walking boots by the front door and put on her slippers. Ten glittery toenails wriggled and peeped out from the soft fabric, and, with a smile, Emily waved ten glittery fingernails in response. She turned to a mirror, which hung above the shoe rack, and studied her reflection. It was almost impossible to believe that the person who stared back had started the day as plain, boring old Emily Avondale. A few hours later, she'd transformed into a head-turning, colourful woman of a certain age. Her new look was better than any feeling she'd ever experienced, and Bridgette's reaction had been even more astonishing.

'Glory be!' Bridgette had exclaimed as Emily and Serena

approached the glamping area and Marjory hurried to join them. 'Vivienne Westwood meets Zandra Rhodes on speed.' With her mouth agog, Bridgette studied Emily from head to toe, then announced, 'You look bloody marvellous. What a transformation.'

Emily was stunned. It wasn't what she'd expected. But neither had she expected to find Bridgette, stark naked, standing by a campfire, burning her bras and smoking a spliff.

'Have you met Norman?' Bridgette waved a smouldering strip of elastic in the direction of a tall older man, who was sitting cross-legged, sucking on a long-handled pipe. He, too, wore only his birthday suit and raised both hands to acknowledge Bridgette's friends.

'Charmed and honoured to meet you all,' Norman said, his pipe dangling. 'Are you by any chance naturists? Would you care to join us in embracing the environment and everything good on this planet?'

'Well, actually, I've got a yoga class to get to,' Emily said, 'but I am so pleased to see that Bridgette has made a new friend.'

Norman looked whimsical. 'Ah, yoga – true change is within; leave the outside as it is.'

'That's a very nice quote,' Emily said.

'Yes, by the great Dalai Lama. I met him when I was in Tibet.'

Amused, Emily looked from Bridgette to Norman. 'Have you asked Norman to your party tomorrow?' she'd whispered.

'I have, and he's accepted, and we're hosting the bash

here, in the area around my tent.' Bridgette grinned. 'And now, I can't wait to be seventy. It is the beginning of a new and enlightened era for me.'

Serena, who'd been silent up until now, spoke up. 'What a great idea,' she said, ignoring Norman and Bridgette's nudity, as though it was perfectly normal for their bossy friend to be naked and smacked off her face at lunchtime on a Saturday. 'Do let us know what the plans are so that we can help with preparations. Will you be asking any other guests?'

'It will be an open house,' Bridgette said.

Marjory nudged Serena. 'You should ask those two nice lads from the penthouse.' She'd been quiet until now, fascinated by Bridgette, unused to seeing her friend so calm and relaxed. Nakedness suited her, and Marjory shook her head in wonderment.

'Er, yes, that's a good idea. Bridgette, would you mind?'

Bridgette grinned, and dropping the last bra into the fire, she turned and hugged her friends. 'The more the merrier, and as long as I have the three of you, my day will be perfect.'

Emily stepped onto the porch. She wondered what on earth Hugo would have to say when he discovered that his wife wasn't returning to Chez Haworth and his surprise birthday party. She'd received a furious voice message from him only a short while ago, informing her in no uncertain terms that Bridgette was to be sobered up and sent home. Emily imagined that the same message had gone to Serena and Marjory's phones too.

As she strode across the hallway, she wondered what

Bridgette would think about her feelings for Yannis. Given her friend's newly found spirit of adventure, Emily believed that Bridgette would probably approve.

Approaching the reception desk, Emily was aware that Danka was dealing with a woman who had both hands balled into fists and appeared to be pleading with Danka.

'I have no sessions available with our massage therapist, Lars. He is very popular. I'm sorry.' Danka was firm.

The guest crossed her arms and sighed. Turning away, she almost collided with Emily. 'Excuse me,' she snapped.

'It's okay.' Emily stopped to let the woman pass.

'Are you the yoga student who had a makeover today?' The woman stared hard, her eyes flickering over every inch of Emily's transformation.

'Er, I've changed my hair colour and bought a new outfit.'

'You look twenty years younger.'

'Oh, thank you.'

The woman stomped off, and Emily saw that Danka was smiling.

'Phillipe has been taking bookings all morning and Lars has no free appointments. You and Marjory are very good for business at Sparadise,' Danka said.

Emily wondered if Danka would say the same about Bridgette. The birthday girl had incensed the runner and his friends with her antics. She would undoubtedly continue to do so if her transition to naturism continued. Was Danka inundated with complaints? Emily decided not to ask.

'We're having a wonderful weekend. Sparadise seems to suit us all.'

'Keep up with your vitamin drinks,' Danka said, 'and you will feel revitalised and renewed.'

Emily opened the door that led to the new extension. She didn't need any of the spa's special vitamin drinks. She was floating on an emotional high, her whole body aglow with anticipation, brought about by her new look and her feelings for Yannis. Her confession of love had shocked Serena and Marjory, but Emily didn't care. Years of frustration over Stephen had fallen away. If her ex-husband could romance a younger love and find happiness, why couldn't Emily?

She'd almost reached the yoga studio when her phone began to ring. Emily was tempted to turn it off, but she recognised the number and, with a sigh, connected the call.

'Hello?' She paused to lean against the pastel-painted wall.

'Mother!' her sons yelled. 'Where the hell have you been? We've been calling you since yesterday evening.'

Emily sighed. 'You know where I am and you know that I am at a spa, celebrating my friend Bridgette's birthday weekend.'

'It's shite,' Joe, her eldest, began. 'You have no right to leave us without any food and no money.'

'You can't just abandon your children,' Jacob, the younger son, whined.

Children? Emily rolled her eyes. 'I'm taking yoga classes,' she said when she felt able to respond.

'What's yoga?' Joe asked.

'That's when you spend an hour trying not to fart,' Jacob said and giggled.

'Oh, for heaven's sake.'

'There's a disaster here. We can't get Sky TV and we've no internet...'

'Netflix and my Xbox won't work,' Jacob moaned.

'Even worse,' Joe said, 'the old fart from Flaxby Manor, Hugo Haworth, has been to the house. He was banging on the door, asking when you're coming home and if we know what rooms you're all staying in.'

Her elder son sounded breathless.

'He was livid and seemed to think that your mate, Bossy Bridgette, has left him.' They both began to snicker. 'As if a bunch of coffin dodgers would make life changes.'

Emily grimaced. She wished her phone had a FaceTime facility, and the pair could see their mouldy oldie mother now. They wouldn't recognise their transformed parent. But having never upgraded her phone in favour of the boys having the most expensive and latest models, it wasn't an option. Emily held her face to the wall as though she was about to bang her head repeatedly.

She hadn't noticed the door to the yoga studio open. Yannis had a concerned expression as he moved along the corridor until he was standing by her side.

'Hello,' Yannis whispered. 'Are you okay? Can I help?'

Emily almost jumped out of her Lycra-covered skin and spun around. 'Goodness, I didn't see you there,' she said. Her free hand flew to her hair, and she rubbed the back of her neck to fiddle with her colourful curls. Her sons, still enraged, continued to shout and argue amongst themselves.

'Is it your family?' Yannis asked.

'Unfortunately, yes. My stupid, spoilt sons.'

Yannis took her phone and held it to his ear. With his free hand, he stroked Emily's face. His touch was soothing.

'Hello,' he said, addressing Joe and Jacob. 'Your mum isn't available at the moment.'

Emily felt her knees give way. Her mouth was dry, and her heart was pounding so fast that she was sure that Yannis must hear it.

'You look beautiful,' he whispered, his fingers tracing the line of her mouth.

'Who the hell is this? Get our mother. We need to speak to her!'

Yannis gave Emily a cheeky wink. 'She is otherwise engaged for the moment. I will hang up now.' He disconnected the phone and dropped it into his pocket. Reaching out to take her hand, he led Emily into the studio and locked the door behind them.

'We have a private session. No one will disturb us,' Yannis said as they slid onto a mat. 'It's time for me to discover more about your dosha.'

Emily didn't give a damn about her dosha and was far more concerned with the prominent bulge in Yannis's shorts, which now pressed against her stomach. She felt muscled arms envelop her in a tender embrace and closed her eyes as soft kisses on her neck stirred long-forgotten desire.

'You are so beautiful,' he said, his hand cupping her breast.

Emily wondered if Yannis was hallucinating. Did he drink the same vitamin drink that the spa ladled out to its guests? It would be impossible for him to feel attraction for a woman of her age. But as she nestled into his broad chest, she let her heart overrule her head.

If only Jo and Jacob could see her now. She pushed a jumble of guilty thoughts to one side as her excitement rose. Yannis's intoxicating touch had electrified every nerve in her body, and she succumbed entirely.

Emily Avondale, the ageing headmistress, hopeless mother, divorced and desperate sixty-something, was hooked on a drug named Yannis.

Robin stood in the centre of the living room in the penthouse and stared at a huge box. Delivered by courier from London, Danka had signed for it and carried it, together with Monika, from reception and carefully placed it on a low table.

'We are intrigued,' Danka said as she straightened up. 'I hope you're not smuggling in contraband.'

'It's a gift for a friend – nothing sinister,' Robin replied.

'Where's your partner?'

'He's in the gym. His trainer says he needs to work harder or his time at Sparadise will be wasted.'

'Stevie likes to indulge. He should take our special vitamin drink; it will help energise him. Guests can't get enough of it.'

'Danka, your special vitamin drink is the last thing either of us would touch.' Robin raised an eyebrow. 'We learnt from our very first stay at Sparadise that too much is addictive.'

'But it makes you feel good.'

'I feel good just by being here.' Robin steered the two women towards the door. 'Thank you both.' He returned to the enormous box and wondered if he should wait for Stevie but, anxious to unveil the item, he picked up a knife and began to circle.

'Hang on!' The door burst open and Stevie fell in, sweating and panting from his exertions with his trainer. Dressed in knee-length shorts and a damp T-shirt that clung to his chubby torso, Stevie was exhausted. 'Oh my, that wretched man. He's had me on circuits until I was so dizzy, I almost collapsed.' He sat down on a sofa and, picking up a magazine, began to fan his face. 'But I've just seen Danka and she said there was a delivery. Is it here?'

'In all its glory.' Robin began to slice through the packing tape.

Very carefully, he opened the outer wrapping then reached in to see an enormous circular hatbox. Stevie jumped up, and together they raised the object and lifted it onto the dining room table.

'The Plumed Chapeau,' Robin whispered.

'Gosh, it's so much bigger than I remember,' Stevie said as he gazed in awe.

'It's perfect but I have my work cut out with alterations to make it appropriate for the occasion. The feathers will have to go.'

The hat covered the table's glass surface, and very gently, Robin lifted it onto a swan-necked polystyrene mannequin head that had also been delivered.

'Does Serena know?'

'No, but she's on her way up. I don't want her to see it,' Robin said.

He disappeared into the bedroom and returned with a white sheet, which he carefully draped over the mannequin.

There was a knock at the door, and Stevie went to answer it. 'Here she is, a vision of loveliness, a delight to the eye.'

'Hardly.' Serena smiled. Her leisure suit was damp and the bikini she wore underneath was wet. 'We've been to see Bridgette and I couldn't resist a quick dip in the lake.'

Stevie shook his head. 'You're fearless. I'd be scared of all those creepy crawlies.'

'I was swimming with ducks waddling beside me and herons searching for fish. It's so tranquil and relaxing.'

'Do you need to change?' Robin asked.

'Yes, I've got clothes with me or I can go back to my room.'

'Nonsense. Use our facilities – we pay enough for them.' Stevie took her bag. 'Go and shower. Have you eaten? I can organise lunch.'

'Something light would be good. I've just left Bridgette, and she was tucking into a delicious chicken Caesar salad.' Serena paused. 'I've never seen Bridgette so hungry. She almost ate the plate.'

'Vitamin drinks,' Robin and Stevie said together.

'Those too. Her neighbour, Norman, seems to have a constant supply.'

'Has she settled into glamping?' Stevie asked.

'I'll say she has. She's gone back to nature. They're like Adam and Eve in the garden of Eden.'

'Has she eaten any forbidden fruit?'

'Anything and everything that she can get her hands on.' Serena chuckled. 'You should wander down and see what they're up to.'

'Perhaps we will. I've never seen the glamping site,' Stevie said.

'If you're free tomorrow, Bridgette is holding her birthday bash. Everyone's invited.'

'A party!' Stevie clapped his hands together. 'How fabulous! What's the dress code? We must decide what to wear.'

'I wouldn't worry too much about clothing. Bridgette is embracing naturism, and as far as I can see, anything goes for the party, but she did mention a tropical theme.'

Stevie frowned. He couldn't possibly be naked and reveal his tubby tummy and man boobs. He was horrified by the thought of letting his nether region hang out too.

Robin came over and put his arm around his partner. 'Don't stress yourself. We will be appropriately covered, I can assure you.'

As Serena turned to head to the bathroom, she noticed the sheet-covered object. 'My goodness, what on earth have you hidden under there? Is it a body?'

'All will be revealed,' Stevie replied and shooed her away.

When Serena stepped onto the terrace, lunch had arrived and was arranged on a table under a large canvas umbrella.

'Come and join us.' Robin stood and pulled out a chair.

'Have some melon. It's delicious,' Stevie said as he forked fruit onto his plate.

'I ought to check my Instagram account. There were no new followers and only a handful of likes when I looked earlier – and there was a horrible comment too.'

'Yes, I saw it.' Robin shook his head. 'You mustn't get upset. Every celebrity has trolls following their account.'

'I think it's one of the guests staying here.'

'Are you sure?' Stevie asked and wiped the juice from his mouth with a napkin.

'Just ignore it, don't reply. I added an Insta-reel an hour ago. Let's have a look and see if there's any traction.'

They picked up their phones and opened Instagram.

Stevie held his head on one side and smiled. 'Great footage,' he said as he studied the images of Serena. She was sitting on a swing in the garden, framed by roses and honeysuckle. A cerise sarong, knotted at the neck in a halter style, clung to her body, the wind catching the edge and lifting it high over her shapely legs.

'Not bad. A hundred plus likes and lots of hearts.' Robin nodded his head in approval.

But Serena wore a face like thunder. As she turned on her phone, the account of @YvettetheChefette instantly filled her screen.

'I don't believe it,' Serena muttered, her eyes wide as she gazed at her enemy.

Holding a large bowl filled with cake mix, a perfectly made-up Yvette held a spoon to her pouting red lips and suggestively flicked her tongue. She wore a cream-coloured, silky, half-cup bra, edged with black lace, matching briefs and a suspender belt supporting the sheerest black stockings. Serena scanned the caption and almost spat out her frustration.

'"I am now a @HankyPankyLingerie girl,"' Serena quoted. 'Yvette has over seven hundred comments and several thousand likes.' She rolled her eyes and sat back in her chair.

'Clever marketing,' Robin said. He, too, had been alerted to the chef's account. 'Whoever is promoting her is doing a great job.'

These weren't the words that Serena wanted to hear. She remained silent, too angry to reply or comment.

Robin watched Serena's fingers as they flexed. The muscles in her arms tensed as she crossed her arms, and he noticed a vein in her neck pulse.

'Calm down,' he said. 'Yvette is a social media expert. Her people know every trick in the book to raise her Instagram profile and divert followers to her cooking business and endorsements.'

'Yes,' Stevie said, 'but we've got a trick of our own, and we think it will outdo your rival.'

Serena was puzzled. She looked at her new friends and studied their faces. 'What have you planned?'

'You'll find out – all in good time.' Robin stood and disappeared into the suite. When he returned, he held a tape measure in his hand. 'Now, Stevie, make notes please.' He reached out and, taking Serena's hands, pulled her to her feet. 'I need a few measurements.'

The two men became business-like as they moved around their model, measuring and assessing, their pencils poised and heads tilted in consideration, then nodding in agreement. Stevie wrote down their findings, and Robin began to sketch, shielding his pad from Serena's curious eyes.

Robin closed his pad with a snap. 'All done. We have work to do, so our living room will be off limits for some time.'

'Gosh, I can't imagine what you two are up to.' Serena reached for her bag and prepared to leave.

'Go and have fun with your friends, chill out and relax, and stop worrying.' Robin led her to the door.

'Thank you for everything that you're doing to help me.' Serena pecked them both on the cheek. 'And I can't wait to see what you have planned.'

The couple stood at the door, their arms linked as they watched Serena move away.

'To work,' they exclaimed, and as they turned back to the suite, Robin reached out for a sign hanging on the handle of the door and flicked it over.

Do Not Disturb.

Chapter Sixteen

It was late afternoon, and many of the residents at Sparadise were not engaged in therapy sessions, outdoor activities, or beauty treatments. They sat on the terrace overlooking the lake, enjoying afternoon tea. They nibbled on wafer-thin sandwiches, dainty cakes, and teas from around the world. The sun was still hot and the heat brought a lazy restfulness to the garden, where sun-worshippers relaxed on loungers, topping up their golden tans.

Beside a coppice of low-hanging trees, Marjory lay in a hammock and rubbed the petals of a dandelion between her fingers. The fluffy sphere reminded her of the fairy wand belonging to her granddaughter, and she waved it in the air to make a wish that her friends were, at that moment, as relaxed and happy as she felt. They were all spending time apart at the spa so the next swimming session at Flaxby pool would be filled with gossip as they debriefed their weekend. But, Marjory reflected, time on her own was the rarest of treats – away from family, work and responsibility. Lying here, at leisure, was the biggest treat of all and Marjory was making the most of it.

Nothing could cloud her contentment, not even the angry phone message she'd received from Hugo Haworth, who, unable to reach his wife, had demanded that the friends return to Flaxby immediately, bringing Bridgette with them. He insisted that they all attend the party that he'd planned the following day.

Marjory stared up at the vast open sky where birds soared overhead.

Suddenly, she blew a raspberry.

'That's what I think of you, Hugo Haworth,' she said, 'and here's another to Reg too.' The vibration on her lips was as satisfying as the gesture she made with her free hand.

There had been no word from Reg since she'd arrived at Sparadise. No messages of warmth, wishing his wife an enjoyable stay. Marjory wondered if Reg even had her mobile number stored on his phone, for he never called her and, as she gently swung, she wondered if he even cared. The only thing he used his phone for was local news on *Life in Lancashire* and an app that published results when his pigeons were racing. She knew he had a race that day, and would have set off early, with his van full of pigeons and paraphernalia, oblivious to his wife and her weekend away.

His only comment, had she the energy to call him, would be, 'You wasted the afternoon lying in a hammock? It doesn't make sense. There are plenty of jobs to be getting on with at home.'

Marjory was worried that Reg would cope on his own and what would their kids think if she left? But most of all, where would she go?

She closed her eyes and breathed in a lungful of delicious woodland-scented air. Time seemed to stand still at Sparadise, and Marjory could hardly believe that they had only been there a little over twenty-four hours. So much had happened. Emily had transformed herself and fallen in love. Bridgette had mellowed and come so far out of her comfort zone that it was anyone's guess whether she would go back into it, and Serena had found a compulsion to resurrect her livelihood in the hope of revitalising her cookery skills.

Marjory thought about the countless photos that Serena was uploading to the internet. It was an odd sort of way to get her cooking career back, but surely, Serena knew what she was doing. As for herself, Marjory didn't recognise the woman who'd arrived expecting nothing more than a dip in the jacuzzi and maybe a visit to the hair salon to top up her colour.

Willie's arrival had been a shock.

Secretly touched that the old fool had driven so far on the off chance of spending time with her, Marjory had to admit that it felt good to have an admirer – someone who genuinely seemed to care. Why on earth he still held a torch for a woman he'd known all these years was a puzzle, but there were lots of strange things happening, not the least of which was that she was swaying three feet above the ground, wearing nothing but her cossie and dreaming of her next session with Lars.

Lars. Massage man with the magical fingers.

He'd awakened Marjory to the beautiful mystery that her body had, until this weekend, never experienced. Orgasms, she now knew, were addictive, and as she twiddled with the stem of the dandelion and pulled on the petals, she began to count off the hours until her next session with the Swedish massage therapist.

'Here you are.'

A voice woke Marjory from her daydream. She peered over the top of the hammock to see Serena stepping carefully over the mossy floor of the thicket. She held a beaker in her hand and held it out.

'Found you. I thought you'd probably be relaxing somewhere and in need of a cool drink.'

The beaker chinked with cubes of ice. Taking a sip, Marjory smiled. 'By heck, that's delicious. Thank you, lass.'

'It's a Sparadise special: lime and lemon with a hint of aniseed.'

'Aye, it's grand. Have any of those special vitamins or herbs been added?'

'No, I watched it being made.'

'Shame,' Marjory said and smiled.

She studied Serena, dressed in a gold one-piece bathing suit with a matching wrap knotted at her waist. Serena looked like a goddess in the soft light, tall and striking, her clear eyes shining, limbs like polished ebony, supple and strong.

'You want to take some photos of yourself in that get-up. You'll have fans galore on t'internet.'

'Hardly,' Serena said. 'If I were thirty years younger,

perhaps, but my cookery rival has the monopoly on glamour shots.'

Marjory sat up. The hammock swayed, and she almost fell out, her drink splashing over her legs. Steadying herself, she wagged her finger at Serena.

'I know nothing about the world of celebrity, but I do know that feeling sorry for yourself never gets anyone anywhere.' She crunched on a cube of ice and continued, 'You are a beautiful woman, as Emily reminded you last night. The years have been kind and, despite the nips and tucks that we know you've had, you set hearts racing when you walk in a room.'

'But you don't understand...' Serena sighed.

'Of course I do. I've sat on my fat backside at the till at the Co-op, listening to folks moan and groan all day, then rushed home to wait hand and foot on a husband who wouldn't care if I was alive or dead.'

'What are you saying?'

'Wake up and smell the roses, girl.' Marjory drained her beaker and dropped it to the ground, then tipped out of the hammock, stumbling as she landed. 'You can't always choose your circumstances, but you can sure as hell choose how you deal with them.'

Serena stared at Marjory.

'In all the years we've been friends, I've seen how you love cooking and teaching others. Who cares about age? It *is* just a number. You can be old at thirty and young at eighty. It's what's in here that matters.' Marjory tapped her heart. 'Look at the four of us. Best of friends who've all had a life-changing event since we got here. Your moment came when you met those two fellas, who, I know, are going to help you beyond your wildest dreams.'

'Do you think so?'

Marjory grabbed Serena's hand. 'I know so. There are no chance encounters in life. Everyone we meet comes into our lives for a reason, and it's up to us to make that reason work in our favour.'

Marjory thought of Willie, his dear old face grinning with love, as he leaned on the handle of his broom in the Civic Centre, watching Marjory polish tables and dust shelves.

Serena began to smile. 'Well, Robin and Stevie are preparing something special for a photoshoot and I think it might be revealed at Bridgette's party tomorrow.'

'Hurrah! Now make sure you stop all this self-doubt and remember just how bloody brilliant you are.' She picked up her robe, draped it over a tree stump, and, linking Serena's arm, marched her out of the thicket. 'Use your years of experience, dazzle in front of the lens and damn well get your cookery career back.'

'Good heavens, Marjory, there must be something in the water at Sparadise. I've never seen or heard you like this before.'

'Aye, it's time I sorted myself out. I've been living in the dark ages and need the same wake-up call as everyone else.'

'You look different.' Serena stopped and studied her friend from top to toe. 'In fact, you're almost as transformed as Emily.'

'I wouldn't go that far,' Marjory said, 'but Lars insisted

that I had one of those colonic irrigate thingies, and I feel at least a stone thinner; this new costume helps too.' Marjory smoothed her hands over the panels of her tummy-tuck elastane swimsuit that shaped and flattened her belly. 'I got it from the boutique that Emily recommended.'

'The colour really suits you and matches your eyes.'

'Aye, the lass in the shop said cornflower blue was perfect for me.'

'You've had a manicure and pedicure too.'

'Yep, Alexandra managed to fit me in earlier. My nails look fab, don't they?' Marjory held up her pearly, pink-tipped fingers and wriggled them. 'I even squeezed fifteen minutes out of Phillipe, the stylist and makeup manager, to give me advice.'

'Crikey, you've done well. I heard he was booked up.'

'Wave money under his nose, and it's surprising how soon his impossible schedule melts away.'

They were nearing the main house, where guests who'd been relaxing had left the garden to get ready for the evening's activities.

'Shall we meet in the bar again before dinner?' Serena asked.

'Yes, I'll let Emily know. She's probably having a rest. She had a long session of yoga this afternoon. It's probably worn her out.'

'Combined with her infatuation with Yannis.'

'I wouldn't worry about that. It'll wear off when she comes to her senses.'

'Do you think Bridgette will put in an appearance?'

'Oh heck, can you imagine if she does? That pink pelican

looked like it had seen much better days. It will hardly cover her assets.'

'She's embracing new things, what if she joins the running squad?'

The two women looked at each other. An image of Bridgette jogging in the buff made them burst into laughter.

'She'd wear a Fitbit, surely?'

'Aye, and one of those peaked caps.'

They giggled as they imagined Bridgette donning a cap and checking her Fitbit as she ordered the runners to line up alongside her naked self.

'Here's your room.' They'd arrived at the annexe. Marjory squeezed Serena's arm. 'I'll see you in a bit, now don't forget what I've said.'

'How could I?' Serena grinned, knowing that she'd have Marjory on her case if she showed any self-pity. 'See you later.'

'Aye, see you soon,' Marjory replied.

Serena unlocked the door to her room and tossed her bag on the bed. Her phone fell onto the carpeted floor and, reaching down, she picked it up and saw that there were several missed calls from Hugo Haworth. An angry voice message instructed Serena to gather Bridgette's belongings, ensure that Bridgette was adequately clothed and brought home to Flaxby Manor at once. Hugo's tone softened when he suggested that his wife had had an 'episode' which he'd put down to her upcoming birthday and the realisation that she'd reached the milestone of seventy years. He rambled on about women's hormones and the associated peculiar behaviour, but Serena had heard enough and ended the call without waiting for Hugo to finish.

She sat on the bed and scrolled down to see if Cornelius had been in touch, but there was neither a message nor a phone call.

'Damn you,' she said and wondered if he was still wandering over the fells. Dodger, she knew, would have given up long ago and turned around and headed for home. The old dog liked neither the heat nor the cold, and his days of lolloping for miles were well and truly over. The Labrador much preferred the comfort of a sagging old sofa in the even temperature of the snug where, nose twitching and tail thumping, he could dream happily of youthful days gone by when rabbits were within easy reach of his paws, and walkies lasted for miles.

'If the mountain doesn't come to Muhammad, then Muhammad must go to the mountain,' Serena said and dialled Cornelius's number.

The phone rang several times and eventually went to answerphone. 'Hi there, this is Cornelius. Sorry, I'm not here to lend an ear, but if you leave a word, you can be sure that I'll hear.'

'Agh…' Serena gritted her teeth. 'Cornelius, why do you have such a stupid message? If you *are* listening to this, could you please let me know that you haven't fallen off a ridge and I don't need to call the mountain rescue team?' She stood up and paced the room. 'This is also to let you know that I am fine and enjoying myself with the girls, but

I've made some decisions and, if you care to cast your eyes on my Instagram account, you'll understand what they are.'

Serena hung up.

Where the hell was Cornelius? He could be so frustrating at times and withdrew into himself for lengthy periods. This episode was one of the longest she remembered, and she had begun to wonder if he would ever get back to work and paint again.

Still, this wasn't the time to be worrying about Cornelius. Marjory was right, and Serena had to focus on herself to get her career back on track. She wandered over to the wardrobe and flicked through the hangers, deciding what she would wear that evening.

She chose a long white dress and lay it on the bed. The dress was a vintage Halston from the seventies with a large collar and rhinestone detail. 'I shall look like Elvis in this.' She smiled as she stroked the soft stretchy fabric.

Her phone pinged, and Serena saw that her Instagram account was attracting interest. The photo she'd uploaded, wearing the gold swimsuit, was getting hits. @LocoLad had made a lewd suggestion that she immediately deleted and @Love2Run was so offensive that she deleted the comment too and blocked his account. Other than a few hearts, the image had done little to engage with followers, though, and with a frustrated sigh, Serena began to dress for dinner.

The modest brick and mortar residence, topped with a tiled roof and occupying three floors, stood out of sight some distance from the main house at Sparadise. An unkempt garden wrapped around the building, with climbing roses and borders overflowing with perennials and weeds. A bicycle with a broken spoke and flat tyre was propped against a shed. At the back, a greenhouse overflowing with plants stood in a sunny spot and a table and chairs sat on a patio beside a whirligig washing line. Lines of bright white tunics, hanging out to dry, fluttered in the breeze.

Chapter Seventeen

The modest brick and mortar residence, topped with a tiled roof and occupying three floors, stood out of sight some distance from the main house at Sparadise. An unkempt garden wrapped around the building, with climbing roses and borders overflowing with perennials and weeds. A bicycle with a broken spoke and flat tyre was propped against a shed. At the back, a greenhouse overflowing with plants stood in a sunny spot and a table and chairs sat on a patio beside a whirligig washing line. Lines of bright white tunics, hanging out to dry, fluttered in the breeze.

A cluttered communal kitchen had dishes stacked in the sink and crumbs littered the surfaces inside the house. Remnants of a sliced loaf lay on an oak chopping board. A corridor led to a sitting room with large sofas and comfortable but ageing chairs facing a wide-screen television. Cream-coloured curtains that had seen better days hung from poles, and sunshine streamed through the gap, highlighting the shabbiness of the room. Over the years, thousands of feet had pounded up the stairs, wearing away the carpet pattern until the weave of swirling roses had faded and frayed.

Rooms led off a passageway on each floor and amongst several names on the first floor, hand-painted door plaques announced Danka, Monika and Alexandra. On the top floor, an attic room had Yannis's name in bold black lettering. Inside the room, posters of the famous Greek football team, Olympiacos, lined one wall, and on another, footballing heroes Leonardo Koutris and Dimitris Nikolaou, wearing their team colours, smiled down. A mattress occupied the centre of the room, covered in part with a traditional woven throw and pillows scrunched in a huddle in the centre.

Emily lay on the mattress and surveyed the possessions.

They were all so reflective of Yannis's spirit and she felt as though she was a student again. Beside the bed, Emily saw a small table cluttered with photos and fat white church candles, burnt down to different heights, alongside a lamp with a meander-patterned paper shade which cast curving shadows over the walls and ceiling. In one corner, a fold-up table held a laptop and several computer games. Wires wound chaotically from multi-socketed plugs.

The staff accommodation at Sparadise was similar to the digs Emily had shared, not far from University of Exeter, where she'd studied for her history degree. As she sat up, Emily thought of Joe and Jacob's rooms at home. The mess and masculine smell were familiar in these surroundings. Draped over every surface, clothes and exercise equipment jumbled together, and plates and a mug lay on the floor.

Two half-full glasses of wine stood beside empty bottles, and she reached down to retrieve one. Handing a glass to a sleepy Yannis, she smiled as he opened his eyes, his fingers touching hers.

'Hello, Emily,' Yannis said. He yawned as he took a sip of the wine.

'Hello, Yannis,' she replied, gazing at his tousled hair and tanned torso. 'I think I ought to be going.'

'Why must you go? Do you not like it here?'

Emily liked Yannis's bedroom very much and was so relaxed and comfortable that she would happily move in. But she didn't want to outstay her welcome and feared that the young man might become bored if she lingered any longer. Earlier, they'd drunk a considerable amount of wine, and her inhibitions had soon evaporated, culminating in Emily flinging her clothing to one side and leaping all over Yannis. Once naked, as their skin moved together, she'd forgotten about their age difference, and Yannis had appeared as fascinated with Emily's body as she did with his.

'Every little line tells a story.' He'd kissed her breasts and stomach, his touch electric. 'I adore your imperfections,' he whispered and ran his hands between her thighs to delve in expertly with his fingers. Emily's release was intense, and time seemed to stand still until she urged him on, their bodies fitting perfectly. Yannis, too, was lost in his ecstasy until they were finally still and snuggled, as close as lovers could be. The young man's energy and stamina soon returned, and with every touch, she was entirely under his spell. Just his smell sent her into a trance, intoxicated with a passion she'd never known before.

Now, as Yannis lay his head across her chest, Emily was conscious that she wore nothing beneath the throw that partially covered their bodies. Should Yannis decide to illuminate the room with the central light, the game would be up. But as she sipped her wine, she pondered the fact that he'd seen every little bit of her, and his ardour hadn't lessened during their lovemaking.

'What are you thinking, my beautiful Emily?' Yannis asked and raised his head to look into her eyes.

'I'm thinking that you have been very kind to me and have made me feel so much better about myself.'

'It is not kind. I like you.' Yannis traced her nipple with his finger. 'Yesterday, you didn't know who you were. Today, you have come alive.'

How true! Emily squirmed under his touch and felt alive in every sense of the word. Not only had her appearance changed, but being desired by Yannis had awakened her after years of a humdrum existence, and no matter what her future held, as she lay in her young lover's arms, Emily never wanted this feeling to end. She put her glass down on the floor then nestled into the pillows, one hand stroking Yannis's soft curls.

In a silver frame, a photograph stood on the bedside table, and she picked it up. 'Are they your parents?' Emily asked as she studied the smiling faces of a couple, similar in age to herself. Their arms were linked as they stood in front of an old three-story building with battered blue shutters framing the windows.

'Yes, my mana and patera.' Yannis rolled onto his stomach and looked at the photograph.

'Is this their home?'

Yannis nodded.

'What a lovely house,' Emily said as she admired the terracotta pots, overflowing with vibrant oleander and bougainvillaea that hung heavy from branches covering the walls, the flowers deep red amongst thick green leaves.

'Have you been to Greece?' Yannis asked.

'Yes, I love the islands. One summer, when I was a student, I travelled around them.'

'But you haven't been back?'

'No, but I hope to one day. Greece is such a beautiful place.'

'I was born in Maxos, on the island of Bessaloniki. It is the jewel in the Ionian crown.'

Yannis lay back and began to describe his home. He explained that the little village was nestled on a peninsula surrounded by the Ionian Sea. The idyllic hamlet could be accessed by a winding road, narrow in the descent, which restricted visitors, as vehicles were limited to cars, carts, and cycles. Seafaring travellers could arrive by boat, and yachts dotted around like diamonds dancing on the sparkling waters lapping gently against the harbour walls.

Yannis was poetic as he spoke. Entranced, Emily was transported to the island and the magic of Maxos as he described the dry, rugged land high above the village where a castle stood, and there, a panoramic view of the peninsula and surrounding sea that was so wonderous, it would take your breath away. Reached by a steep path, he told her that the Venetian army built the castle of Maxos in the late fifteenth century to protect villagers from pirate raids. The prominent structure was partially hidden by vegetation, and as Yannis described the trees, Emily could almost smell the cypress and pine. He described the Venetian buildings that remained, and Emily, as a historian, was fascinated.

'You like to swim?' Yannis asked.

'Oh, very much. I swim every week with my friends. I love the water.'

Yannis described the warm turquoise waters and a pale sandy beach which stretched in front of a row of waterfront bars and a café. Brightly coloured awnings provided shade for day-trippers who wandered around the village before enjoying a leisurely lunch.

'There is a horseshoe-shaped beach, accessible by a set of uneven steps from my parents' home.' Yannis smiled. 'It is quite private. When I was growing up, I spent all my days with my friends, playing on that beach.'

'It sounds like paradise,' Emily said. 'Why would you want to leave it?'

'There is no money in Maxos unless you have a bar, but only a few visitors can reach the village even then. No coaches or big vehicles can negotiate the steep road.'

'What do your parents do?'

'They rent out a couple of rooms in summer, mostly to backpackers. My father helps with sheep and goats on a farm in the hills. My mother cleans and waits table at the café when there is work. It's a hard life. They are getting old and when they die, the house will be mine, but it is falling apart. It is uninhabitable in places and needs a great deal of money for repairs.'

'How did you become a yoga teacher?'

'I didn't want to do what my parents did and live with hardship, so I studied in Athens, gained my qualifications, then came to Britain to look for work.'

But Yannis had edited his story.

He didn't tell Emily that he'd romanced a woman who was on holiday in Maxos. Single and somewhat older than Yannis, the woman taught yoga in Athens and ran a successful business. When her holiday came to an end, she invited him to stay with her and, living in her home and at her expense and guidance, he studied hatha yoga and ultimately gained his teaching qualification.

'Why did you come to Britain?'

'The money is good here. Everyone wants to come to Britain. When I was nineteen, there was a downturn in the Greek economy, and things were tough. It was hard to make a living.'

Emily remembered hearing about the financial collapse of 2009 in Greece and understood that it must have been a challenging time for a young man starting out in life.

But Yannis had also not told Emily that the woman had kicked him out when she found him in bed with one of her yoga students. Furious at his betrayal and forbidding him to darken her door again, she threw his belongings onto the street from the top storey window of her house.

'So, Britain has been good to you?' Emily asked.

'Yes and no.' Yannis wriggled up the bed and put his arm around her shoulder.

'What do you mean?'

'I have travelled back and forth from Greece in my time here, and I've travelled in Europe. Now, in 2018, while we are part of the EU, it is easy. But when Britain leaves the EU, it will not be so easy.'

'You don't have to worry about that at present, surely?' she said.

Yannis pulled on the throw, and Emily gasped as he pounced on her and began to make love to her.

'No, my beautiful Emily,' he said. 'The only thing I have to worry about is making you happy.'

Happy was an understatement.

Emily was happier than she could ever remember as she gave herself to Yannis. She couldn't wait to confide in her friends and hoped that they'd all understand. This time at the spa had been a revelation and now, with her new image, she felt attractive, confident, sexually awake, and even powerful. The years seemed to have slipped away, and once more, she felt as young as Yannis. His hands were bold, and his body felt hard as he expertly touched her. She gave in to caresses that smoothed away her doubts, and as she listened to tender words, Emily stopped worrying about her past. Feeling very much in love, she knew that the present was all that mattered.

The day drew to a close at Sparadise, and the glamping site surrounding Bridgette's and Norman's tents glowed in the comforting light from Norman's campfire. As daylight began to fade, it was as though Mother Nature had flicked a switch with the stars twinkling in the heavens. The temperature was still high thanks to the heat that had blazed since dawn, and in the cool of the lake, two submerged bodies lazed about, enjoying the soft silky water as it embraced their naked skin.

Bridgette spread herself across the inflated pelican, and Norman lay on a Lilo. His hands and feet splashed gently, creating ripples, and his wide-open eyes stared up. The tranquil lake was calm and glassy, reflecting the clouds in the sky. Bridgette scanned the edge of the water where a heron was performing. The bird's long beak was poised at an angle as its stick-like legs prowled in the shallows, patiently stalking its prey.

'Herons have wonderful eyesight, even at dusk,' she said as the bird suddenly dived down, emerging with a flash of silver in its beak, the snared fish wriggling furiously.

'Vision is a gift. We must use it wisely.' Norman, still staring at the star-studded sky, was tracing the outline of the plough with one finger.

As he rambled on about nature and all of God's creations, Bridgette adjusted her weight and sighed contentedly. Gently propelling her feet and hands, she began to circle. She'd had the most enjoyable day, and now, feeling very relaxed, was happy to play about in the water with her new friend.

'Not heading in for dinner tonight?' Norman asked.

'No, I won't to go up to the house tonight,' Bridgette replied. 'I know that the girls will understand. We all agreed that while here, we would respect each other and do our own thing when we felt like it.'

'You have good friends.'

'The very best. I don't know what I'd do without them.' Bridgette thought fondly of Serena, Emily and Marjory and hoped that they were enjoying themselves as much as she was. 'Shall we ask Danka for room service again?'

'I have a few sausages we could roast over the fire and a couple of potatoes that will bake in the cinders. I'm sure I could rustle up a tin of beans too.'

'Lovely,' Bridgette said. 'I feel like a grown-up girl guide.'

'Won't your friends miss you?'

'The girls will guess that I won't be joining them tonight and will all have had their treatments today and are probably exhausted. They can save their energy for the party tomorrow.'

'Ah, the party.' Norman rolled off the Lilo and began to tread water. 'Are you all set?'

'Yes, Danka has my instructions. Her team will be here in the afternoon to set up. I shall ask folk to wander over in the early evening when their sessions have finished.'

'Clothed or unclothed?'

'Come as you like.' Bridgette giggled. 'I certainly will.'

'I've been to a few parties in my time. Swimming with polar bears in the Antarctic for my fiftieth is probably up there with the best. There was a cave climb in New Zealand which ended with a crowd of us racing down the rapids at Lake Taupo's Tongariro River and drinking champagne in a lagoon at the bottom to celebrate my sixtieth.'

Bridgette smiled. 'All naturist parties?'

'Naturally,' Norman said and nodded.

'How wonderful to confidently live a life that includes such adventure.'

They'd reached their tents, and Norman tidied away the inflatables. He handed Bridgette a towel and blanket then stoked the campfire.

'What was your career?' Bridgette asked.

'Top secret, dear lady.' Norman tapped his nose with a finger. 'After the French Foreign Legion, I was MI5 trained, with counterintelligence, abroad for most of my life on missions.'

'Oh, I see.' Bridgette didn't see at all but felt that the nature of Norman's work didn't include a disclosure. 'Did you marry and have any family?'

'Married many times, broken hearts across the globe, more children than the United Colours of Benetton.'

'Crikey.' Bridgette tried to imagine Norman as a globe-trotting lothario.

'What about you, any kids?'

'We have a son, Ralph. He lives in Abu Dhabi. He works for the British Embassy in the commercial section.'

'Grandchildren?'

'No.' Bridgette smiled as she thought of her son. Ralph was a bachelor who came back to the family home each Christmas and, to date, there was no sign of a partner. 'I've enjoyed travelling too,' she said as she watched Norman prepare their meal. 'I'm a trained horticulturist and have been lucky enough to host talks on cruises around the world.'

'A gardener!' Norman exclaimed. 'No wonder you feel so close to nature. I'm surprised you haven't ditched your outer layers long before now.' He speared a fat sausage with a toasting fork and held it close to the fire.

Bridgette would normally have bristled at the inadequate description of her talent. Over the years, she'd won four gold medals from the Royal Horticultural Society, including best historical garden and best in show, and she'd exhibited at Chelsea and Hampton Court flower shows and was a trained botanical guide. Her garden at Flaxby Manor attracted keen horticulturists from far and wide during open days in summer. She knew her cruise ship talks were lively and entertaining, with plenty of personal anecdotes. Still, as she stared into the flames and Norman heated beans in a pan, she realised that the company she kept was generally stuffy and pretentious. Cruise passengers were often too busy keeping up appearances and bagging a seat at the captain's table to worry about getting their hands dirty in good, honest soil, and at the shows, there was an air of competitive elitism that only the well-off could enjoy.

Here, Bridgette had suddenly felt released from all the snobbery of her day-to-day life. This knowledge meant that she didn't have to prove anything anymore. Going back to nature with Norman was forcing her to evaluate what mattered in life. Hugo's paralyzingly boring party at Flaxby Manor tomorrow was not on her agenda. Neither was the upcoming time she would spend entertaining day visitors who could afford the exorbitant entrance fee to her garden.

'An aperitif before dinner?' Norman asked and held out

a glass of their favourite vitamin drink. 'I've added a drop of rum to warm your cockles.'

'Lovely jubbly,' Bridgette said and took the drink.

'Tell me about your talks,' Norman said as he sat down.

'Oh, you'd probably be bored with most of the topics.' Bridgette smiled and took a long swallow. She reeled off several titles that included, *Behind the Scenes at Hampton Court* and *Top Tips for a Tip Top Garden*. Sensing that Norman was glazing over, she added, 'You'd probably enjoy a talk called *The Plant Hunters*.'

Norman sat forward and studied her with interest.

'It's about the transnational discoverers who brought exotic plants from all over the world to our shores.'

'That sounds right up my street,' Norman said.

'I make most of it up, but the audience seems to enjoy it.'

Norman turned his head. 'I think I can hear the phone ringing in your tent. Shall I fetch it?'

'No, Norman, let it ring. It will only be Hugo, having a fit and ordering me to return.' Bridgette's cheeks were flushed and her eyes sparkled. 'I've got a feeling he may well turn up and try to take me back to Flaxby. I've told Danka that he must not be admitted to Sparadise under any circumstances. He'll only spoil my weekend.'

Norman stood. 'I will not allow that to happen. Rest assured that you are safe while in my presence.' Soldier-like, he sprang to Bridgette's side. 'Top-up?' he asked and took Bridgette's empty glass.

'Only if you'll join me.'

Norman swayed slightly. 'I'm already a couple ahead of you.'

'Lovely,' she replied as Norman leapt into the air and kicked his heels, narrowly missing the open flames.

'Do be careful.' Bridgette, now equally as relaxed, grabbed her blanket and, grinning senselessly, pulled it around her shoulders. Then, stretching her naked legs and wriggling her stubby toes, watched the sausages sizzling on a skillet. 'We don't want roasted testicles on the menu tonight,' she said and collapsed in a heap of giggles as the ringtone from her phone in her tent began again. 'Not unless they're Hugo's...'

Chapter Eighteen

Marjory was in her room. She stood by an open wardrobe and tried to decide what she would wear that evening. There was only one good dress on the rail. It seemed pretty drab, and she wished she'd treated herself to some new clothes for the weekend. Before they'd arrived, she'd felt that the clothes in her suitcase would suffice, but now she wanted something special to go with her newly made-up face and energised body.

The shirtwaister that hung limply looked dowdy and, in truth, Marjory knew that she'd exhausted it during the many occasions when she'd worn it. It had an annual outing when she accompanied Reg to the Royal Pigeon Racing Association Show of the Year, a two-day event held in Blackpool and said to be the largest gathering of pigeon fanciers in Great Britain. Marjory considered the event the most boring two days of her life, but for Reg, it was the highlight of his year as he rubbed shoulders with fellow fanciers. The brotherhood saw pigeons change hands for large sums of money, and Reg spent many nervous hours competing in different classes with his pigeons. The 'Crufts' of the pigeon world, his dream was to be the best in the show. Marjory would like to see his favourite pigeon, Polly, in a nice, tasty pie rather than entered in the Supreme Champion Class, and instead of trailing around the trade stands, where eager punters could buy anything from a bag of corn to a velvet-lined, oak-crafted loft, Marjory made the most of her weekend and took herself off to the sights of Blackpool. She enjoyed eating fish and chips out of a takeaway box on the promenade while watching pensioners dozing in deckchairs on the beach and having her destiny told on the pier by a canny fortune-teller.

The woman gave readings in a little wooden hut hung with signed photographs of celebrities who'd appeared at the theatre on the pier. She had told Marjory to cross her palm with a twenty-pound note, and in return, stared into a crystal ball.

'I see feathers flying,' she said, 'and there's a man, known to you, with his heart set on a bird.'

Marjory considered the horoscope reading a complete waste of money. It was hardly clairvoyance to know that the pigeon show was in town. Reg's heart had always belonged to the wretched pigeon Polly, his prize-winning bird.

She was lost in her thoughts when the door was flung open and Emily came bursting into their room.

'By heck!' Marjory jumped. 'Is there a fire somewhere?'

'Oh, sorry.' Emily threw her key on the bed and began to peel her Lycra layers away.

'Are you in a hurry?' Marjory asked as she watched her friend hastily undress.

'Yes, I'm meeting Yannis, and he's going to cook for me.'

'What, in the yoga studio?' Marjory was puzzled as she followed Emily into the bathroom.

'No, silly. He lives in the staff house and there's a kitchen there. He's gone to the local shop to buy ingredients. I've come back for a shower.'

'You're spending a lot of time with that lad.'

'I'm sorry, do you mind?'

'No, we all agreed before we left that we could do our own thing. After all, we see each other all the time at home.'

'Oh, how I adore you.' Emily gave Marjory a hug. 'I may never get another opportunity to be with Yannis and he is the most divine human I've ever met.'

As Emily showered, Marjory raised an eyebrow. Emily had a love bite on the top of her breast and, judging by the faint scratch marks on her bottom, she'd been indulging in far more than a discussion of what Yannis might cook for dinner.

'He's making a Greek meal,' Emily said as she dried herself. 'Moussaka and a bottle of Assyrtiko, which is one of the best wines from Greece. We've been drinking it all afternoon. Yannis had a case tucked away, which he said was for an exceptional occasion.'

'Very nice,' Marjory said. She secretly thought the occasion was Yannis's celebration of banging an old broad daft enough to get involved with a toy boy but she decided to keep her thoughts to herself.

'I know what you are thinking – that it will all end in

tears, but I am having the first bit of fun that I've had in years.'

'Aye, lass, I know.'

Marjory watched Emily dress in another new outfit of loose-fitting cerise-coloured yoga trousers and a gorgeous pink lace-edged vest. She knew that, given her own experiences at the spa, she had no right to judge what Emily should or shouldn't do. Clearly in her element, and no doubt blinded by the best sex she'd ever experienced, Emily had blossomed. Surely she was entitled to a weekend of pleasure?

Marjory reflected on her own events. Should she have joined Willie in his motorhome and, if she had, could she live with the aftermath? Marjory already knew in her heart that Willie was more than a one-night stand.

'You look grand.' Marjory sat up. She watched Emily fluff her hair into the pretty style that Phillipe had cleverly cut.

'What are you doing this evening?' Emily asked and slipped her feet into a pair of silver jewel-encrusted sandals.

'I'm having dinner with Serena and Bridgette.'

'That should be fun, especially if Bridgette decides to bare all. What are you going to wear?'

Marjory pulled her dress from its hanger 'I don't know, but I haven't much choice. Everything I have is so frumpy that I feel like the oldest swinger in town.'

'I think Sparadise suits you. Have you done something differently?'

Marjory explained that she, too, had been paying attention to her appearance and experimenting with makeup, but with the boutique now closed, she'd have to stick with her boring old shirtwaister.

'Oh, no, you don't,' Emily said. 'I have the perfect thing.' She spun around and opened her suitcase. 'I've only worn this once because Joe and Jacob said I looked ridiculous when I wore it at Christmas.' She shook out a bright red silky jumpsuit. 'It's a bit big for me, but I was going to scrunch it in with a belt.'

'I could never wear anything like that…' Marjory's eyes were wide as she studied the gorgeous outfit that Emily laid out on the bed.

'Yes, you can. I won't wear it; it doesn't go with my new style for leisurewear. Try it on.'

'I can't wear something so flashy at my age… or could I?' she asked and looked dubiously at the clinging fabric. 'I'd need to wear my big pants.'

'You'll need some shoes too. Those old slingbacks won't do at all.' Emily rummaged further into her case and brought out a pair of black patent Louboutins. The stunning shoes had a plexiglass heel, studded to look like diamonds and the designer's signature red sole.

'By heck. I couldn't possibly wear them.'

'Why not? We have the same size feet. My sons would collapse if they knew how much these beauties cost. It was an impulse buy before I came away. They were nagging me to pay for a holiday to the Caribbean, to some music festival on an island called Bequia that they'd set their sights on.' Emily shook her head. 'They've done nothing to earn themselves a holiday and sooner than pay for them to go, I thought, "sod it," and treated myself. But now, I don't think I shall ever wear them.'

Minutes later, Marjory wobbled around the room in her new outfit. She stood shakily in her heels and stared at her reflection in a mirror. 'Blimey,' she gasped, not recognising the woman who stared back. 'This would put the proverbial cat amongst Polly and her wretched pigeons.' She grinned and thought of parading around at the pigeon fancier's show. 'I bloody love it!'

The jumpsuit, cut with a flattering 'V', showed plenty of Marjory's cleavage, and elbow-length sleeves covered the loose flesh at the top of her arms. Long in the leg, the fabric was flattering and combined with the designer heels, her body appeared elongated and slim.

Emily hugged her friend. 'The outfit is perfect. You look amazing and I hope that you feel as happy as I do tonight.' Emily's eyes had filled.

'Get away with you.' Marjory felt close to tears herself. The stranger in the mirror looked wonderful and appeared so much younger than her actual age. Reg would never recognise her, but would he even notice? Emotion welled up in Marjory's chest as though years of subdued frustrations were coming to the boil and threatening to spill over. *Oh, Willie!* she silently sighed. *What have I done? You offered me happiness and I turned you away…*

Pulling herself together and not wanting to spoil her makeup, Marjory gave Emily an affectionate shove. 'Now, I want you to go and find that young stud and have the night of your life.'

'Thank you, my precious friend.' Emily leaned in and

kissed Marjory on each cheek. 'You have a lovely evening too.'

———————

'Wow!' Stevie exclaimed as Serena floated into the bar. Her white gown fell gracefully to the floor, accentuating her curves as it clung to her body. The huge collar, edged with twinkling rhinestones, emphasised Serena's long neck. Every head turned as she strolled across the room.

Robin stood and patted a space on the banquette beside Stevie. 'Vintage Halston. It's perfect.' He kissed her on both cheeks. 'I think this calls for champagne.'

Stevie grinned and admired Serena from top to toe. 'Very Elvis,' he said, nodding his head in approval.

'Are your friends joining us this evening?' Robin asked when he'd ordered their drinks.

'Marjory should be here soon, Emily seems to have gone on the missing list, and I'm not sure about Bridgette.'

'Do tell us.' Stevie held his fingers together as if in prayer. 'What are the girls getting up to?'

Serena updated the couple on Emily's newly transformed appearance and her earlier confession of love for Yannis.

'I love a good romance,' Stevie said. The champagne had arrived and he held his foaming glass. 'To love, at whatever age,' he toasted.

'And Bridgette?' Robin was curious.

'She won't answer her phone, so I went to her tent to ask if she was joining us for dinner.'

'What did you find?' Stevie sat forward, anxious to know more.

'Not something that you'd want to post on Instagram. Bridgette and Norman were leisurely prancing around the campfire, holding a pink plastic pelican between them, who appeared to be dancing too.'

'Crazy,' Stevie breathed.

'Were they clothed?' Robin asked.

'Not a stitch, although Norman wore a bandana and Bridgette had a rubber cap on her head – the colourful flowers appeared to be drooping, though, like the rest of her.' She smiled. 'I never thought I'd see the day when Bossy Bridgette let her hair down, but I'm hardly surprised. I think this may have been coming for some time and Sparadise is the release she needed.'

'She seems to be doing more than just letting her hair down,' Stevie said. 'Are they at it, do you think?'

'If you mean are they having sex, no, I don't think so. The pair are so stoned I don't think either Bridgette or Norman would be capable of indulging in anything that required too much exertion.'

'Does Bridgette have a husband at home?' Robin sipped his drink, his manicured fingers elegant around the glass.

'She has a husband named Hugo, who, having found out that his wife has taken up naturism, is apoplectic with rage and keeps calling us all, demanding that we take her back to Flaxby Manor.'

'How exciting.' Stevie shook his head. 'Do you think he'll turn up for the party tomorrow?'

'No, I think Bridgette has banned Hugo from the

premises, hence his demands that we return with her.' The trio was so engrossed in their conversation that they hadn't noticed Marjory strut into the room.

The group of runners, gathered at the bar, were open-mouthed when they saw Marjory.

'Hello everyone,' she said and gave them a wave.

The bald runner tipped his head back and an unkind smile spread slowly over his face. He stared at Marjory's outfit and shook his head. 'Would you look… at… that. Nothing a good diet wouldn't sort out.'

'Look as much as you like because I don't need a diet,' Marjory retorted. 'The only carrots worth having are in a diamond.' She gripped a borrowed clutch from Emily, just large enough for her lipstick and phone, and kept her free hand on her hip as she determinedly placed one Louboutin in front of the other and made her way to Serena.

Marjory stood by the banquette, wobbling precariously in her heels. 'Good evening everyone. Is there a spare place at this party?'

Serena stood up. 'Marjory… my goodness, you look fabulous.'

'If you can't beat them, join them.' Marjory puffed out her cheeks. 'Budge up. My feet are bleedin' killing me and I'm so hungry I could faint.'

Chapter Nineteen

E mily hurried back to the staff house. She couldn't wait to be with Yannis again. Each moment apart felt like forever, and with the weekend already rushing by, every hour was precious. Racing through the yard, she noticed that the greenhouse was brightly lit and a pungent smell from masses of leafy green plants filled her nostrils.

Entering the kitchen, she was surprised that no one was there. She flicked a switch to illuminate an overhead strip light that cast a harsh brightness, emphasising every dingy nook and cranny. A bottle of Yannis's wine stood on the cluttered table. Picking it up, she opened the fridge and, moving a lump of dubious-looking cheese to one side, placed it on a shelf to cool.

'He must still be at the shop,' she said to herself, her thoughts running away as she imagined Yannis's extravagance with the money she'd given him to buy supplies. She stood by the sink, which was overflowing with dirty pots and pans, and ran the tap. The water was cold. Filling a kettle, Emily set it to boil and began to tidy the room. She didn't want anything to spoil their romantic dinner, and although she knew that Yannis would insist that he do all this on his return, she thought that she would save him the job.

Knowing that the house was empty, with all the residential staff either busy at work or out for the evening, Emily felt comfortable with the chores. Her mothering instinct had taken over, and, as if preparing an evening for her sons, she cleaned and polished until the place looked spic and span.

Admiring her handiwork, Emily ignored a dozen missed calls from Joe and Jacob and checked the time on her phone. Yannis had been gone for some time and must surely walk through the door at any moment. She rooted about in a cupboard and found a handful of household candles. There were matches, too, and she placed them on a plate in the middle of the table.

As the candles flickered to life, she opened the fridge and took out the bottle, turned off the light and pulled a chair to sit down, then poured a glass of wine.

Nervous with anticipation, Emily waited for her lover.

Dinner with Robin and Stevie was a thoroughly entertaining affair. Flushed with champagne and hilarious anecdotes, Marjory and Serena sat comfortably in the bar, both nursing a coffee as they listened to how the couple had met and set up their business.

'It was Robin who started the business. I came along several years later. You tell the story, Robin,' Stevie urged, looking lovingly at his partner.

Robin crossed his legs. He placed his fingers, pyramid style, on his chest and smiled. 'I was fortunate to have a mentor, and she wore my hats to every event she attended.'

He explained that a famous magazine editor enabled Robin to leave his little workshop on the top floor of his mother's house in Dulwich and set up on his own, eventually with a Knightsbridge address.

'She has been a massive inspiration,' Robin said, 'and still is, helping me to work with some of the main fashion houses.'

'He's designed hats for lots of celebrities. Pop stars too.' Stevie had a satisfied smile and held his shoulders back as he waited for their reaction. 'Tell them about royalty. You know, *the* wedding.'

'I've been lucky enough to design creations for royalty, and several have been rather eye-catching.'

'Of course, your hats are genius, and we all remember *that* wedding,' Serena joined in.

'By heck, do you mean the Mad Hatter's Tea Party Hats?' Marjory frowned. 'Even I remember those creations. The little lasses wearing them were front page on all the papers in the Co-op.'

'So, how did you two meet?' Serena looked from one to the other.

'Stevie was an intern. He'd studied at the London College of Fashion, and I can tell you that it was love at first sight.' Robin reached out and took his partner's hand. 'But he is very talented and has his own portfolio of famous names too.'

'Everyone said it wouldn't last because Robin is somewhat older, but we've been married for seven wonderful years. I don't know how he puts up with me.'

'I indulge him, and he loves to be indulged, which is why we spend large amounts of time far from the maddening crowd in London, hidden away at Sparadise.'

'The camera never lies, does it, darling?' Stevie turned to Serena. 'I look enormous in photos and need to slim down every so often, which is why the press call us by that horrible nickname.'

'Aye, Fatman and Robin are a bit cruel, but I've been called worse.' Marjory thought of some of the abuse she'd received while working at the Co-op, mainly dealt out when dealing with teenage shoplifters or Saturday night drunks.

As she was talking, Marjory's phone buzzed. Reaching into her bag, she flicked it open and glanced at the text on the screen.

The passion wagon is at the back of the building beside the woods. Come out, Cinderella, and meet your prince!

Marjory read the words then closed the phone. Her heart had begun to pound, and her hand shook as she snapped the clasp on the clutch. The silly old fool! Willie had returned and parked up. What on earth would folk say if they knew he was here and looking for her?

Marjory stood up. 'I'm ever so sorry, everyone, it's been a great evening, but I've had a phone call that needs answering.' She drained the last of her coffee.

'Is everything alright?' Serena looked concerned.

'Aye, right as rain, nowt I can't deal with.'

Robin and Stevie were on their feet.

'Thank you for a lovely evening, and if I don't come back, I'll see you in the morning. We have a big day tomorrow with Bridgette's party to look forward to.'

'If you can, do join us for a night cap,' Robin said, 'but if you don't return, sleep well.'

'Sweet dreams.' Serena gave Marjory a kiss on her cheek.

'Don't let the bedbugs bite,' Stevie called out.

As Marjory began to walk away, she passed the team from Lancashire Automotives. The sales manager, still sporting a black eye, looked up and let out a low wolf-whistle. The youngest, his face covered in patches of cream as green as grass, glanced in Marjory's direction.

The group of runners had gathered at the corner of the bar, sipping non-alcoholic beer and sparkling water.

'Past your bedtime?' a jogger called out.

Determined not to rise to the bait, Marjory gripped her clutch and held her head high.

'Mutton dressed as lamb…' the leader of the group said, loud enough for all to hear.

Marjory felt her blood boil. It was tempting to retaliate with an equally abusive remark and wipe the smug expression off his face, then follow it up with a kick in the crotch with the point of a Louboutin. But her phone was buzzing again. Fearing that Willie might walk into the spa in his moleskins and muddy boots, she glared at the runner and kept moving.

Danka sat at the desk in reception. She looked up from a

computer screen when she saw Marjory come into the hall. 'Wow, Mrs Ecclestone, I didn't recognise you. How glamorous you look this evening.'

'Thank you, Danka.' Marjory tried hard not to appear flustered. 'I've had a big dinner and am just popping out for a breath of fresh air.'

'It's a lovely evening for it.' Danka smiled.

Marjory teetered as her heels clicked on the tiles of the porch. 'Bleedin' hell, the gravel will bugger up the heels and Emily will kill me,' she mumbled. Grabbing a coat peg to balance herself, she removed her Louboutins and placed them on the shoe rack.

Opening the heavy oak door, Marjory stepped onto the drive.

'Ouch! Willie, where the bleedin' hell are you?' The gravel was sharp underfoot, so she darted back and donned a pair of Wellingtons.

Setting off again, Marjory crept around the side of the building, crouching low in the shadows in an attempt to dodge the security lights. Eventually, she made out the shape of a vehicle parked under a thicket of trees to one side of the garden. A fluffy white head popped up from the passenger seat, and two pink paws scrabbled at the window as she got closer. Willie's Westie wore a scarlet bandana.

'Keep it down, Fred.' She could hear Willie soothing his dog.

'Open up, you old fool,' Marjory hissed.

She'd reached the motorhome and had every intention of giving Willie a good telling off and sending him on his way, but as the side door slid back, she stared incredulously, and her mouth dropped open as she slapped a hand to her cheek.

'Blimey, Willie,' Marjory gasped.

'Climb aboard, Cinderella.' Willie, clean-shaven and dressed in an evening suit, crisp white shirt, scarlet bow tie and tuxedo, held out his hand. 'Your magical mystery tour awaits...'

Willie led her into the candlelit motorhome. Champagne on ice sat in a silver bucket on a linen-covered table, and the scent of fresh flowers overpowered the small space. A bed was covered in silk sheets, and a heart-shaped box of chocolates lay on a pillow. It was the most enormous box she'd ever seen.

'What on earth?' she whispered as Willie quietly closed the door, then poured the champagne and handed her a sparkling cut-glass goblet.

'To Marge, my beautiful Cinderella.' Tears glistened in the corners of his wise old eyes as he took in the sight of the decadently dressed woman before him. 'You look beautiful.'

Marjory was lost for words as she tasted the ice-cold drink. It was delicious, and her heart pounded as the bubbles popped on her tongue.

'Oh, Willie,' she sighed and sank on the bed.

'Oh, Marge,' Willie replied as he glanced down at her feet. 'How did you know that Wellies are my biggest turn-on?'

Chapter Twenty

Bridgette had eaten a substantial supper, which to her surprise, tasted very good. The potato was crisp outside, and light and fluffy within, the sausages oozed juice and flavour and the beans, with a dash of Worcestershire sauce, had been the perfect accompaniment that satisfied her food craving.

As the sky darkened and night set in, Norman produced a bag of marshmallows and, taking his long-handled fork, began to toast them on the fire.

'Something sweet, Empress?' he said as he pointed the fork in her direction, and she eased the warm gooey mass onto her fingers and began to lick.

'Mmm, delicious,' Bridgette murmured, her mouth full as she took another. A slight chill breezed in from the lake, and Bridgette pulled the blanket closer around her shoulders. She felt the damp air, dewy on her skin as her bare feet touched the grass.

'I think I might turn in,' she said and began to ease

herself up from her deckchair. 'It's been a long day and I suddenly feel exhausted.'

Norman leapt to his feet and, stretching out a hand, helped Bridgette negotiate the tricky procedure of deckchair dancing as she carefully manoeuvred herself up.

'Good idea,' Norman said as they stepped over guy lines. 'You'll need all your strength for your big day tomorrow.'

'Yes, I can't wait. I think it's going to be my most memorable birthday yet.'

'Sleep well, Empress,' Norman said as they reached Bridgette's tent, and he leaned over to unzip the opening. 'Sweet dreams.'

As Norman wandered away, Bridgette hoped her dreams didn't involve her last glimpse of Norman. His testicles, hanging like cow's udders, were hardly conducive to a good night's rest, but perhaps the sway of swinging flesh would send her off to sleep, like a boat gently bobbing on the sea.

It was cosy in her tent. The fairy lights were illuminated and gave an inviting glow, and the atmosphere was warm, the canvas having absorbed the day's heat. The housekeeper had placed a little ladder by the bed to enable Bridgette to climb easily onto her mattress, and the woman's kindness touched her. On a table, her phone lit up. She could see that there was a string of messages from Hugo.

'Oh, do stop worrying, you silly fool,' Bridgette sighed as she turned the phone over. 'Get off to the golf club where you belong and complain to your cronies because I've stopped listening.'

Bridgette threw her blanket off and ran her hands over her body. She felt marvellous in her nakedness, and the feeling of freedom, combined with the delicious vitamin drinks and swimming in the lake, had given her a euphoria that a good night's sleep would heighten.

There was only one problem, and it involved her ears.

Having submerged herself in the lake, she now had water in her ears, creating an annoying sloshing sound. It would be impossible to sleep if it continued. She held her hands to cover her ears, and suddenly, the sound stopped.

'Bugger, I can't sleep with my hands in that position all night,' she mumbled and looked around for something to help. Her rubber swimming cap lay on a suitcase, and the vibrant colours caught her eye. 'A perfect solution,' she said and slid off the bed, pulling it firmly over her head, smoothing the floppy flower adornments until her ears lay flat against her scalp.

She padded over to the ladder and, stepping onto the rungs, climbed back into bed. As she lay snuggled under the light summer duvet, she stretched out her arms and wriggled her toes.

'Ah,' she sighed. 'Deep breaths in and hold it...' She remembered a talk on mindful meditation at Flaxby WI and how it could induce a restful snooze. But as Bridgette's eyes closed and her body began to lull itself into La La Land, she heard whispering through the thin rubber of her cap, and it came from outside the tent. Someone was gasping.

Her eyes popped open, her senses suddenly alert.

'Ahhh!' The gasping turned into a strange, strangled moan, and she could hear a man cry out.

Bridgette threw back the duvet and slid out of bed, landing with a thud.

'Ouch!' she exclaimed, wincing as her bottom met the rough coconut matting. Lifting the flap on the tent, she eased out and crept in the direction of the cries. Her heart was pounding as her eyes adjusted to the clear moonlit night. Was Norman alright? Had he been hurt? Was there an intruder within the grounds? Questions flooded her mind as she moved stealthily forward, strangely unafraid of what she might find.

A flash of something white was visible up ahead, and as she got closer, Bridgette realised that it was a tunic. The uniform of the staff at the spa, which at that moment was being tugged tightly over the bare breasts of Monika, the beautician. A man was pulling on a pair of shorts, his half-covered buttocks pale in the moonlight. As he turned, Bridgette blinked. Wasn't that the young yoga instructor named Yannis?

Bridgette stopped in her tracks. The pair were oblivious to the onlooker and had begun to giggle again.

'You must get back to your cougar,' Monika said as she straightened her clothing.

'Don't call her that,' Yannis replied. 'She's just lonely and I am fulfilling her fantasies.'

'All part of the job?'

'Isn't it always?'

Yannis had grabbed Monika's arm and they hurried into the night. As Bridgette crept forward, she saw them break apart when they reached the garden gate, and the pair went in separate directions.

'Young hearts,' she said and smiled to herself, turning to return to her bed.

But as she turned, something huge, shadowy, and dangerous loomed ahead.

Bridgette's eyes were wide with fear, and her heart pounded as she tried to back away. Whatever was coming towards her was getting closer and, in the moonlight, she could see hot moist breath steaming from the bulk. The earth beneath her bare feet shuddered as the creature came closer.

'N... N... Norman!' she cried out and began to run. She was gasping as her blood pressure soared. Bridgette's plump little legs were no match for whatever was in pursuit, and the creature was almost upon her. 'Norman!' she screamed as his tent came into view. *'Help me!'*

'Empress! I'm here,' Norman raced forward, silhouetted by the embers of his fire. 'Oh, hell, someone must have left the top gate open in the fields. It's a bull!' He reached out, and as Bridgette fell into his arms, she felt Norman's fingers tearing at the cap on her head. Time seemed to stand still as the object flew through the night and landed at the feet of the most giant, most ferocious bull they had ever seen. Suddenly, as if shot, the bull stopped in his tracks and, thrusting his head down, caught the cap on his nose and violently shook it. Then, suddenly calm, the creature chewed on a cud of grass and swishing his tail, emptied his bowels and turned to meander away.

'A b… b… bull…' Bridgette was trembling and could barely speak.

Norman muttered, 'I don't know what upset it, perhaps the rubber flowers on your cap?'

Such was the relief of both Bridgette and Norman that they simultaneously let out a sigh. Still entwined and gripping one another, they turned to go back to their tents. But as they altered their route, neither saw the guy lines threaded like mines under their feet. In seconds, Bridgette's little toes had become tangled and, unable to keep her balance, she careered through the air, taking Norman with her and landing with a crash on a deckchair.

A loud crack pierced the night air as though petrol had been poured on the fire. 'Agh!' Bridgette screamed as white-hot pain seared through her arm.

'Oohhhh!' Norman yelled as he fell on top of her, his weight crushing her little body.

The last thing Bridgette remembered before she passed out was feeling a man's naked skin against her own, an experience that hadn't occurred for a great many years, and as she drifted into oblivion, she wondered what Hugo would have to say.

Chapter Twenty-One

Yannis sat with Emily at the table in the kitchen of the staff house, their glasses almost empty and two plates pushed to one side.

'I hope that you liked the dinner?' Yannis asked, reaching out to touch her hair and curl it around his finger.

'Er, yes, it was good.' Emily was hesitant.

Yannis had eventually returned to the house with a chilled lasagne. It was unfortunate that the local shop hadn't stocked any of the ingredients for him to make moussaka, and, given the length of time that he'd been gone, Emily doubted that there would have been time to assemble such a dish.

'The shop was so busy. I waited for ages, but the lasagne was almost as good as my mana's recipe for moussaka.' Yannis leaned in and began to lick Emily's ear.

Emily thought that Yannis's mana couldn't have been a very good cook if her son highly rated the pale brown mush that she'd primarily left on her plate. But she had little appetite for the hurried meal – her desire was for Yannis, and she longed for him to suggest that they go up to his attic room and settle down for the night.

Yannis picked up the bottle on the table and, lifting it, drained the last of the wine into his glass. 'It's on nights like this that I wish I were back in Bessaloniki, sitting on the terrace of my mana and patera's house in Maxos.'

Taking Emily's hands, his eyes shone as he described the sun sinking over the horizon, casting an orange and gold light that sparkled on the indigo waters of the Ionian Sea. Mesmerised, he would stare at the dark shape of the peninsula and breathe in the sweet smell of cypress and pine as shades of red and pink splintered the sky and beads of twinkling lights threaded through the trees in the tiny village.

'It sounds like a wonderful place. You paint such a vivid picture, and I can almost imagine what it would be like to be there.'

'It is magical, my Emily.' Yannis swept his hand across the room. 'So much more than anything we could have here.'

Emily noted that Yannis used the plural when talking about his future and her heart melted like chocolate in the sun. She moved closer, gripping his hands.

'I want to take you there. It is as beautiful as you, and you will blossom in the warmth and charm of the island.'

'Oh, Yannis, but we can go.' Emily was excited. Her mind was awhirl with images of walking together with Yannis along the cobbled pathways and drinking in the scents of oleander, juniper, myrtle, and geraniums as they overflowed from window boxes and flower pots. Locals would wave, their weathered faces smiling as they acknowledged the happy couple so very much in love.

'We will swim in the tranquil waters and bathe in the shallows; the sea is so good and restoring.' His eyes were alight, and he took hold of her shoulders. 'Imagine, my Emily, we can practice our yoga early in the morning, before the heat becomes intense and make love as the sun rises, then embrace each new day.'

Emily's eyes were closed. She could almost hear the waves and feel the sun on her skin. 'Oh, Yannis, how soon can we go?'

Yannis pulled her closer. 'It takes money. Maxos is so small – there is no work for me and we would struggle to survive.'

Emily hadn't envisaged anything more than a holiday, but she suddenly realised that Yannis was discussing a future where they would be together on the island. Intrigued and flattered beyond her wildest dreams, she asked, 'How much money?'

'The only way we could live would be to do up my parents' home. They are old, and it is bequeathed to me, and as long as they have a room there, it would be possible.'

'But what would you do with the property?'

'I would turn it into a yoga retreat. The building is perfect, with large rooms overlooking the bay and plenty of accommodation that can be upgraded.'

Emily could feel his excitement. He'd given this idea a great deal of thought.

'The town would embrace such a project,' he continued.

'It would bring tourism to the area. We could collect guests from the airport in a personalised vehicle that easily negotiates the steep incline.'

'A good website would help attract bookings and word of mouth would spread.' Emily was getting carried away too. 'We could use local produce and ensure that everyone benefits from a healthy Greek diet.'

'You like my idea?' Yannis gripped her shoulders and held her at arm's length.

'It's a wonderful dream.'

'Yes, but an impossible one.' His hands dropped and his head dipped. 'To live a life like that we need money to make money.'

'But I have money.'

Yannis looked up. He flicked his hair away from his face and shook his head as if he didn't understand.

'I have plenty of savings which we could use to live on while the project is planned, and my house in Flaxby is worth quite a bit. There's no mortgage on it.'

'But what about your sons?'

'What about them?' Emily almost snapped. 'Joe and Jacob are lazy and ungrateful and I'm tired of supporting them. It's time they took responsibility for themselves. They could always come and visit us. It might do them good.'

'There would always be a home with us for your family.' He put his hands under her shoulders and lifted her to his knee, nestling her body into his.

Emily thought that Yannis might retract that kind offer if he spent so much as a day with Joe and Jacob, but now, she felt a giddiness in her tummy and a lightness in her chest.

Could this be happening? Was Emily Avondale's boring old life about to change beyond her wildest dreams? Her mouth felt dry as she turned to Yannis. Licking her lips, she said, 'I'm serious, Yannis, I have the money and you have the location.'

'Together, my Emily, we have the love to make it happen.'

They covered each other in kisses. Emily was almost hysterical with excitement as she thought about how her life might transform.

'But we must make plans.' Yannis had become severe.

'Yes, of course.'

'This must happen as soon as possible.'

'I have no reason to delay. I can leave whenever you like.'

'Shall we go and look for flights?'

'Why not?'

'My mana and petera will love you!' Yannis cried out as he swept Emily into his arms and carried her up the stairs to his room.

Emily hardly dared contemplate what his parents would say when the prodigal son returned, unannounced, with a woman old enough to be his mana. But as Yannis grabbed his laptop, for once in her dull, lonely life, she didn't care what anyone thought.

In the penthouse, three heads huddled together, bent low as they examined a drawing in a large leatherbound notebook. Shoulder to shoulder, Robin, Stevie and Serena considered each careful sweep of the artist's pen and the gentle curves of the model that had been drawn to demonstrate how the newly adapted Plumed Chapeau was to be worn.

'It's brilliant but I'm not sure I can carry it off.' Serena glanced nervously at the others to see what they thought.

'Of course you can,' Stevie said. 'If you can wear a dress like the one you're wearing now, you can wear anything. We've designed the entire show-stopper as a bespoke piece for you at Bridgette's birthday bash.'

Serena cleared her throat. 'Do you really think I can wear something as outrageous as this?' She picked up a pencil and pointed to the drawing. 'I mean, the swimsuit barely covers my body and with the hat towering above my head, I may well fall flat on my face.'

'You have the presence of Naomi Campbell. You can carry anything off, it just takes confidence,' Robin said.

'I can hardly believe you're going to so much trouble to reveal this incredible hat tomorrow.' Serena directed a hesitant nod towards the drawing.

Robin stood up. 'It works both ways, my darling. You want exposure on Instagram to get your cookery career back, and we want to launch something head-turning that will be picked up in the press.'

'You can never have too much press.' Stevie stood too.

'I don't have any so the slightest whiff of a column inch would be greatly received.' Serena looked up at her new friends.

'Our people are working on it as we speak.' Robin

winked. 'They've sent everything I requested, and plans are in place, so stop worrying.'

'And this will give your rival something to think about. Let's have that nightcap we promised. I fancy something creamy.'

The two men disappeared to root through the minibar in the next room.

Serena flicked on her phone. @YvettetheChefette had been posting all day, and as reluctant as she was to study the images, Serena found that she couldn't help herself. There were more lingerie shots of the young chef draped around a variety of kitchen equipment. A video that showed Yvette doing anything but prep food with a rolling pin made Serena gasp. The ever-increasing hits and followers were mind-boggling to watch. The sponsors must be over the moon with the publicity, Serena thought as she gritted her teeth and flicked through the posts. The #HankyPankyLingerie girl had certainly earned her keep.

Serena sat back in her seat and tapped the pencil in her hand as she glanced around the suite. The boys had a lot riding on their prodigy the next day, and she was doubtful that she could carry it off. Bridgette's party was the perfect setting to perform the stunt, but would Serena have the courage to do it? She flicked her phone open again and searched for any news from Cornelius. She longed for some reassuring words and his soft voice instilling confidence. But there was nothing. No call or message. She wondered if he had written an email and searched her inbox too. But Cornelius was nowhere to be seen. Serena took a deep breath and counted to ten. She must not get annoyed with him. It would disturb her sleep if she were angry, and she badly needed to look her best the next day.

'Drinks,' Stevie announced and came bounding into the room, followed by Robin carrying a tray.

'Let's go out to the balcony.' Robin moved towards the doors. 'It's still warm and we can study the stars.'

Together they stepped outside. Robin placed chunks of ice in a tumbler and poured a strawberry-flavoured creamy drink loaded with whisky. He handed it to Stevie.

'Oh, here's half a stone weight gain just looking at this divine concoction,' Stevie said as he pushed a straw into the pink mix and began to suck. 'It's very yummy.' He offered the glass to Serena. 'Would you like a taste?'

'No, thank you, I'll decline.'

'Will you join me for a brandy?' Robin held a bottle of expensive cognac and poured a measure into a balloon glass.

'No, I want to keep a clear head for tomorrow.'

'What a beautiful night. Just look at all the different shapes that the stars are making. What does it all mean?' Stevie asked as he stared up at the sky.

Serena held onto the railing and breathed in the warm sweet air drifting up from the countryside. She listened as Robin began to answer Stevie's question, and she looked around, her eyes resting on the glass-like lake under the silvery moon.

'In earlier times the stars were the inspiration for story-tellers. People also used the sky as a calendar and as the seasons changed, they noticed a correlation between different times of the year.'

He continued to explain why observatories were built, but his voice faded as a commotion suddenly caught Serena's attention on the other side of the garden.

'Something's wrong. Look, there are people in the glamping area.'

The trio moved closer to the handrail, squinting as their eyes adjusted to the darkness. Flashes of white were moving about close to a pair of tents.

'I think it's the staff.' Robin leaned over as far as he could. A cloud moved away from the moon then, allowing light to illuminate the scene. A huddle of white tunics was crouching down, and a woman was issuing instructions.

'It's Danka,' Stevie said. 'I wonder what she's doing down there at this time of night?'

'Oh, Lord, they're beside Bridgette's tent.' Serena's hands were clammy as she gripped the railing.

Suddenly, a siren wailed and flashing lights, a lightning bolt of blue, flew across the driveway below.

'My goodness!' Stevie's hand flew to his throat.

'Bridgette may be hurt. I must go!' Serena cried out and began to run.

'We're coming too.' Stevie followed in hot pursuit with Robin alongside.

'Please let Bridgette be alright,' Serena said as they reached the stairs. 'I should have spent more time with her, not left her alone in her tent.' She hitched up her dress then hurried down the first flight.

Stevie, who still held a drink in his hand, was right behind Serena but suddenly, he stumbled. Robin reached out to steady his partner and took the glass, which was now empty, the contents an abstract painting all over Stevie's white linen shirt.

'Keep calm, I'm sure Danka has everything in hand,' Robin said as they hurried to the front door.

Serena pounded across the drive and saw that an ambulance had come to a stop by an old motorhome parked under a thicket of trees. Security lights lit up the area. As the trio squeezed through a gap between the vehicles to reach the garden gate, the motorhome curtains were suddenly pulled back and a face stared out of the window, eyes blinking in the harsh unnatural light.

'Marjory!' Serena gasped as she saw her friend. 'Whatever are you doing in there?'

A fluffy white dog appeared and began to jump up and down, and Marjory pushed it out of the way. As she mouthed words and gesticulated wildly, Serena could see that Marjory's shoulders were naked. She didn't appear to be clothed.

'I don't know what you're saying, but come quickly. I think Bridgette is hurt,' Serena shouted. She eased her way through, and as she got to the gate, a hand reached out and caught her arm.

It was Emily, her face white. Yannis stood behind her.

'Serena, what is it?' Emily implored, her eyes blinking as she looked towards the tents. 'Is it Bridgette?' Yannis tried to soothe Emily and hold her back, but she broke away and grabbed Serena's hand.

'Wait for me!' Marjory suddenly appeared beside them. She wore a pair of moleskin trousers and a worn checked shirt. Her candyfloss hair was fluffed up. Emily and

Serena's eyebrows rose, and their mouths fell open as Marjory took Serena's free hand.

'Don't ask,' Marjory said. 'I didn't have time to get back into that fancy jumpsuit and these were the only things to hand...'

Gripping hands, the three friends set off.

'We shouldn't have left Bridgette on her own,' Serena repeated. 'Why on earth didn't we share the tent with her? Then none of this would be happening.'

'We will deal with whatever *has* happened once we know what we're dealing with.' Emily, the schoolmistress, was calm.

They headed towards the tents where Danka stood and watched the paramedics at work.

'How is she?' Serena asked.

'It took a long time for the ambulance to arrive, but they are dealing with her now,' Danka said, a frown creasing her smooth brow.

Marjory had begun to sob, 'Please, please let Bossy Bridgette be alright,' she cried as together, they saw Bridgette lifted onto a stretcher and driven away into the night.

Chapter Twenty-Two

I n the calm sanctity of the penthouse, Sunday morning began with a restorative breakfast for the traumatised group who'd witnessed the scenes from the night before. Robin and Stevie had arranged for room service to provide a substantial spread and set up on a table under an umbrella on the terrace. Slowly, one by one, Serena, Marjory and Emily made their way to the suite and now sat together, napkins on their laps.

'I thought she was dead,' Marjory said as she poured cream onto a pile of pancakes topped with strawberries and blueberries.

'She was so pale,' Emily said in a hushed tone as she buttered a slice of wholemeal toast. 'I thought she'd stopped breathing.'

'Bridgette must have been in a great deal of pain to have passed out like that.' Stevie was munching on a cooked breakfast, his plate piled high.

'That's not what the doctor said in A&E when she was

wheeled in.' Serena had her elbows on the table and rested her chin on her hands as she watched the others. 'It seems that she was so smacked off her face on her vitamin and rum concoction that she'd simply fallen asleep.'

Robin and Stevie had insisted that they accompany the friends to the hospital. With Danka at the wheel of the Sparadise courtesy vehicle, they'd followed the ambulance. Bridgette had Norman by her side and was monitored throughout the journey. Two hours had passed as they anxiously waited, but then, assured by hospital staff that their friend would be alright, they'd left with Norman wrapped in a blanket, and returned to Sparadise in the early hours.

'Poor Bridgette.' Emily ignored Serena. 'What a terrible day for her and with her birthday party too.'

'I'm sure she'll be back for that. They were only keeping her in for observation while the substances cleared out of her body.' Serena reached for a cup and poured coffee.

'Yes, but a fracture is agony. Surely she'll have her arm in plaster?' Emily looked at the faces around the table.

'I loved having plaster on my arm when I was little,' Stevie said between mouthfuls of mushrooms and black pudding. 'Everyone wrote things in different coloured pens and drew little pictures all over it. I felt like the most popular kid in school.'

'She's seventy,' Serena, Emily and Marjory stated flatly, staring at Stevie.

'Oops, I forgot –you ladies are so youthful and full of fun.'

'Flattery will get you everywhere,' Marjory stood and

dabbed at her lips with her napkin. 'I hate to break the party up, but I've got my last session with the magical massage therapist and I don't want to be late.'

'Not the only session you've been having.' Serena raised her eyebrows as she stared at Marjory, whose face had flushed crimson. 'So, tell us, who was in the passion wagon with you? It couldn't have been the Westie dog that got you all worked up?'

'I think the trousers and shirt were too big for the dog.' Emily giggled.

'Nowt to do with any of you if I have an admirer.' Marjory's fingers began to ball her napkin.

'I think I know who it is,' Serena teased. 'Could the mystery man be a certain caretaker from Flaxby Community Centre by any chance?'

Stevie's eyes lit up. 'Do tell. I love illicit romance.'

'He's been batting his broom at you for years. I can't imagine why you've never climbed on board before now,' Serena said as she smiled.

'Don't come a knocking when the motorhome is rocking.' Emily laughed out loud. 'You've discovered sex at sixty-eight, which is curious considering you live at number fifty.' She dodged Marjory's swipe at her head with her napkin.

'Tell us more,' Serena insisted.

'There's nothing to tell so you can keep your crude thoughts to yourselves.' Marjory moved away, but as she glanced at Serena, a smile had formed on her lips, and she gave her a wink.

'Your secret will always be safe with us,' Serena called

out to Marjory's retreating figure. 'What happens at Sparadise stays at Sparadise.'

'Does anyone know how Norman is today?' Emily asked as Robin came into the room.

'Norman is currently swimming, alone, in the lake,' Robin said. 'But you will be interested to know that he's made news in the local online paper.' He opened his phone and searched until he found the website for *Life in Lancashire*. A headline stated:

Blame the Bull! Says Naturist Norman

The article told how two naturists staying at Sparadise, a luxury spa located in the Forest of Bowland, had been so scared by an incident with a raging bull in the middle of the night that they'd ended up in the A&E department of the local hospital. Norman's partner, an elderly woman in her seventies, whom an anonymous source said didn't wish to be named, had suffered a broken arm but was expected to make a full recovery.

'I knew we shouldn't have let Norman ride with Bridgette in the ambulance,' Serena said.

'Especially as he refused to put his clothes on.' Emily shook her head.

'It's a wonder he wasn't arrested for indecent exposure.' Stevie stared at the photograph that a keen young journalist had taken. The journalist had been in A & E hoping for a story on a slow news day. The photograph showed Norman, his lower half covered by Bridgette's stretcher, eyes wide, hair wild, and mouth open as he stared into the lens.

'Goodness, Bridgette won't like that, "an elderly woman in her seventies," and she isn't Norman's partner,' Serena said. 'I'm sure they're nothing more than friends, but let's hope that Hugo hasn't seen it.'

'Well, it's hardly going to make the nationals. I can't imagine that anyone actually reads stuff like this,' Robin said.

Emily stood up. 'I must go. I have a yoga session and like Marjory, I don't want to be late.'

'Yes, we have things to do too.' Robin looked at Stevie. 'Are you going to give me a hand to make sure everything's in place?'

'Lead on.' Stevie followed Robin into the lounge.

Serena sat alone at the breakfast table. She'd booked a facial and, glancing at her watch, decided she should make a move as she too didn't want to be late. It might be sensible to have a word with Danka and make sure that everything was ready for the party since Bridgette might not be feeling well enough to check last-minute arrangements. Reaching for her phone, she searched for messages. There was still no word from Cornelius, despite her text asking him to call and assure her that he was okay and hadn't got lost on a fell.

Drawn irresistibly to Instagram, she studied her account. The latest image of Serena wearing the white dress included the hashtag "Halston". It had gained a few more followers and likes. Serena smiled when she read, "I'm all shook up!" from @LocoLad, but her face turned to stone as she noted a comment from an Instagram user who called themselves @RunningFree.

'*Time for Elvis to leave the building,*' the comment read. Had the lead runner renamed himself and opened a new account?

Serena instantly blocked him.

With a sigh, she closed her phone. The account for @SaucySerena paled compared to @YvettetheChefette's popularity, and no matter how hard she tried not to be annoyed, Serena secretly seethed. Robin and Stevie were kindly helping her, but Serena knew that their efforts of posing her in a hat and posting it on social media would hardly rock the world. Time was running out, and the weekend was almost over.

She would be returning home tomorrow to an empty house if Cornelius was out on the fells. Hopefully daft old Dodger would keep her company. It was hardly the dazzling world of celebrity cooking that she craved. The ancient Aga in her cottage kitchen was no match for the fabulous backdrop of Sparadise.

'We're all set,' Stevie announced as he stepped onto the terrace and looked at his watch. 'You need to shake a lovely leg and go and have your facial.'

'I'm on my way.'

'We've also arranged for Phillipe to do your makeup – no arguments,' he said, cutting Serena off as she was about to object. 'We've pulled a few favours. Everyone wants to book him, but he's yours for a full hour.'

'You're both very kind, but I'm still unsure of wearing such an outfit at my age. I don't think I can do this.'

'Nonsense. We'll hear no more.'

Stevie took hold of Serena's hand, then marched her out of the suite and down the stairs to the spa, where Monika was waiting for them.

'Let's get this party started.' Stevie blew a kiss and left Serena with Monika.

'Time to get you glammed up for the party. Are you ready?'

Serena glanced at a clock on the wall. Her big entrance was getting closer. 'As ready as I'll ever be,' she said and, with an anxious feeling in the pit of her stomach, allowed herself to be led away.

———

Emily sat at the table in the corner of Yannis's room and stared at the screen on his laptop. A confirmation had just arrived from an airline. She could barely believe her eyes as her fingers flew over the keyboard and two boarding passes appeared for a direct flight from Manchester to Bessaloniki, leaving the following evening.

'All confirmed,' she announced, wetting her lips. Her eyes were bright and her tummy fluttered with excitement. An adventure was about to begin! Emily wanted to run across the room to leap all over Yannis, but he was suddenly by her side.

'This is good.' Yannis punched the air then leaned down to hug her.

'Don't you think you ought to tell the management that you're going?' Emily asked.

Yannis had moved away and was busy taking posters down from the walls. 'It's easier this way, less complicated. I will leave a note for Danka to read tomorrow after we have gone. She may only try and stop me; I am very well-liked here.'

Yannis was aware of his popularity and, although he knew that his sudden departure would upset the rotas and bookings at the spa, his concern was more personal. He didn't care about leaving them in the lurch. Yannis was far more worried about Monika's reaction. Although liberal and broad-minded, she would be furious when she found out he was heading to Greece with Emily. It was a dream that they'd discussed during their on-off relationship, but Monika had no money to make the dream come true. She accepted his short-lived flings, as long as they didn't last, but Yannis had made promises to her that he couldn't keep.

He knew he had to leave with Emily before Monika found out. Emily's gold waited for him at the end of his Bessaloniki rainbow, and the retired headteacher had more than enough to keep them in style for some time. He smiled as he considered the amount of money they'd have when her house sold.

Emily saw Yannis smile. *How content he looks*, she thought, delighted that he felt the same way she did. Happy and in love and about to begin a new journey in life. During the yoga class that morning, Emily had felt secretly smug as she stretched and bent her body. The rest of the students would be green with envy if they knew her plans, and it had been all she could do not to blow kisses to Yannis as he led the class.

She forwarded the airline confirmation to her phone and several messages popped up on the screen from Joe and Jacob. There were countless missed calls too.

There was also a new voice message from Hugo.

Emily sighed. Hugo could be so difficult. He always got in the way when the friends gathered at Flaxby Manor for coffee and a natter. Pompous and interfering, Emily wondered how Bridgette put up with him. But Hugo wasn't her problem, and she had no intention of listening to his rant. Emily scanned the angry messages from her sons and decided to wait and phone Joe and Jacob as soon as she arrived in Greece. If they knew she was leaving, they would only try and stop her.

Emily went back to the laptop and saved the details of a local estate agent in Flaxby. She might contact them and felt sure that Serena, who had a set of keys to the house, would step up and be there for the agent to value the property. Joe and Jacob would have plenty of notice, and she would make sure that they had a deposit and at least three months' rent for somewhere new to live.

Still, for now, as she watched Yannis, she needed nothing more than her suitcase of clothes. Their love for each other would get them through whatever complications might arise.

'Bridgette will be back from the hospital soon,' Emily said as she helped Yannis gather his belongings and sort them into suitcases. 'She might need help to get ready for her party and I really can't miss it. I won't be seeing her for a long time.'

'Of course, my beautiful Emily.' Yannis took her in his

arms. 'She is your friend. It is good – we will go to the party tonight and wish her well.' He leaned down, his lips brushing against her own.

'She will have a very happy birthday,' Emily replied as Yannis's hands moved to encircle her, 'but she will never be as happy as I am now.'

248

Chapter Twenty-Three

B ridgette sat in the back of a vehicle that Danka had kindly sent to the hospital to bring the injured guest back to Sparadise. The driver, Edmond, helped to oversee valet parking at Sparadise. He was a nervous man with a comb-over hairstyle and beady eyes that constantly checked the rearview mirror as he drove through the countryside and along the roads that led to the spa. It was another hot day and Edmond kept the air-conditioning in the car on its coldest setting, but this had little to do with the temperature outside. Edmond was far more concerned with the temperature inside the vehicle. Any heat caused his passenger to fling her blanket to one side, and the sight of her naked seventy-year-old breasts bobbing about on his back seat was most unsettling.

Edmond was aware of his passenger's age because of the constant stream of conversation she was engaged in on her mobile. In the short time that she'd travelled with him, he felt he knew her quite well. The woman was staying at the spa, and during the night, she'd had an accident. Edmond was trying to piece together snippets of conversation and had gathered that her injury had something to do with a man called Norman and a raging bull. He thought she seemed remarkably calm given that her arm was encased in plaster and held in place with a sling. But as she sipped on a vitamin drink that the spa manager had handed to him to ensure that the guest was hydrated, the woman appeared pain free and perfectly relaxed. She'd spoken at length to the manager to ensure that preparations for a birthday party were well underway. Now the conversation with a new caller had become heated and piqued the driver's interest.

'Hugo, if you turn up at Sparadise, I will have you removed from the premises.' Bridgette's tone was firm. Her conversation was on loudspeaker, and the driver tilted his head back to ensure he didn't miss anything.

'Blast and damn, woman!' Hugo shouted. 'I demand that you make a U-turn and return to Flaxby Manor immediately!'

'Not happening,' Bridgette said, sipping her drink as she gazed out of the window.

'I know all about your games. I've had Marjory Ecclestone's husband, Reg, here all morning. He had the Life in Lancashire app on his phone, and I have to say,' Hugo paused and spluttered, 'I am appalled by the article and shocked by your behaviour with this nutter called Norman. It says you are *his partner*?'

Edmond, intrigued, made a mental note to go online and find the article as soon as he stopped driving.

'Norman is just a friend. He has shown me how to live an alternative life and I must tell you that I am loving it.'

'Listen, old girl,' Hugo's tone softened. 'It's your hormones. Reaching the big seven-O has upset your balance. You're a little unstable now, but we can get you to Doctor Shipman as soon as you come home.'

'For the umpteenth time, Hugo, I'm not coming home today.'

'You will feel better when you're back on firm territory,' Hugo soothed, ignoring his wife's reply. 'There's still time to get back for the party I've arranged. It will do you good to be with all your friends – people who understand you.'

'I am not going to sit around all afternoon with your cronies. I am having my party at Sparadise and that's an end to it.'

'I don't know who's put you up to this; I can only imagine it's the company you keep. I always knew your swimming class on Wednesday was a dangerous environment.'

Edmond frowned. He wondered if Bridgette was in a terrorist organisation that secretly met in an underground pool. Hugo droned on and Bridgette glazed over as she studied the cows in a neighbouring field.

'I've even had those two surly Avondale youths on my doorstep, demanding that I drive them over to the spa to rescue their mother.' Hugo sounded short of breath. 'If I could get hold of that artist fellow who wanders aimlessly over the fells and lives with Serena, I'd get him to talk some sense into you all.'

'Have you finished, dear?' Bridgette asked.

'No, I bloody well haven't! I hope you've got some clothes on. I'll chop this Norman's balls off for the influence he's having on you.'

'Calm down. You know what Doctor Shipman says about your blood pressure.'

Edmond, who didn't like Hugo's aggressive manner, nodded his head in approval. He admired his passenger.

'What would your son think about your behaviour?' Hugo said, throwing an underhanded blow.

'He'd probably applaud. Our dear Ralph is hardly a saint in Abu Dhabi. Has it ever crossed your mind that, at forty, he has never married or brought a partner home?'

Hugo had no desire to listen to his wife discuss their son's salacious sex life. She seemed fully clued-up on the topic, and in anger, he yelled, 'BRIDGETTE, I ORDER YOU TO COME HOME.'

Hugo was hysterical and his voice vibrated off the ceiling of the cab. The driver winced and, losing concentration, swerved to one side of the road to avoid an oncoming vehicle.

'Goodbye, Hugo,' Bridgette said. She turned her phone off then tipped her drink back and drained the last drop.

They were passing a line of motorbikes, parked neatly beside a roadside café and, undisturbed by Edmond's erratic driving, Bridgette leaned forward to tap him on the shoulder. 'I say, do you think you might pull over? This is a lovely spot by the river. Ideal for some light refreshment, if you'd care to join me?'

Edmond stopped the car and rushed to help Bridgette out. She'd wrapped the hospital blanket around her body, and her plastered arm, secure in its sling, lay comfortably by her side.

'Allow me.' Edmond felt sorry for the woman, who had a brute of a husband, and he carefully guided Bridgette to a table. When a young girl arrived to take their order, Bridgette ordered a milkshake and chocolate cake.

'Got a sweet tooth with all that swimming?' the girl asked. She gave Bridgette a knowing wink. 'We all enjoyed your performance on Friday. Have you been overdoing it?' She nodded towards Bridgette's plaster cast.

'It's nothing to worry about,' Bridgette said and smiled.

Their refreshments arrived, and, companionably, they sat side by side, watching the river flow as birds swooped overhead in a translucent blue sky. When Bridgette took a credit card out of her phone case to pay for Edmond's cheeseburger and chips, his admiration rose.

'Sparadise please,' Bridgette said and stood up. 'But before we go, there's one thing that I'd like to do…'

'She's back!' Emily shouted as she stood on the driveway at Sparadise.

A car appeared at the gates and began to travel down the private road towards the main building.

Marjory, who sat on the porch in the shade, held up her hand to acknowledge Emily. She turned to study Serena. 'You look good. Has Phillipe been working his magic?'

'Yes, he certainly has. Robin and Stevie insisted that I

look my best for the party.' Serena touched her heavily made-up face.

They both looked up as the car got closer and Emily ran towards it.

Flushed from her massage with Lars, Marjory ran her fingers through her tangled hair, then stood up and straightened her robe. 'Let's get Bridgette settled. I hope she's not in too much pain.'

Having been informed by Edmond that Bridgette was only a few minutes away, Danka had gathered the friends to greet her, and she joined them as the vehicle crunched across the gravel and came to a stop at the front of the house.

'Does she need a wheelchair?' Emily, dwarfed by Serena and Danka, stood on her tiptoes to get a better look.

'No, that won't be necessary,' Danka said. She nodded to Edmond, and as he opened his door and climbed out, they both went to help Bridgette.

'Sing up,' Marjory said as she gave Emily and Serena a nudge. 'It is her birthday – let's welcome her back.'

'Happy birthday to you,' the three friends began to sing, 'happy birthday to you, happy birthday dear Bridgette, happy birthday to you!'

'Hello, my dears,' Bridgette's voice called out. 'How wonderful! Are you all ready for my party?'

With Danka on one side and the driver on the other, Bridgette was manoeuvred out of the car.

'Here, have these.' Emily dropped down and gently slid a pair of slippers onto Bridgette's feet. As she straightened up, she stared at Bridgette's hair. 'Gosh, you're all wet. Has something happened?'

'Not at all. We've had a perfect drive, haven't we, Edmond?'

Edmond, thrilled to be on first name terms with his passenger, nodded and grinned. 'Yes, Bridgette, we certainly have.'

Emily's brow was puckered. She'd noticed that his hair was wet too.

'By heck, it's good to see you.' Marjory touched Bridgette's free arm. 'We've been worried that you wouldn't make it back for your party.'

Serena stepped forward and gently hugged Bridgette. 'Happy birthday, Bridgette. Thank goodness you aren't more seriously injured – the attack by the bull could have been fatal.'

'Aye,' Marjory said. 'Are you going to complain about a wild animal roaming loose on the premises?'

'No, there's nothing to worry about. I am sure that the bull is safely back in his field.' Bridgette pulled her arm out of the sling and held it up. The bracelet of wooden beads was visible on her wrist. 'It was my own fault for wandering out of my tent so late at night when the bull was having a nocturnal stroll, but I didn't break my beads.' She smiled.

Marjory and Serena looked at each other, eyebrows raised. Bridgette seemed remarkably calm for someone of her years who'd experienced a nasty fall and spent the night in hospital. But when Danka took an empty bottle of vitamin drink from Bridgette's free hand, they nodded, understanding the reason for her serene demeanour.

'What's that writing on your plaster?' Emily frowned and as she leaned in, the various squiggles became clear. 'There's drawings of motorbikes and someone's signed their name "Flying Tiger." Who is "Frisco Pete" and why have you got a drawing of a winged skull by his name?'

The three friends looked at Bridgette.

'We had a pit stop for refreshments and things...' She flapped her hand, dismissing the question, then patted her wet hair. 'I'm so happy you missed me and hope it wasn't boring around here while I was gone.'

Emily, who was anything but bored, looked away, and Marjory flushed.

'You've only been gone for a few hours,' Serena said.

As they turned to go into the house, a group of runners came into view. They were jogging towards the garden, and the leader called out when he saw Bridgette.

'Fallen out of your cot in the nursing home?' he smirked and nodded towards Bridgette's sling. 'Bones get very brittle at your age; you need to be more careful.'

Bridgette stopped and glared at the man, who was now only a few feet away. Grabbing the edge of her blanket, she whipped it away from her naked body. 'Room for one more in your pack?' she asked, a wicked gleam in her eye. 'Matron says a jog would do me good.'

The group of runners began to laugh and applaud. But their leader was horrified by the sight of Bridgette's plump little body as she jiggled up and down.

'The best contraception for old people is nudity!' he shouted.

Unfortunately, he wasn't concentrating and suddenly stumbled. His teammates began to giggle as they saw him spin, almost head over heels. Humiliated, he straightened up, then spun on his Nikes and ran as fast as he could in the opposite direction.

Serena rolled her eyes. 'Behave yourself,' she said and picked the blanket up, covering Bridgette.

They all stopped by the desk in the hall and Bridgette spoke to Danka. 'Please put Edmond's fare on my bill and add fifty pounds for his trouble,' she said and turned to Edmond. 'Thank you for driving safely. I enjoyed our ride.'

'The pleasure was all mine.' Edmond gave a bow.

'Now, I must insist that you all go and get ready.' Bridgette's tone was bossy. 'I don't need any assistance and as you can see, I'm as fit as a fiddle and looking forward to the celebrations.' She moved to the front door, gripping her blanket tightly. 'Please have a rest this afternoon if you need it and arrive no later than six.'

Bridgette disappeared towards the garden and glamping area beyond, and Marjory looked at Emily and Serena. 'Have you sorted the cake?'

Emily and Serena glanced at each other. 'Yes, it's ready.'

'And I've got her gift from all of us. It's wrapped,' Emily said and smiled.

'But what about her *special gift*?' Marjory whispered and bit on her lip. 'I'm not so sure it will be special anymore…'

'Too late to change it now,' Serena said.

'Stop worrying. It will be her best birthday ever.' Emily

took their arms and, linking them with her own, led them away. 'Come on, let's get this show on the road.'

In the study at Flaxby Manor, Hugo Howarth was beside himself with rage. Pacing, he stared through leaded glass windows to the grounds of his family home where, at the entrance to a maze, a gardener balanced precariously on a ladder and clipped a shrub into the shape of a bird. Had Bridgette been here, Hugo knew that she would have been close by, calling out orders to the gardener as he wielded his sharpened blades. Bridgette would be dressed in gardening dungarees and a battered straw hat, standing as tall as her little frame would allow. She would check every clip of his shears and secateurs until the bird was perfect.

But Bridgette wasn't here. She was prancing around in the altogether in the middle of nowhere, hypnotised by some madman named Norman. Hugo wondered how the devil the man had managed to entice Bridgette to take up naturism. For reasons far beyond Hugo's comprehension, she was embracing the lifestyle and, he feared, making a terrible fool of herself.

A laptop was open on Hugo's desk, the article from *Life in Lancashire* clearly visible. 'Pah!' he exclaimed and closed the lid with a swipe of his hand. Thank goodness Bridgette's face wasn't shown in the photograph. Since the journalist hadn't managed to get her name, Hugo might save face at the golf club.

He had cancelled the party, pretending that Bridgette

was too unwell with a heavy cold. Hugo explained to the guests that the celebration was postponed until his wife was better. The platters of food, delivered earlier that morning, lay stacked in boxes in the kitchen. It had been too late to put the caterers off, costing Hugo a pretty penny, which enraged him even more. Bridgette had maintained a wilful streak throughout their marriage. It seemed to Hugo that Bridgette thought she had something to prove. He knew she'd been bullied about her height when she was younger and still heard occasional jibes behind her back. But at seventy, wasn't it about time Bridgette knuckled down and accepted her life as it was? No point in looking for change when the grim reaper could knock on your door at any moment.

Staring out of the window, Hugo knew he probably spent too much of his time on the golf course. Occasionally, he gave up golf to accompany Bridgette on her cruise ship excursions, and he enjoyed the glamour of being the partner of a guest speaker. But she'd been adamant that her big birthday bash be spent without him, with her close female friends, and his efforts to persuade her otherwise had been fruitless.

Hugo felt helpless as he looked at the carefully laid lawns and tidy pathways surrounded by deep herbaceous borders that Bridgette had so lovingly tended over the years. He adored his wife and longed to see her, fully clothed in a pretty summer dress, welcoming visitors to their open days. She would stroll alongside fascinated horticulturists as they enquired about the soil's acidity and how she managed to grow such giant hydrangeas.

Hugo had served in the Lancashire regiment and had seen active service in Aden in the Middle East in his twenties. Now, as he twiddled his moustache and watched a sprinkler dampen Bridgette's favourite rose bed, the old campaigner felt the blood boil in his veins. War wasn't won when troops stayed in their barracks far away from the frontline.

Suddenly, the gardener teetered on his ladder and accidentally clipped the bird's tail, sending foliage flying. Hugo banged on the window with his fist. The man spun around in fright and, with a horrified expression, fell to the ground.

'Damnation! You've buggered the bird!' Hugo yelled as the leafy tail fluttered to the ground. Oblivious to the man's injuries, he continued, 'This would never have happened if Bridgette were here.'

It was no good, he told himself as he turned away from the window. If Bridgette wouldn't come back, he would have to go to her. The rebellion must be quelled. Hugo hoped that other alienated Flaxby family members would march alongside.

A clock on the mantlepiece chimed three o'clock as Hugo reached for his phone and began to dial.

'Reg?' he roared when Reg Ecclestone picked up. 'Get back here! It's time to pull away from your pigeons and take action. Be at mine within the hour for an evening assault.'

His next call was to Emily's house, and Hugo was about to hang up when one of the boys answered.

'Hello?' Joe was hesitant, unused to a landline. 'Who is it?'

'Stir your stumps, young Avondale. We're going to rescue your mother, gather your brother and get to Flaxby Manor, pronto. Operation "Bring Back Our Women" is about to commence.'

'But we won't all fit in your car,' Joe whined.

'We'll split into teams and get a taxi too for the homeward journey.'

Unable to locate Cornelius, Hugo left a long-winded message for Serena's partner. 'If you can't get here on time, make your own way to the target,' he concluded before slamming the phone down.

Hugo stomped into the hallway and stared into a gilt-framed mirror. He wore navy corduroy trousers and a white polo shirt with a red cashmere sweater slung over his shoulders.

'Patriotic fighting colours,' he told his reflection and, grabbing a walking stick from a stand, turned in his polished leather brogues. 'Let battle commence!' he cried and marched out of the manor.

Chapter Twenty-Four

B ridgette spent a leisurely afternoon being pampered. She'd reunited with a bereft Norman and assured him that her broken arm was nothing to worry about and it wouldn't impede her enjoyment of the evening ahead. Consoled by her confidence, Norman went off to help with preparations for the party.

Danka had arranged a portable massage table, and Bridgette succumbed to the pleasure of a facial and mini massage in the comfort of her tent. While staff busied themselves outside, Bridgette luxuriated under the calm and soothing fingers of Danka, who worked on the birthday girl's muscles using hot stones and experienced hands.

'That massage was utter heaven,' Bridgette said as she turned over and lay on her back. 'Marjory swears by Lars, but you have magic fingers too.'

'Lars looks after certain clients with specific needs.'

'Will he be coming to the party?'

'Unlikely. He keeps a very low profile, but one never

knows.' She prepared lotions for Bridgette's facial. 'Look after your arm. Keep it supported.' Danka gently tucked a pillow under the plaster cast, then applied an exfoliating scrub to Bridgette's face and asked her client if she'd enjoyed her time at Sparadise.

'Yes, it has changed my life.' Bridgette closed her eyes. 'I realise that I was ready for change but didn't expect it to happen so quickly. I don't think I can go back to my old ways.'

'You like being a naturist?'

'It's the best thing I've ever experienced. I feel so confident.'

Bridgette sighed with pleasure as Danka lightly pummelled her skin. In truth, she knew that the confidence she was experiencing was because she no longer cared what anyone thought of her size. Shedding her clothes had shredded the hang-ups of a lifetime, and she knew she would never feel belittled again. Being small was empowering, and being naked and small made her deliriously happy.

'Is it better than sex?' Danka placed slices of cucumber over Bridgette's eyes.

'Oh, hell, yes. Anything is better than sex with Hugo. Digging a deep, earthy trough for potatoes gives me more pleasure than his attempts at passion these days.'

As Danka continued with the facial, Bridgette felt sleepy. She thought of her husband and his occasional foray into her bedroom. It usually followed a heavy drinking session at the golf club, and after a few grunts and groans, was soon over. Often, Bridgette hardly woke and could get back to sleep within minutes or finish a chapter of whatever book she was reading.

But it hadn't always been like that. Bridgette had enjoyed the physical side of her marriage, and it had lasted for many years, but as they got older, she'd liked it less.

Now, naturism gave her a feeling of freedom. The high that she felt was as close as Bridgette got to the days when every nerve in her body was electrified by lovemaking. It was a sensation that she didn't intend to let slip away when her time at Sparadise came to an end.

'All done,' Danka whispered and eased the bed into a sitting position. 'Phillipe is here to do your hair and makeup and Monika is ready for your manicure.'

'How good it is to be pampered. I shall look so much younger with a bit of slap on my face and my hair in a tidy style.'

'Are you dressing for the party?' Danka asked as she put away her lotions and potions.

'Of course,' Bridgette said with a smile. 'I shall be wearing my birthday suit.'

Marjory was enjoying the last couple of hours of relaxing by the pool. She'd been joined by Serena and Emily, who were excited about Bridgette's party.

'I can't have a swim,' Serena said as she lay back on a lounger. 'I mustn't ruin my makeup.'

'What are you going to wear?' Emily asked.

'Robin and Stevie have concocted an outfit they want to

photograph me in and post on Instagram.'

'So you're still pushing for a higher profile?'

'Yes, if it helps get me back in the culinary world.'

'What about you?' Emily touched Marjory's knee. 'Are you going to wear my jumpsuit again?'

'Aye, if that's ok. It's a damn sight smarter than my sagging old dress.'

'Of course, you look fabulous in it.'

'Aren't we lucky?' Serena suddenly said and began to sit up. 'This weekend has been so enjoyable. I know we haven't spent much time together but I feel that we've all benefitted from being here.'

'I think that meeting new people has been enlightening. Each of us has been enriched by the experience,' Emily said.

'We'll have plenty to talk about when we go home. Is Yannis escorting you to the party?' Marjory asked Emily.

'Yes, he is.' Emily stood. 'I'd better go and find him. He was busy when I slipped away.'

'I must get ready too. The boys want me to meet them in the penthouse.'

'Well you two lasses go and get your glad rags on and I'll meet you at the birthday bash.' Marjory turned to look out through the large glass windows and noted the other guests outside making the most of the late afternoon sunshine. The lads from Lancashire Automotives were playing croquet on the lawn and egging each other on as balls flew through hoops and points were scored. The youngest still wore a familiar layer of green gunk on sections of his skin and she hoped, for his sake, that the acne treatment was working.

Yoga students had laid their mats out on the grass and practised positions that they'd learnt in Yannis's class that morning. Their bendy bodies and multi-coloured outfits reminded Marjory of vibrant flowers planted in a vivid border.

She looked up to see the group of runners standing in a circle on the terrace. Their leader stood in the middle, issuing commands. As if on an army assault course, they all began to jog around him, stopping only to do star jumps and squats.

'By heck, if I was to squat, I'd never get up.' Marjory chuckled. She thought of Bridgette and wondered if her friend would be clothed for the party; surely, she wouldn't prance around starkers? But Bossy Bridgette was a determined soul, and if she wanted to go all beads, bangles and Buddhist, there was nothing anyone could do that would stop her.

As she continued to stare out, Marjory thought about Reg. She'd had no contact with her husband since she'd left the house on Friday morning. He'd made no effort to get in touch and find out if she was enjoying herself and Marjory had no desire to call and enlighten him. Marjory thought of her evening of passion with Willie and felt a deep stab of guilt. It had never been in her nature to be unfaithful. What would Reg do if he knew about Willie?

'But all he cares about are his bleedin' pigeons.' She sighed as a bird flew past a window, dipping low, eyes trained on the ground below.

Willie was bombarding her with text messages and insisting that they meet up again. The daft old fool was besotted. Marjory's face softened as she remembered all the kind touches he'd put in place to make sure that she enjoyed her evening. With chocolates and champagne, his candlelit home on wheels had felt like a five-star hotel, including the silk sheets. Willie's sexual appetite had been both a shock and a delightful surprise, and she'd enjoyed every moment. With her elderly lover raring to go again after their first bout of passion, Marjory had asked what his secret was.

'Just the sight of you, my darlin',' Willie said with a gleam in his eye. 'And the help of a little blue tablet.'

'Drugs?' Marjory's eyes were wide.

'Aye, if you can call 'em that. I got 'em over the counter at the chemist.'

Suddenly, Marjory sat up. Willie's words had dropped like a bomb. 'Sod it!' she exclaimed as she realised that bleach-blonde Jean was employed part-time at the chemist. Flaxby's biggest gossip knew that Willie and Marjory worked together at the Civic Centre on Saturday mornings and it wouldn't take Jean long to work out the reason for Willie's purchase at the chemist.

Marjory gripped her robe and thought about her dilemma.

Jean's other part-time job was behind the bar at the Flaxby Arms, which was Reg's local, and Marjory was aware that after two halves of cider, Jean's tongue would be as loose as a goose. Reg may soon know of his wife's brief encounter with Willie.

'Oh hell,' Marjory said as she eased herself off her comfortable chair. 'What *am* I to do?' She picked up her robe and put it on, then put her feet into her slippers. 'Well, if the cat's out of the bag,' she told herself as she wandered out of the spa and headed for her room, 'I may as well make the most of Bridgette's party.'

'Showtime!' Stevie exclaimed. 'Serena, you look A.M.A.Z.I.N.G.'

'I don't think I can walk in these heels *and* balance the hat at the same time.' Serena's wide eyes peered out from the brim of the Plumed Chapeau.

'Of course you can,' Robin said. 'The hat has tiny weights. Be confident and walk tall. This is your moment.'

'Everything is in place. We have our team ready to film at the glamping site,' Stevie assured her, 'and your entrance will go out live on YouTube and Instagram.'

The three stood in the living room of the penthouse.

'Don't panic,' Robin said and together with Stevie removed the hat from Serena's head and placed it carefully on the table. 'As soon as you see the camera, the years will melt away and it will be just like live TV again and *Wake Up with Serena!*'

'I do hope you're right.' Serena slipped out of her heels and, picking up a silk kimono, slipped it over the designer swimsuit that Robin had couriered in from a fashion house in London.

Stevie looked at the Rolex on his wrist. 'We have fifteen minutes and then we're off. I think we have time for some bubbles.'

A bottle of champagne sat on ice, and Stevie poured three glasses.

'To our beautiful Serena and the future.' Robin smiled at them both and took a sip of his drink.

Serena wanted to knock her drink back in one. Anything to help quiet the nerves that were bouncing about in her stomach. An hour ago, she'd checked the latest posts on her Instagram account and, to her continued dismay, saw that her hits had hardly increased. @YvettetheChefette, on the other hand, was steadily notching them up. Posed in her Sunday best, which consisted of a maid's outfit with the scantiest skirt, teeny lace apron and a minuscule corset-style bodice, she carried a tray of roast beef with two Yorkshire puddings strategically covering her breasts.

'Do you like my puddings?' the young chef had captioned the photograph.

Serena scowled. A steady stream of comments, hearts and likes poured in as she stared at Yvette's glossy balloon-like lips, which, if they contained any more collagen, would surely burst.

Stevie took the phone out of Serena's hand. 'Put that away and leave everything to us. We want you to enjoy yourself.'

'Are you ready?' Robin asked.

'I'm ready,' she replied. Taking a deep breath, she thrust her shoulders back, raised her chin and smiled.

'Lights, camera and... ACTION!' Stevie called out, and as if heading for a state event at the palace of Bossy Bridgette, he opened the door, and they made their way to the garden.

Chapter Twenty-Five

I t was late afternoon at the glamping site at Sparadise, and after hours of activity, the staff had left to freshen up before joining the party. As Bridgette stepped out of her tent, she gasped when she looked around at the final preparations.

'It's like a tropical wonderland,' she said, momentarily forgetting all else as she clutched her injured arm to her chest and began to move forward in short, hesitant strides.

Danka, who had followed Bridgette, walked alongside. 'You like it?'

'It's fabulous,' Bridgette breathed.

'You wanted a Polynesian theme and I think, together with the caterers, we've managed to create this.'

'One of my happiest cruises was in Hawaii and the islands and today, on my seventieth birthday, I feel like I've stepped onto my own island of joy.'

Bridgette's eyebrows rose as she stared at the activity in the area sloping from the tents to the lake. Neatly mown, the grass was covered with hay bales, ensconced in fabric throws patterned with sea turtles and white hibiscus. The bales were grouped around free-standing firepits and, strung from tropical flower-covered posts, pretty lanterns and fairy lights twinkled in the blue sky. Bridgette grinned when she saw weighted arches of pink balloons, fluttering as they caught the breeze. Banners announcing 'Happy Birthday Bridgette' reached as far as her eye could see, and an exotically themed bar, surrounded by inflatable palm trees, made a central display. Tiki-style, it had a palm-thatched roof covered by plastic parrots. Tall stools for thirsty customers were lined along the bar. A chalkboard displayed an extensive list with a selection of cocktails, and on the counter, gallon jars were full of ready-mixed Mai Thais.

'We'll light the area as it gets dark,' Danka said and pointed to tall torches surrounding the setting. More torches were clustered by a platform on the lake where a band was setting up their instruments. 'They will play Hawaiian folk music as the guests arrive and when it's time for dancing, they will have the music for the hula dance.'

'How splendid.' Bridgette's eyes sparkled, enhanced by a shimmery sapphire powder, which Phillipe had told her would complement the coral shade on her lips.

'I have something for you.' Danka opened her bag and pulled out a package. 'Please, take it.'

Taking great care, Bridgette pulled at the straw-like twine and lifted a sheet of brown paper. Inside the parcel lay layers of raffia. Bridgette shook it out and smiled.

'A grass skirt!' she exclaimed as she examined the strands decorated with bougainvillaea flowers.

'I know you don't want to wear anything on your skin, but this will enhance your body. Please, try it on.'

Danka took the ties and wrapped the skirt around Bridgette's waist. The gift was flattering. It covered Bridgette's tummy and fell to her knees.

'You should wear this too.' Danka pulled out a floral lei and placed it around Bridgette's neck. The lei gave minimal cover to Bridgette's breasts. 'I have a lei for all your guests. It is a powerful symbol of love, friendship and celebration and, most of all, you honour your guests when you give a lei.'

'Danka, you have made me so happy.' Bridgette plucked a flower from her lei and tucked it behind her ear. 'How different I feel from when I arrived at Sparadise. I have a sense of well-being that I've never felt before.'

'We have aids to help you reach your point of happiness, but fundamentally, the change is within. You, by yourself, have achieved that.'

Tears pricked the corners of Bridgette's eyes, and blinking them back, she stared at Danka. Then, perching on her toes and stretching up, kissed her softly on her cheek.

'Thank you,' Bridgette whispered. 'Finally, I like who I am. It has taken seventy years and a stay at Sparadise for me to be able to say that.'

'Now go and enjoy your party,' Danka said as she smiled and gently pushed Bridgette away.

Bridgette watched the young woman move through the grounds and thought that amongst Danka's aids, there was one person who had helped her reach her happy aura. Breathing in the heat of the summer evening and admiring the backdrop of the lake, so perfect for her party, against the vivid red and orange sky, she set off in search of Norman.

'Norman, are you there?' she asked as she reached his tent.

'At your service, Empress,' he called out.

A hand pulled the canvas flap to one side, and suddenly, a body leapt out. The abrupt movement of Norman, springing from his tent, alarmed Bridgette, and she jumped back.

'Good God, Norman! You made me jump. Is that you under that scary disguise?'

He wore a long hardwood hand-carved Polynesian battle mask, stained in dark earthy tones.

'Indeed,' Norman said and eased the mask from his face. 'This is to protect you and ward off evil spirits. I want to keep it to hand.'

Bridgette stared at Norman's flushed face. 'Well, I don't think we'll be needing it, thank you, but it is a kind thought.'

'I got it when I was ambushed on the Polynesian islands; a tribal leader gave it to me by way of thanks.'

'Well, that's nice.' Bridgette was beginning to wonder about Norman's fascinating life. Was there a place on earth that he hadn't visited or been involved in some rebellion?

'Your skirt is eye-catching,' Norman said and studied Bridgette's strands of raffia. 'Are you comfortable in clothing?'

'It's hardly clothing,' Bridgette said as she took his arm,

'and I can't imagine there will be much left of it as the party progresses.' She fluttered her eyelashes and smiled. 'Shall we help ourselves to a cocktail before the guests descend?'

'Lead on, lovely lady.'

The party was in full swing when Marjory arrived. 'By heck, I wasn't expecting this,' she said as a waiter, wearing a grass skirt and little else, held out a Blue Hawaii.

'Aloha,' the waiter said as Marjory took the cocktail.

''Ello... a,' she replied. Taking a sip, she licked her lips and tasted pineapple and coconut. The blue curacao matched her hair and was laced with rum. The drink was sweet and refreshing and, as she sucked on her straw, Marjory saw Bridgette approaching.

Her friend, glamorously made-up, with wooden beads around her wrist and ankles, wore a finely threaded grass skirt and held out a garland of flowers with her free hand.

'Shaka, Marjory,' Bridgette said.

'Eh?' Marjory looked puzzled.

'Shaka is a Hawaiian greeting and means "hang loose".'

'Oh, aye, I shall be doing that, especially if I stay on the Blue Hawaiis.'

'You can also say, "Aloha" which means "hello".'

'Aloha, shaka and happy birthday Bridgette.' Marjory kissed her friend and dipped her head as Bridgette held out a lei. 'Oh, that's lovely and it goes with my outfit.'

The green and white flowers wound into Marjory's lei were a perfect match for the ankle-length muumuu that she'd borrowed from Danka. Sparadise had an extensive selection of fancy-dress outfits that guests could use, and Marjory's dress was kaftan style in palm tree-printed fabric.

'Let's enjoy ourselves and mix with everyone,' Bridgette said and took Marjory's arm.

Stepping onto the lawn, Phillipe made an entrance accompanied by Monika and Alexandra. He wore a Hawaiian shirt and shorts, and gold chains shone from his neck as Phillipe postured and posed, teeth gleaming. Monika and Alexandra, both pretty in shoestring strap dresses patterned with orchids, had matching flowers in their hair.

The lawn was full of people.

Everyone from the retreat had accepted Bridgette's invitation and come to her party. The students from the yoga class, in colourful sarongs, ran across the grass to chat to Bridgette and wish her a happy birthday. Heads turned and knowing glances were exchanged as they saw their tutor arrive, and Marjory looked to see what had diverted their attention.

'Cooee... Marjory, Bridgette!' Emily called out as she appeared with Yannis.

Oblivious to the stares from the students, Emily was vibrantly dressed in a lilac vest with lacey straps, complemented by a long multi-coloured wraparound silk skirt. It swished as she moved. Her shining hair reflected in the sunset, and her face had a luminous glow that Marjory thought could only come from a surge of happiness within.

'My goodness, you do look a pair,' Marjory said.

'A pair of what?' Emily giggled.

'A pair very much in love,' Bridgette added.

Emily tilted her face up to look into her lover's eyes. 'But we are, aren't we, darling Yannis?'

'You are irresistible,' he replied and touched her nose with his finger. 'My little Emily, the beat of my heart.'

Marjory and Bridgette watched the show of adoration.

Yannis, handsome in a tight white T-shirt and faded ripped jeans, had his hand cupped to Emily's chin and began to kiss her. Embarrassed, Marjory dipped her head and was pleased to see that Emily had abandoned her walking boots for a pair of silvery sandals. Yannis wore thongs on his feet, his skin tanned and nails a perfect white.

'I'm off to the bar,' Marjory said. 'Can I get everyone a drink?'

'Nothing for me,' Bridgette said.

'Yes, please, can we have what you're having?' Emily had managed to tear herself away from Yannis's eager lips.

'Two Blue Hawaiis coming right up.' Marjory left Bridgette with Emily and Yannis and eased through the crowd that had gathered.

The sun, high above the lake, had started its descent and, silhouetted, the band played south sea island tunes while guests danced the hula. White clouds puffed above the glassy water, and gentle waves lapped the edge.

The Lancashire Automotives team, entering into the spirit of things, all wore leis over floral shirts.

'Aloha!' they called out as Marjory went by.

''Ello!' she replied and was pleased to see that the youngest lad had removed the green cream from his face. His skin was now clear and healthy. 'It worked!' she called out and pointed to his face. He replied with a thumbs-up and a wide grin.

His boss, the sales manager, cocky in a straw hat and Bermuda shorts, was leaning back under a limbo pole and attempting to writhe under it. As he wriggled his shoulders, he suddenly fell flat, and Marjory winced. With his bruised eye and lump on his forehead, she wondered if he'd be adding a strained spine to his list of injuries.

Guests lined the bar as Marjory approached.

As staff served beer and cocktails to keep up with the demand, a bald man wearing a lei and surfing shorts shoved in front of Marjory, holding his glass for a refill.

'Oy, Bruce Willis, I was here first,' she said, recognising the runner who had been so rude throughout their stay. Gritting her teeth, she jerked her knee into the back of his leg.

As he stumbled, his head spun around, and their eyes met. To stop himself from falling, he suddenly reached out.

'Damn,' Marjory said as she felt a warm, clammy hand grip her own. 'Up you come,' she tugged hard, and in seconds he was back on his feet.

'Thank you,' the runner said.

'You can thank me by ordering some drinks.' Given that she was the reason for his fall, Marjory didn't know why he thanked her.

'No, I mean, thank *you*, and your friends.'

'Eh?'

'I owe you all an apology. I have been exceptionally rude throughout your stay.'

'Well, I can't deny that.'

'My running group think I have been cruel and ageist and have given me quite a telling off. On reflection, they are absolutely right. In truth, I think you are all marvellous and a credit to the older generation. In fact, my friends and I have decided to call you the "Sparettes".'

Marjory leaned in. She wasn't sure that she had heard the man correctly. 'Sparettes?'

'The name suits you perfectly. It's a compliment.'

'Er, right, okay, thank you.'

'I feel very humbled,' he said and nodded towards the lake where Bridgette was dancing with Norman. 'I've been so mean to your friend and despite that, she invited us to the party.'

'Well, we all love a party.'

His chin began to tremble and he was unable to meet Marjory's gaze. 'I was unfairly critical over the weekend and am so sorry for the way I behaved.'

Marjory wondered if the man was several cocktails ahead of her.

'My name is Barry, by the way.'

'Pleased to meet you, Barry.'

'Shall I get your drinks for you?'

Marjory was about to reply when she heard a roll of drums. The guests became silent and turned as a procession entered the party.

Abandoning her position at the bar, Marjory ran forward to grab Bridgette's free hand and pull her across the lawn to stand with Emily. Emily, letting go of Yannis, placed her hand on Bridgette's shoulder. The three friends stood together, eagerly staring ahead to see what was happening.

A camera crew appeared and began to film as two well-muscled hunks, wearing tight chequered trousers and tall chef's hats, came in to view, carrying flaming torches. Behind them, a woman of height, wearing the most elevated of heels encrusted with precious stones, stepped forward. Dazzled by her shoes, the crowd let their eyes travel up her endless thighs to rest on a pearlized swimsuit with cut-away sides. A halter top, revealing a glimpse of firm breasts, dipped low at the front, where a colossal jewel nestled in her belly button.

A photographer ran ahead, his long lens zooming in on Serena.

'Oh my...' Marjory breathed. 'She's a goddess.'

'But her hat,' Bridgette whispered, her mouth open and eyes wide. 'It's incredible!'

Serena's elegant arms reached up, and her hands touched a circular silver brim, wider than her body. The Plumed Chapeau, now recreated as Le Chapeau Gâteau, was tiered and shaped like a giant birthday cake. Covered in silver silk to emulate edible frosting, it glittered with an array of tiny candles that dazzled in the setting sun. A train glided out from Serena's body beneath the hat. The fabric was as delicate as a ribbon of icing and caught the gentle wind, hovering magically.

The crowd gasped at the sight, spellbound by Serena. Guests pointed to their phones, fingers quickly clicking as they took photos. With her shoulders thrown back, Serena beamed as the camera rolled. Then, holding up her hand to catch the band's attention, Serena swept her arm to one side, and the band struck up a Polynesian version of 'Happy Birthday.'

As everyone sang, Robin and Stevie appeared. They pushed a trolley forward until they reached Bridgette. Serena stood alongside, and the light from the candles on Le Chapeau Gâteau cast a glowing circle over the trolly, which held the most enormous cake that the birthday girl had ever seen.

'Oh, goodness,' Bridgette exclaimed, her free hand flying to her open mouth. 'What on earth…'

'Oh, heck. This could go horribly wrong.' Marjory winced and gripped Emily's hand.

As the crowd joined in with the birthday song, the top layer of the cake suddenly burst open. A naked man appeared wearing a flower blossom to cover his modesty.

'Oh my.' Bridgette's eyes were like saucers as the handsome young man bounced out of the cake-shaped decorated box. Muscles pumped on his oiled body as he strutted and paraded before her.

'Happy birthday,' Emily and Marjory sang nervously as the man swaggered around Bridgette. Marjory scraped her hand through her hair, and Emily chewed at her lip. But their fears soon vanished as Bridgette, entering into the spirit of things, began a hula, and called out that everyone was to join in.

'We needn't have worried,' Emily said and breathed a sigh of relief.

'Aye, the naked birthday cake has gone down well.'

'How on earth are those candles on Serena's hat burning so brightly?'

'Battery operated, Emily. Keep up.' Marjory shook her head.

Now the party was in full swing as the band played loudly and lanterns were lit. Firepits glowed and drinks flowed as staff from the spa merged with the revellers. Delicious aromas from the hog roast drifted across the garden as guests tucked in.

Serena, hatless and wearing a shimmering kimono over her swimsuit, gathered Emily and Marjory. Together, they presented Bridgette with another beautiful birthday cake, creatively made by the chefs at Sparadise. Shaped like the Emperor Bell, the sugar paste cake was topped with seventy candles.

'Oh, I shall set fire to my skirt if I'm not careful.' Bridgette giggled as she leaned over and took several breaths to blow all the candles out.

'Make a wish,' Emily called out.

'I wish that our precious friendship lasts forever and that you all are as happy as I am tonight,' Bridgette said and hugged them.

The guests cheered and applauded, and everyone burst into song.

For she's a jolly good fellow, for she's a jolly good fellow.

Norman came forward. To their surprise, the friends noticed that he was wearing a grass skirt.

'May I?' Norman asked and took Bridgette's hands to lead her into the crowd. He began to sing, *'Do, do, do, come on and do the conga!'*

The band picked up the tune, and in moments everyone formed a line behind Norman, hands holding tight to swaying hips. They headed off to snake around the lawn and along the edge of the lake. Arms and legs flew out as voices rang out in the night, *'Dance that conga till you drop, we're never gonna stop!'*

'Oh, I shall have to stop for a moment,' Bridgette said, laughing as she flopped down onto a hay bale. She held onto her plaster cast and adjusted the sling. 'I haven't danced like that for years.'

'The night is still young, Empress. Shall I get you a drink?' Norman stood before her.

Bridgette shook her head. 'No, my dear. I've no further need for stimulants. I'm high on life.'

'Then you shall dance some more.' Norman tugged Bridgette back to her feet. He called out to the crowd, 'Are we ready?'

'Yes!' they roared in response.

'This is something I taught the crew when I was held captive on a Somalian pirate ship.' Norman took up his position as the band began to play. With Bridgette doing her best to keep up, he began an energetic rendition of the Macarena.

'Hey, Macarena!' everyone sang as they surrounded Bridgette.

'Happy birthday dear Bridgette!' Serena, Marjory and Emily, feet dancing and arms pumping, called out to their friend.

Chapter Twenty-Six

I n the Forest of Bowland, the country lanes were busy
with vehicles snaking their way home. The area
provided a peaceful and remote landscape, and after a fun-
filled day, tourists and day-trippers left the area designated
as a place of outstanding natural beauty. Bird twitchers
who'd been studying rare wildlife took to their transport,
and groups of cyclists gathered, elated from the challenging
landscape. Hikers rambled along the riverside, running
parallel to the road, admiring the distant fells studded like
quilts and laced with centuries-old stone-built walls.

Heading along the winding route that led to Sparadise,
Hugo sat in the driver's seat of his Jaguar four-door S-Type.
With his foot hard on the saloon's sporty accelerator and
hands gripped to the steering wheel, his eyes gleamed,
unaware of hazards ahead.

'Bloody cyclists!' Hugo roared as he overtook a trio of
Lycra-clad bodies and swerved from oncoming traffic.

'They should all be banned; no place for wheel-spinners on today's thoroughfares.'

In the back seat, Joe and Jacob swivelled around to stare wide-eyed at the heap of cycles, riders still attached and wheels revolving, that lay upturned in a ditch. The angry cyclists raised gloved fists and screamed curses as Hugo's car sped away. Speechless, the brothers gripped their seats and sank into the tan leather. Joe ran his fingers through his mop of limp hair while Jacob closed his eyes and bounced his knee nervously up and down.

Reg, perched on the passenger seat beside Hugo, sucked on an empty pipe. Occasionally, he scratched at wisps of grey hair that stuck out from under his battered old cap. 'They'll have action cameras on their helmets to capture footage of that incident,' Reg said as he stared out of the window where fields and rivers flashed by.

'Make 'em pay road tax, then they can argue about the right to be hogging the road.' Hugo's face was red and his brow damp with sweat. 'If I had bull bars I'd run them off.'

'I agree they're a menace, but one of the first things I learnt from my training as a bus driver was to be courteous to cyclists. Most drivers don't want to end up in court.'

'Pah!' Hugo snorted, dismissing Reg's warning.

Ahead, parked in a lay-by beside a river, a mobile refreshment van was open. A café alongside had closed for the day, but the van still served food to a group of bikers enjoying warm pies and burgers after their day out. Hugo had no choice but to slow down as he negotiated past the Harleys, Ducatis and Hondas.

'Can we stop?' Joe asked, his eyes looking longingly at the food. 'We haven't eaten for days.'

'Our mother didn't leave us any money to buy food,' Jacob whined.

'You lads should have come to me,' said Reg. 'Marjory left enough food to feed five thousand.'

'There's no time.' Hugo didn't like the look of the bikers and was reluctant to stop. With their gleaming chrome, tattooed limbs, chains, and the hairiest faces he'd ever seen, he decided against unloading his odd-looking party. 'We're not out for a picnic. I've made our mission quite clear.'

'I may faint,' Joe said and rubbed his stomach.

'I shall wait in the car while you do what you have to do,' Jacob grumbled.

'You two must man up.' Hugo glared in the rearview mirror where the sallow-faced brothers stared back. 'Are you men or mice? Do you want to put an end to your mother's nonsense and get her back at home where she belongs to look after you both?'

The brothers didn't reply and slunk further into their seats. They were silent for the rest of the journey. Reg, too, had little to say. He'd been unable to stop Marjory from coming on this trip. Now, after hearing a rumour circulating in the pub, he knew he needed to talk to his wife sooner rather than later. He had no intention of discussing his business with Hugo Haworth, who was the most obnoxious, toffee-nosed old fart that Reg ever had the displeasure of meeting. But Hugo had a car and had prompted this trip, and Reg, not wanting to fork out for a taxi, had jumped at the opportunity to grab a lift.

As they continued, Hugo's driving didn't improve.

Jacob had bitten his fingernails down to the quick, and Joe was almost in tears. Reg had sucked so hard on his pipe that he'd dislodged one of his front teeth, and now it wobbled precariously. Hugo was oblivious to a raging farmer whose sheep he'd almost run over, and he ignored every stop sign and junction. It was only a miracle that kept his car on the road. Incensed drivers hooted and swore when the Jaguar roared past, paying no heed to road signs or speed restrictions.

'This must be the place.' Hugo slowed the car to squint through the windscreen. 'No point in announcing our arrival,' he said and turned the Jaguar's lights off.

His passengers breathed a collective sigh of relief as the main gates of Sparadise came into view.

'Mind the tree!' Reg yelled as a vast, impenetrable shape suddenly reared up, and Hugo swerved recklessly to one side.

'I don't want to die.' Jacob choked back a sob and held tight to his trembling brother.

'I'll slip her in where no one can see us,' Hugo mumbled and with the lights from the main house guiding him to the retreat, he cruised around the side of the building and parked under a thicket of trees.

Reg climbed out and, having been rigid with fear for many miles, stamped his feet to bring circulation back to his limbs. He hoped there was a bar open. Only a pint and a whisky chaser would settle his jangling nerves.

'The plan is to move as one troop.' Hugo held a rug in one hand and his walking stick in the other and indicated that they should progress slowly forward. 'We keep together and when we see the targets, we round the gals up, negotiating them into a corner, then talk some sense into them.'

'I'll enjoy seeing you round my Marjory up. You'll need a posse of cowboys with large lassoes.'

'Mum is stick thin – she weighs nothing,' Joe said. He'd perked up, suddenly getting into the spirit of things. 'We can lift her between us.'

'Leave Bridgette to me, I'll deal with my wife,' Hugo whispered. They were approaching the gate to the garden. 'She'll be half-cut, celebrating her birthday. I know how to manage that sort of thing.'

In truth, Hugo feared that Bridgette would be starkers, and he intended to cover her with a blanket as soon as he saw her. He didn't want Reg sodding Ecclestone taking tales of Bridgette's nudity and debauchery back to the Flaxby Arms.

'There's a lot of noise coming from over there.' Jacob, crouched low, had gone ahead and found a route through the garden. 'Look, there's tents and lights and music.'

The group stood together and stared into the distance. Through the dimness, the scene ahead was bright, and a torchlit path led to the party.

'Follow me.' Hugo held his walking stick high and, with the rug draped over his shoulder, moved as swiftly forward as his seventy-five-year-old legs would allow.

'Bloody hell!' Reg uttered as they reached the edge of the lawn. His eyes were like saucers as he took in the scene.

'Wow, how cool…' Joe said, open-mouthed.

'OMG, this is awesome.' Jacob gave a slow disbelieving shake of his head. His feet moved as though detached from his brain.

Hugo was stunned.

The music was loud and a party was in full flow beyond an archway of inflated balloons. Speechless, Hugo stared at the tropical scene. Inflatable palm trees and a tiki bar were positioned alongside firepits. Smoke twirled heavenward from a hog roasting on a spit. Lanterns lit up the sky and fairy lights strung above seemed to dance in time with the band. Banners and balloons were everywhere, and a massive crowd of people, dressed in an assortment of clothing, including grass skirts, Bermuda shorts and colourful shirts, danced in a circle. Many had plastic parrots attached to their shoulders, and everyone wore a lei around their neck with flowers in their hair.

'Man, this is so sweet,' Joe said, his nostrils twitching as he caught the fragrant and earthy whiff of a spliff, carried by a warm breeze.

But Hugo was not to be deterred. 'Attention! Long live the Queen!'

He charged forward and they all followed.

But as they approached the party, Joe unexpectedly stumbled and, reaching out to save himself, grabbed an archway of balloons. The balloons teetered towards a flaming torch and then exploded.

Ear-splitting booms, like gunfire, ricocheted, and as women screamed, guests held their hands over their heads and dived for cover. Hugo, propelled by Reg clutching him in a manic attempt to get away from the balloon fireworks, fell to the ground.

He shook his head to gain composure, gripped his stick and looked up.

Bridgette, with her hands on her hips, eyes bulging, and lips curled back in disgust, stood over him.

'Bridgette!' Hugo croaked. 'I've come to rescue you.'

Chapter Twenty-Seven

A s Hugo stared at his wife, almost naked in the skimpiest grass skirt he'd ever seen, he leaned on his hands and began to struggle to his feet.

'Bridgette, you have to stop this nonsense,' Hugo began, reaching for the blanket to cover her. 'You'll catch your death of cold out here and your place is with me in the warmth of Flaxby Manor.'

But as Hugo stood up, a sudden movement caught his eye and before he could protect himself, a wild figure wearing a dark hardwood hand-carved Polynesian battle mask leapt out of the darkness.

'I'll save you, Empress!' the figure cried out and, in an instance, felled Hugo.

'What in God's name?' Hugo yelled as he grappled with the half-naked man.

The Lancashire Automotives team, who had been enjoying Blue Hawaiis and the best version of the conga that they'd ever experienced, rushed forward as the fight began. As dust flew and the two bodies tangled, the sales manager started betting odds with Norman as the favourite. Hands slapped as deals were done, and the youngest rep jumped up and down.

But Norman's enthusiasm to be a hero was no match for army-trained self-defence expert Hugo. In minutes, his mask was off, and his body was pinned on the floor while Hugo, one foot triumphantly on Norman's chest, towered over him. Hugo's arm was raised, and his walking stick ready, but just as he was about to bring it down on Norman's head, Bridgette stepped forward and, with her free arm, balled her fist and punched Hugo hard in the stomach.

'Don't you dare!' Bridgette shouted at Hugo. Her eyes were wide as she turned to Norman, astonished that the international man of mystery, the self-proclaimed hero, cowered in a ball under Hugo's leather brogue.

'B... bloody hell, old girl... there was no need for that.' Hugo staggered back. Doubled up, he gasped for breath and leaned heavily on his stick. 'Just look at you, all naked and broken.'

'I may have broken my arm, but my nakedness is my choice and naturism a way of life that I intend to continue living.'

'But...'

'There will be no "buts" about anything Hugo. You have gate-crashed my party, but you're not going to spoil it and I insist that you pick up your blanket and leave.'

Hugo buckled under Bridgette's telling off. 'Come on, old girl, you don't really mean it.' He took her free arm and gently pulled her to one side. When he was sure that no one could hear them, he gave a weak, pensive smile. 'Bridgette, I adore you and love you with all my heart. I realise that I haven't been the best of husbands in recent years and I would do anything to change that and make you happy.'

Bridgette stared at Hugo and felt her heart begin to melt. The old fool had come all this way and stood up for her, fighting to protect her honour. In the soft light of the torchlit garden she saw the handsome man she'd fallen in love with so many years ago. She sighed as Hugo took her hand and began to softly stroke her skin.

'I'm sorry if I've upset you, but this weekend has been life-changing and I'm not sure if I can go back to the way we were.'

'You don't have to. We can make changes,' Hugo pleaded.

'But I'm taking a leap of faith as I step into the next decade and I don't think that you *can* change to my new lifestyle...'

Before Hugo had time to reply, they became aware of a scuffle behind them and turned to see Reg push through the crowd and extend a hand to Hugo's opponent.

'Hello, Norman, what are you doing here?' Reg said as he tugged the man to his feet. 'I didn't recognise you without your clothes.'

Marjory, who had until now stayed back from the fray, wondered if Danka had been spicing up the Blue Hawaiis.

Surely she was seeing things. Was that Reg, helping Norman to his feet, holding his cap in his free hand? Bustling her way through the spectators and the Lancashire Automotives team, many of whom were dismayed by Norman's poor performance and the fight's result, she stood in front of her husband.

'What's to do here, Reg?' Marjory asked.

''Ello, to you too, Marjory. You've got some fancy get-up on.' Reg studied her from top to toe, taking in the pretty tropical dress that flattered her figure and the orchid in her hair.

'I want to know how you're so familiar with Norman.'

'He's a passenger on my bus route,' Reg said, glancing at Norman. 'He works behind the counter at the garden centre in Hamilton. He plants and packs the plants. I've known him for years.'

Norman, who'd heard Reg's comment, was now more exposed than his nakedness could make him. Conscious that everyone else had heard too, he picked up his mask and, with his head bent and shoulders down, began to slink away.

But Bridgette stepped forward and took Norman's arm. 'Norman, my dear, could you be kind enough to ask the band to start playing again and ensure that guests have drinks and continue to enjoy my party?'

'Empress, it will be my pleasure.' Norman brushed dust off his skin and gave a slight bow. With a furtive, sidelong glance at Reg and Hugo, he moved away.

Hugo, still livid, wanted to kick Norman in the buttocks,

but he held back, not wishing to further antagonise Bridgette.

'Who's looking after your pigeons?' Marjory asked Reg. She raised her eyebrow and folded her arms.

'A friend.' Reg made no effort to elaborate. He reached up and fiddled with his loose tooth.

'What have you done?' Marjory leaned in, peering at Reg's mouth. 'Your tooth is hanging.'

'It's nothing,' Reg said and glared at Hugo. He took his cap in both hands and seemed nervous as he began to twist the tweed fabric. After a hesitant cough, he said, 'Marjory, we need to talk.'

The music started up and, with no fight to watch or scenes of husbands being battered by the birthday girl, the guests drifted back to the party. Serena, who'd been dancing with Robin and Stevie, came forward and put her arm around Marjory.

'Is everything alright?' she asked.

'Aye, don't dash off, Reg has something he needs to get off his chest and, as it will be gossiped about all over Flaxby before daybreak, you may as well hear it here first.'

Reg looked flummoxed. 'Er, I didn't want it to come out like this,' he said, scratching his chin and scraping a hand through his hair. 'But Marjory is right, folk will all know soon enough.'

Aware of onlookers, including Bridgette and Hugo, Marjory took a gulp and, straightening her back, glared at her husband. 'Go on then, Reg, get on with it.'

'I'm sorry, Marjory, it's all around the pub. Folk are talking.'

Marjory closed her eyes. That was that then. News of her dalliance with Willie had made the headlines. Bleached-blonde Jean couldn't keep her big mouth shut. Marjory would be the laughingstock at the Co-op, too, now that everyone knew.

For a moment, absorbed in her thoughts, Marjory didn't hear what Reg had said.

'Are you listening to me?' Reg leaned in and shook Marjory's arm. 'I said, *I'm leaving you*. I've fallen for someone else.'

'Eh?' Marjory opened her eyes. What had Reg just said? *'You're* leaving *me?'*

'I'm sorry lass, b... but it's j... just happened and we both feel the same way.' Reg was stuttering and stumbling over his words.

Marjory suddenly relaxed and her arms fell to her sides. She felt Serena's hand stroke her shoulder. 'Oh, I see, there's someone else,' Marjory whispered.

Reg began to ramble on about his new love and how their passion for pigeons had brought them together and that they could no longer hide their feelings for each other.

'Very well, if that's what you want.' Marjory dabbed at the corner of her eye.

Reg stepped back. 'Thanks for being so understanding,' he said, brow furrowed. He hadn't expected Marjory to be so meek.

Marjory nodded and took the tissue that Robin had magically placed before her. Stevie held out a Blue Hawaii and told her to take a sip for the shock. Bridgette had picked up Hugo's blanket and draped it around Marjory.

But Marjory was struggling to hide her emotions.

Reg's news had indeed been a shock. *Halle-bloody-luah!* she secretly sang to herself. Of all the things! Never in a month of Sundays had she expected dull and dismal old Reg to show an ounce of emotion for anything but his pigeons, and out of nowhere, he'd just announced that he was leaving her!

Marjory felt as though she had won the lottery. Suddenly all her anxieties about a life without Reg seemed to melt away. His affair was the key she needed to unlock the door to the rest of her life. She'd have no guilt when news of their parting got out.

'Are you okay?' Serena asked, her voice soft, her hand still caressing her friend's shoulders.

Marjory was more than okay. She was bloody ecstatic. Wait until she told Willie! Her dreams of a life on the open road with Willie and his Westie were about to become a reality.

But she knew that now wasn't the time to show her feelings. Not until she'd had every penny she could get out of Reg to fund her newfound freedom.

'It's a terrible shock, but I'll be alright.' Marjory dabbed at her eyes again as she saw Reg, head bowed, walking away.

'Reg, just a minute,' Marjory called out. 'Who is your new love? At least tell me the name of the woman I've lost you to.'

Marjory couldn't imagine that Reg would have met anyone in Flaxby. There wasn't a woman alive in the town who would give the boring old git a second glance. It had to be someone from the pigeon fancier's show. Someone with a brain as feathered as the birds they both adored. He'd probably been chatted up when Marjory was out in Blackpool enjoying her fish and chips. She remembered the fortune-teller's reading. Feathers would certainly fly. She'd said that Reg's heart belonged to a bird, but Marjory never thought it would be human.

'Is it someone I know?' she asked.

'Aye, lass, I think you might. Her name is Jean.'

'JEAN?' Marjory spat the word out. *'Jean?* You can't mean bleached-blonde Jean, who'll never see a size sixteen again and likes leggings that make her thighs look like crumpets?'

'There's no need to be like that…'

Marjory shrugged Serena's hand away and, replicating Bridgette's earlier action, balled her fist and threw herself forward to swing a stiff jab at Reg's stomach followed by an uppercut to his jaw.

Reg shrieked as Marjory missed and his loose tooth spun into the air. For protection, he hurled himself on Hugo, but his ally fought him off with his stick.

'Whoa!' Stevie and Robin cried out, and before Marjory's punches could connect, they had hold of her shoulders and pulled her away.

'You two-faced little shite. You can have her!' Marjory wriggled about to try and break away from the strong hands holding her back. 'And you'd better ask the tooth fairy for a solicitor – you'll be needing one!'

After a few moments, Marjory regained her composure and Robin and Stevie let go. She ran her hands over her dress, then patted her hair. 'But I'll be consulting a solicitor too as soon as I get back, so don't think you'll get off lightly.'

Reg, unsure of Marjory's next intentions, and with no wish to be on the receiving end of her fist as he searched for his tooth, began to move away. 'I'll be waiting by the car,' he told Hugo, and in seconds had disappeared.

Bridgette and Serena stood on either side of their friend. Hugo, bemused by the proceedings, leaned heavily on his stick. They all turned as a couple hurried across the lawn towards them. It was Emily, holding tightly onto Yannis.

'Bloody hell...' Hugo spluttered and shook his head as he stared in horror at the mature woman, a vividly violet vision, and her youthful toy boy. A waiter passed by with a tray of drinks and Hugo reached for a glass. Without looking at the green cocktail, he downed it in one.

'Marjory, I just heard the news. I am *so* sorry! You must be devastated. Reg is an absolute bastard, and you must hate him.' Emily held Yannis's well-muscled arm and wrapped it around her body as if to protect herself.

'Aye, something like that.' Marjory tilted her head back and finished the drink that Stevie had given her. 'I never saw that coming. *Jean!* Of all people.'

'Do you know her?' Emily blinked rapidly.

'Aye, she's always in the Co-op buying groceries.'

'Gosh that will make things difficult for you.'

'A couple of tins of baked beans slapped around each earhole should encourage her to shop at the Spar. It's fine, really.'

In truth, it was more than satisfactory, and Marjory

noticed that Serena had nudged Bridgette, and now, they both looked at her with perceptive smiles.

'I expect you'll be updating your friend Willie with this recent turn of events?' Bridgette asked, her grin widening. She fiddled with the flower lei around her neck where the blooms covered her bosom.

'Well, I might just do that.' Marjory nodded her head, but before the discussion could gain traction, there was a rustle behind the group.

Hugo, his neck stretched, appeared to be enjoying the tête-à-tête. He turned as newcomers appeared. 'Ah, the Avondales are here,' he said, addressing Emily's sons, 'and you've obviously found the bar, but have you found your mother?'

Everyone stood back as Joe and Jacob joined the group. The brothers, each wearing a lei, had tall glasses of beer in their hands and silly smiles on their faces.

'No, not yet, but this is some party,' Joe said as he watched Monika and Alexandra, both still attached to Phillipe, stroll over to wish Bridgette a happy birthday. The straps on Monika's dress had slipped, revealing plenty of pert breast and Joe, eyes glued, took a big gulp of his beer. As she tilted her head to one side to smile at Joe, the orchid in her hair fell to the ground and Jacob, in a rush to pick it up, nearly fell over his brother who reached the flower before him.

Besotted by the pretty girl, neither Joe nor Jacob had looked at the people gathered nor paid any attention to the couple standing beside Marjory.

Emily, heart-thumping, froze. She gripped Yannis even

tighter and squeezed her eyes closed to shut out the sight of her sons as they fawned over Monika.

'Perhaps these ladies can help you to locate her?' Hugo grabbed another drink and nodded towards Bridgette, Serena and Marjory.

Jacob dragged his eyes away from Monika. 'She's not at the party. We've looked everywhere.'

'She must be in her room,' Joe said. 'Can anyone tell us which room Emily Avondale is booked into?'

The two boys looked from one to the other, searching the group's faces, hoping for an answer. When they saw Bridgette, they both snapped their heads away at the sight of her partial nakedness and their glance fell on Emily and Yannis. But there was no recognition of the woman gripping the younger man.

Bridgette, Serena and Marjory were motionless. They stared at Emily and waited for her to come forward, but Emily was rooted to the spot.

Yannis spoke up. He looked puzzled. 'Emily? These boys... they are your boys?'

'You know where our mother is?' Joe looked hopeful.

'But she's here.' Yannis loosened his arm and gently pushed Emily forward.

Emily, eyes still closed, began to nod her head.

'*Mum?*' Joe and Jacob were incredulous. Their mouths hung open, eyes agog. Joe's hand was still on his drink, but the glass had slipped, and as the contents ran over his T-shirt, he was oblivious to the sticky brown stain that slowly spread over the fabric and dripped onto his jeans.

'*Mum?*' they repeated, waiting for Emily to speak.

Emily took a deep breath and opened her eyes. She took hold of Yannis's hand and wrapped his arm over her shoulder.

'Hello, both. What brings you to Sparadise?'

Chapter Twenty-Eight

Joe and Jacob were speechless. They paled as they stared at the dazzlingly dressed woman before them. Neither could recognise in her flame-red bob, streaked with lilac and orange, the long, scraggly grey hair they were used to. The radiant makeup and smooth skin were nothing like their mother's worn and weary face. Nor did her lilac vest and rainbow-coloured skirt share any resemblance with the dull and drab clothes she always wore.

Emily removed Yannis's arm and held out her hands, but the boys shrank back, their expressions horrified as they stared at the glittery polish on her manicured nails.

They looked as though they'd seen a ghost.

Joe began to gag as he caught sight of Emily's feet in a pair of silver, jewel-encrusted sandals. 'W… where are your walking boots?' His voice was shrill and face ashen.

Jacob reached blindly, dropping his drink to the floor. 'Mum, that can't be you… what the hell have you done?'

'You look like someone else.' Joe slowly shook his head as he gaped at his mother.

'You're too old to do this.'

'You'll make us a laughingstock at home.'

'You look like a drag queen.'

'It's grotesque.'

'It's disgusting.' Jacob glowered and almost spat the words.

Emily stared at her sons. Neither had the good grace to compliment her makeover or courage to change, and her transformation had fallen on rocky ground. By the expression on their faces, it was unlikely to ever be well received.

Bridgette, Serena, and Marjory stood anxiously waiting to see what their friend would do next. Phillipe, Alexandra, and Monika seemed mildly amused. Hugo frowned and tilted his head, his eyes narrow as he tried to connect this colourful woman with the haggard headmistress he thought he knew. Stevie held onto Robin's arm. His eyes were bright as he waited for the next instalment of the scene playing out before them. Barry, curious to see where the birthday girl had got to, strolled over and joined the group. He was about to apologise to Bridgette for his appalling behaviour and thank her for her excellent hospitality but stopped when he saw Emily's expression.

Yannis sensed that Emily was shocked. He stepped forward and protectively put his arm around her and looked at the boys. 'These are your sons?'

Emily merely nodded, unable to speak.

'Hello Joe and Jacob,' Yannis said.

'Who the hell are you?' Joe's face contorted as he took in the sight of this handsome, model-like man whose arm was resting with familiarity on his mother's bare and bony shoulders.

'My name is Yannis, and I teach yoga to the students at Sparadise.'

'Students?' Joe sneered. 'Most of the residents here are old enough to be locked up in a nursing home.'

'Or an asylum,' Jacob added, staring at Emily with horror.

'What the hell have you done to yourself?' Joe asked. 'You really do look ridiculous. Are you ill?'

'I think you should go and get changed. We're here to take you home. Hugo is giving us a lift.'

'Could one of your friends help you to gather your things?' Joe looked towards Bridgette, his eyebrows raised.

'You'll feel much better when you're at home and things get back to normal. Whatever normal is for old people.'

For a split second, no one spoke. All eyes rested on Emily as they waited to see what she would do, and they didn't have long to wait.

'ENOUGH!' Emily exclaimed, her hands flying to her ears. 'How dare you two talk to me like this?' She walked towards them. Her face was tense and her eyes narrowed. 'What the hell do you think you're doing, turning up uninvited at Bridgette's party with chips on your shoulders the size of boulders?'

'W… we—' Joe stuttered and stumbled back.

'What makes you think you have the right to tell *me* what to do?' she continued as her eyes popped and chin jutted out. 'You are both the most selfish and lazy offspring that ever lived, and I am sick to death of your ungrateful ways and condescending attitude.'

'Atta girl,' Phillipe said, his eyes glazed as he drew heavily and puffed out smoke rings.

'B... but—' Jacob began.

'But nothing! I'm not listening, and you are *not* to tell me what to do.'

As she turned, Yannis moved forward, and they fell into each other's arms. He kissed the top of her head and began to caress her back.

'You can't be serious,' Jacob whispered, the pitch of his voice rising in disbelief as he watched his mother being comforted.

'Who is this? This... this... yoga man,' Joe asked. 'What is he to you?'

Emily dropped her hands to her sides and turned to stare at them both. 'He's my lover.'

'Oh God...'

'Ugh!'

Monika began to giggle and Yannis, suddenly anxious, shot her a warning look.

'And there's something else you should know.' Emily stood tall now, her head back, body confident, as she moved in for the kill. 'I'm selling the house and leaving Flaxby. Yannis and I are going to Greece to live on an island named Bessaloniki.'

There was a collective gasp as everyone heard Emily's words. They stared at the couple, wide-eyed and shocked. Like a slow-motion film, time seemed suspended while, in the background, the party continued. Dancers swayed to the music; drinkers were merry at the bar, and diners stood around the barbecue pit, enjoying thick, meaty chunks of roast pork.

Then Monika let out a blood-curdling scream and ran towards Yannis. 'You bastard!' she screeched, 'You no good lying bastard!' She hammered her hands on his chest and her fingers clawed at his skin.

'Let go, get off me!' Yannis, whose strength far outweighed the vigour flamed by Monika's anger, yanked her away and held her at arm's length.

But Monika, still furious, continued to kick and lash out. 'You pig! You promised *me* we would go to live in Greece and set up a yoga school at your parents' house.'

'Calm down, dear.' Bridgette moved towards the young girl and with her free hand peeled Monika from Yannis. 'It's no good upsetting yourself. It can all be sorted out, but not like this.'

Phillipe, now alert, pushed Alexandra towards Monika. 'Help me to deal with her,' he said with a firm nod, and together, they led the distraught girl away.

Monika was still furious and screamed oaths into the night. Yannis was the devil himself. 'I hope you rot in hell with the decrepit old cow you've conned for her money!'

Serena, Marjory, and Bridgette looked at each other, their eyes fearful as they heard Monika's words.

'I think it's true,' Serena whispered as they moved towards Emily to comfort her.

But, to their amazement, Emily was back in Yannis's

arms, and he was stroking her hair and soothing her with encouraging words.

'Monika is deranged. She is obsessed with me. I am sorry you had to witness that.'

'It's okay.' Emily's voice was soft.

'I have always had to warn her off. She won't leave me alone – it is hard when a person is so consumed and out of control.'

'I understand.'

'You must believe me when I say I have never given her any reason to think of me in any other way but as a work colleague.'

Bridgette stopped in her tracks. Had she just heard Yannis tell Emily that there was no romantic connection between him and Monika? Serena and Marjory, seeing Bridgette's expression, raised their eyebrows at her.

'I'll tell you later,' Bridgette whispered.

Joe and Jacob, still close by, had heard enough.

'You're disgusting,' Joe called out. 'You won't be able to get rid of us.'

'We're sitting tenants,' Jacob said. 'We'll *never* move out!'

Bridgette raised her hand. 'I think it would be best if you two young men went home now. Nothing will be resolved in this atmosphere and everyone needs to calm down.'

Joe's face contorted as he stared down at Bridgette and held a hand to his eyes to shield himself from her nakedness.

'Hugo!' Bossy Bridgette was back in town.

Hugo, intrigued to see what was going to happen next, spun around to stare at his wife.

'Stop gawping,' Bridgette said. 'Take these young men home immediately.'

'Yes, of course, dear.' Hugo leapt to attention and, forgetting the reason for his trip, took his stick and poked Joe and Jacob. 'Follow me, men!'

Without a backward glance at their mother, the brothers muttered curses as they were marched away.

Bridgette watched them go then turned to look at her friends. 'Now, even after all this activity, the night is still young. Can we please get back to my party?'

Chapter Twenty-Nine

S erena and Marjory stood side by side and watched Bridgette. As the birthday girl moved away, she was joined by Barry, and they now appeared to be the best of friends as he indicated that Bridgette might join his running buddies grouped at the tiki bar. They could hear cheers of 'happy birthday' as Bridgette climbed onto a stool. The yoga students, who'd been sitting by a firepit, stood up and went to the bar to congratulate Bridgette.

'Are you going to join in?' Serena asked Marjory and motioned towards the activity surrounding Bridgette.

'No, I'm nipping to my room in a minute. I've got a phone call to make.'

'Are you upset by Reg turning up and making his announcement?' Serena examined Marjory's face but deduced that her friend looked relieved. Marjory's smile was wide, and she seemed cheerful despite being told that her husband was leaving her.

'I expect I'll get over it, but I wonder if Emily will get over Monika's outburst?'

Serena and Marjory stared at Emily and Yannis. The couple sat together on a straw bale, heads bowed, holding hands and deep in conversation.

'Do you think we should have a word with Emily?' Marjory asked. 'Bridgette seems to know something about Yannis and Emily's idea to sell up and move to Greece seems bonkers to me.'

'Let's wait until we hear what Bridgette has to say. There's no rush, it's probably just infatuation. It will take Emily a while to sort out her house sale, if she does intend to go ahead with their plans, but I very much doubt that she will.'

'Aye, driven to desperation by those two daft sons,' Marjory sighed. 'Once the magic of Sparadise wears off, she'll come to her senses and see Yannis in a different light.'

'Yes, Flaxby on a cold wet Monday might not keep the love affair alive.'

'Talking of love affairs, where's your Cornelius these days?' Marjory raised an eyebrow and turned to look at Serena. 'You never mention him. Is he still drifting about the fells with his dippy dog?'

'I have no idea. He hasn't called but at least he's not dropped off a precipice as I am receiving texts from Dodger, and I don't think it's the dog's lumpy paws that are pressing the keys on Cornelius's phone.'

'That's odd. Still, you know that he's up and about, but it would be nice if he could see everything that's happened to you since you hooked up with the Haines lads.'

'I'm not sure that anything *has* happened.'

'Eh? Are you barking?' Marjory lightly punched Serena's arm. 'I bet you've got a virus raging on that insta thingy, what with the camera crew and everything.'

'Hardly. I don't think my posts will go viral. Social media isn't into mature women like me prancing about in next to nothing.' Serena dropped her hands and stared at her nails. 'I think Robin and Stevie's idea to get my cookery career back has fallen rather flat.'

'How do you know? Have you checked whatever it is that you check?'

'Stevie has my phone and refuses to let me see it, so things must be pretty bad.' Serena sighed. 'No doubt the trolls are out in force, cursing and bad-mouthing me.'

'Trolls?' Marjory was puzzled. She remembered the ugly little dolls with masses of frizzy hair from her grandchildren's picture books.

'The boys have put the hat somewhere safe. I ought to go and find them.' Serena cast her eyes into the distance, scanning the party for Robin and Stevie.

'Isn't that the hat over there?'

Marjory pointed to an area to the side of the bar where the camera team had set up lights. Le Chapeau Gâteau lay on a tall stand against a designer-logoed background, printed with social media hashtags in large red lettering.

#HainesHats, *#SaucySerena* and *#Sparadise*.

The hat looked magnificent. Like a luscious, layered cake. On either side of the backdrop, two large screens showed a film of Serena entering the birthday party, wearing the hat and her stunning outfit.

A queue had formed, and guests giggled as they took turns to stand beneath the candlelit novelty hat and snap their photographs. Phones clicked as everyone recorded their moment and posted it to their followers.

'I think you should get your shapely arse over there as fast as possible. Aren't you missing out on an opportunity to be photographed?' Marjory gave Serena a shove.

'Goodness, yes, it does look like something might be happening.'

Serena craned her neck to get a better look. She took hold of Marjory's arm, and noting that Emily and Yannis were still deep in conversation and oblivious to the events on the other side of the lawn, they moved away and hurried over to Robin and Stevie.

'Ah, here she is,' Stevie greeted Serena. As Marjory stepped back, he led Serena onto the carpeted area. 'Ladies and gentlemen, please make way for the latest addition to Haines Hats, our new millinery model, the very beautiful Serena.'

Serena took Stevie's hand, and they moved towards the hat.

'New millinery model?' she whispered as cameras clicked and eager faces watched Serena take her position next to Le Chapeau Gâteau.

'Why not? You're a natural and Robin has a great vision for you for the coming season.'

'But, surely, I'm too old?'

'Oh, please.' Stevie ignored Serena's protestations. He turned to the line of guests that had gathered around the hat. 'If you would like to be photographed wearing Le

Chapeau Gâteau, do step up,' he said, encouraging people to come forward. 'Haines Hats have printed postcards of Le Chapeau Gâteau and Serena will be happy to personally sign her autograph.'

Marjory stepped away. She chuckled to herself as she left the crowd of folk eager to get their picture taken with Serena. Perhaps the tide was turning for the talented chef at last.

Treading carefully around the firepits, burst balloons and bales of hay, Marjory could hear Bridgette laughing as she sat at the bar, regaling Barry and his buddies with tales of her talks on the high seas when *It's a Jungle Out There!* and *The Great Gardens of Guyana* were, for many travellers, one of the highlights of their Caribbean cruise. Marjory wondered if *Naturism and Nature* would be entering Bridgette's long list of talks. She knew that if Bridgette had her way, Flaxby Manor's open days would soon be asking visitors to step out of their comfortable clothing in the car park and enjoy *Blooms in the Buff with Bridgette*. God only knew what Hugo would do if Bridgette insisted on keeping up with her new way of life.

A dancing couple, not seeing Marjory, almost fell into her as she crossed the grass.

'Hi, have you had a good time?' Danka asked.

Beautiful in a red bikini and grass skirt, Danka was dancing with a man dressed in a white sheet. Toga-like, the fabric draped attractively around his tall frame. It reached to his knees, and as Marjory looked from his head to his feet, she was mesmerised by the man's long toes, tanned with perfect half-moon nails the colour of opals.

'By heck.' Marjory drew a breath, her hand fluttering to her heart and she realised that the man before her was Lars.

'You want to dance with us?' Danka asked.

'Er, no, thank you.' Marjory felt her face and neck flush and could feel sweat break out on her forehead. She had never seen any part of Lars other than his feet and felt acutely embarrassed as she recognised his digits.

'Come,' Danka encouraged. 'Come and play with us.'

Marjory gulped. She'd done more than enough 'playing' with Lars throughout her stay. The thought of any action, in the middle of a field, filled her with horror.

'It's very kind of you,' she began, her gaze on Danka, eliminating Lars from her view, 'but I have to make a phone call.'

'What a shame,' Danka said and winked. 'We would love to have you join us.'

'Aye, perhaps another time...' Marjory's slingbacks couldn't move fast enough as she hurried across the grass and undid the garden gate. 'Blimey,' she mumbled to herself as she went through the rose garden and around the side of the house. 'First Reg causing mayhem, and now Lars getting me all hot and bothered.'

Suddenly, a little white dog wearing a scarlet bandana ran out from under a thicket of trees. Startled, Marjory jumped back. The dog wagged its stumpy tail and began to bark.

'Bleedin' hell, Fred, where's your dad?' Marjory said, recognising Willie's Westie as the animal pawed Marjory's sandal.

'Here I am, Marge!'

Willie stepped out of the shadows. He carried a bouquet of red roses and wore a clean chequered shirt and freshly-pressed moleskin trousers.

'Oh, you made me jump.'

'Jump into my wagon and I'll take you to paradise,' Willie said and leaned in to peck Marjory on the cheek. 'I'm parked up at the side.'

'We need to talk,' Marjory said.

As she took the flowers, her face broke into a beatific smile. Never, in all her life, had anyone bought her such a magnificent bouquet.

'I'm all ears.' Willie grinned too.

'Woof, woof,' Fred agreed and wagged his tail.

'Brace yourself, old lad. That trip to paradise might be sooner than you think.' She took Willie's arm. 'Waggons roll!'

The party continued, and at midnight concluded with a spectacular display of fireworks as rockets of light shot into the sky and fell like brilliant confetti, illuminating the silvery lake. The pyrotechnics created an impressive show, but then the band began to pack away their instruments, the caterers removed the remaining food and drink, Sparadise staff doused the torches, and the evening came to an end.

Bridgette, weary but elated, stood by the tiki bar, and said goodbye to everyone as they made their way back to their rooms. Leis circled her neck as grateful partygoers returned the gesture of friendship. The plaster on her cast was covered in printed messages, birthday greetings and get well wishes.

'You made our weekend, you and your Sparettes,' the Lancashire Automotive sales manager called out. He was unsteady after an evening of Blue Hawaiis and limbo dancing and was supported by the youngest member of his team.

'Same place, same time next year?' The yoga students chorused. They waved goodnight to Bridgette. 'We had a blast,' they said as they smiled and nodded their thanks to the birthday girl.

'Wouldn't that be nice,' Bridgette replied as she watched them move towards the main house, their arms looped in a happy huddle.

'May this be the happiest of birthdays and may you have many, many more.'

Bridgette turned. Barry and his running buddies had waited patiently to say their goodbyes. As the spokesperson for the group, he came forward and reached out.

'Thank you,' Barry said as Bridgette offered her free hand. 'I want to wish you a wonderful year ahead but most of all, I apologise again. I think you're an inspiration.'

'Oh, come now…'

'I hope I have half your energy and courage when I get to seventy. You seem to have made a big change to your life, as though you have found a new spiritual path and you've shared your journey with us all tonight by inviting us to your party.'

'I'm just pleased you've had a jolly time.' Bridgette nodded and smiled at the group of expectant faces.

'My behaviour has been unforgiveable,' Barry said.

'Oh, what nonsense. I would probably have done exactly the same if I witnessed four silly old women getting up to no good.'

'No, you wouldn't.' Barry was firm. 'You and your Sparette friends are amazing. Good luck, Bridgette, and may all your birthday dreams come true. It's been an honour to know you.'

Bridgette watched the runners walk away. One or two had their arms around each other, and others joked that they might struggle to rise for their final early morning jog. Touched by Barry's words, tears pricked at the corner of her eyes. Wiping them away, she turned to cross the deserted lawn and stepped uncertainly over plastic glasses and debris from the party. Most of the guests were checking out in the morning, and there would be a significant turnover of rooms. Housekeeping would have their hands full.

From the thicket of trees, branches danced like moving silhouettes, and Bridgette looked up to gaze at the inky sky, where moonlight peeked out from slow-shifting clouds to join a sprinkling of stars high above the lake.

'Empress? Are you there?'

'I'm here, Norman dear. I'm admiring the beautiful night and standing just in front of the bar.'

Out of the shadows, Norman came forward. His steps were hesitant, and he held a blanket in his arms as his eyes scanned the darkness to find Bridgette.

'I didn't want you to stumble on your way back to your tent and I thought you might be cold.'

'How kind.' Bridgette stopped as Norman wrapped the

blanket around her shoulders. She reached out and took his arm. 'Where did you get to? I didn't see you at the fireworks.'

'I... I wasn't sure you'd want to see me.'

They had reached a firepit, where the last dying embers glowed, and sparks still crackled. Bridgette stopped and turned to face Norman. 'Why? What on earth do you mean?'

'That man... Reg... the bus driver.'

'What about him?'

'He blew my cover.'

'What cover?'

'I might not be the person you think I am.' Norman hung his head. His whole body appeared to shrink, and he couldn't look Bridgette in the eye. 'You must be embarrassed by what people will say.'

'My dear Norman, do you really think I give a hoot anymore about anything anyone says?' She placed a finger under his chin and raised it. 'Look at me. Look what you've done.'

'What do you mean?'

'You've given me a new lease on life – a confidence about my height and my body and a reason to live for many more years.' Bridgette smiled as she continued, 'People may laugh or feel disdain for naturism, but who cares? I certainly don't anymore. I have never felt so free or so happy as I have over these last few days.'

'I'm pleased for you.'

'Nudity is such a leveller. It's made me reflect and I couldn't care less if your imagination is fertile. You have kept me entertained for hours and given me a great deal of pleasure.'

'I have?'

'Yes.' Bridgette tugged on Norman's goatee and, perched on tiptoe, pulled his face down to reach her own. 'I owe you a great deal, my friend.'

She pursed her little lips and softly kissed him.

'Empress…' Norman whispered.

'Now, it's getting very late, and our beds await us.'

Bridgette tucked her free hand back into the crook of Norman's arm and they set off.

'What a wonderful night,' Bridgette said as she gazed up at the sky.

Norman, now confident once more, held his body upright as he carefully guided and looked down at the woman on his arm. 'Wonderful, indeed, my Empress.'

When Bridgette got back to her tent, she said goodnight to Norman, and he disappeared into the night, his footsteps soft on the damp, dewy grass.

'Such a dear man,' she said to herself.

As she prepared for bed, Bridgette wondered how the weekend would have turned out had she not met Norman. Would she have kicked up a fuss about sleeping in a tent and been bossy with the staff when she went for her treatments, demanding the best of everything? Bridgette was sure she would never have approved of Robin and Stevie, the Haines Hats hijackers who had nabbed her penthouse suite and she was confident she'd have lost her temper with Emily as she swooned over a younger man. Marjory, too, would have received a ticking off for her behaviour with the massage therapist, and Bridgette would have told Serena to get dressed, put more clothes on and stop moaning about her rival.

But Norman, dear Norman, in such a short space of time, had shown her a way of life that she'd embraced. It was as though naturism had been waiting for her. With the lifestyle at her fingertips, she shed not only her clothing but her inhibitions too, allowing herself to look at life quite clearly and embrace it for the wondrous phenomenon that it was.

'Never again will the petty injustices be a priority,' she said as she stepped onto the ladder and climbed into bed. 'I will not live with memories of being bullied, nor get bogged down with the day-to-day trivia, nor worry about my height. Instead, I will live my life wearing nothing but a smile.'

Bridgette snuggled under her duvet and, to her surprise, she saw a small but beautifully wrapped package on the pillow. Wondering what on earth it could be, she pulled at the pretty pink ribbon and very gently slid the wrapping paper away. Lifting the lid on a neat leather box, she held her breath as her tiny fingers wrapped around a beautiful chain. Hanging from the chain lay four gold hearts, and on each, a name was engraved.

Bridgette, Serena, Emily, Marjory. A gold bar between the hearts also had an engraving, *Friends Forever*.

She fastened the necklace around her neck and sat for

some time, her fingers caressing each heart as she thought about the individuals inscribed on the gold. Friendship isn't something that just miraculously happens, she contemplated, and remembered their weekly outings to the pool and their time in the pub afterwards. Despite their different backgrounds, they'd been drawn together for a reason. With Serena, Marjory and Emily, she'd put the world to rights, shared highs and lows and in doing so, they'd subconsciously helped each other. Bridgette wondered if she'd taken them for granted and realised how important the three women were to her. Friendship, even more so at their age, is a bond, she mused, an invisible cord of comfort and support. If any of them were to find themselves in trouble or lost in life, Bridgette vowed that she would sail through any storm, climb any mountain or crawl over broken glass to help them.

'What a wonderful weekend this has been.' Bridgette snuggled into the soft downy duvet and sighed with pleasure. The necklace was smooth and warm as her little fingers held on tight, and closing her eyes, the birthday girl fell into a deep and peaceful sleep.

Chapter Thirty

As Bridgette slept soundly in her tent, Marjory snuggled up to Willie and Fred in their motorhome, and Emily lay in Yannis's arms in the attic room of the staff house, Robin and Stevie rose extra early in the penthouse, and invited Serena to join them.

Serena, who hadn't slept a wink, was silent as she sat on a sofa and watched the two men carefully place Le Chapeau Gâteau back in its gigantic box and neatly arrange the veil in sheets of tissue. Serena was acutely aware of everything in the room as her eyes travelled from the fine furnishings to the abstract wall hangings. Anything to distract her from the ultimate question that would soon be on their lips.

'Are we ready?' Stevie finally asked the question.

Robin sat down next to Serena. 'Yes, I think the time has come.'

'I don't think I'll ever be ready, but let's get on with it.'

'We'll have a look at Instagram first,' Stevie said.

'I think I'm going to be sick.' Serena crossed her arms. 'This has all been a terrible mistake. We should never have started to post any pictures, let alone a video of me parading about in a ridiculously brief swimsuit and a novelty hat that looks like a cake. I'm far too old and way past it. I haven't a hope of resurrecting my cookery career and the trolls are going to have a field day.'

'For heaven's sake, calm down. You're letting your imagination run away. Let Stevie and me take the first look.'

Serena closed her eyes. She heard fingers tapping on screens as Robin and Stevie opened her Instagram account.

'Oh, my. I never ever expected that…' Stevie gasped.

'Good grief, how on earth…' Robin clasped a hand to his mouth.

'Oh no, is it really *so* bad?' Serena's face crumpled. 'Have I made a complete fool of myself?'

Stevie and Robin stared at each other. Both were unable to speak.

'Well, it's not what we anticipated,' Robin finally said.

'No, darling.' Stevie took a deep breath. 'The response has been…'

'ABSOLUTELY, UNBELIEVABLY OVERWHELMING!' Robin shouted out and leapt to his feet.

'What? Is it good or bad?' She looked from one to the other. '*Please* tell me.'

Stevie thrust out his phone. 'You're an Instagram sensation! You've received thousands of new followers since these posts went live and they're increasing by the minute – just look at the comments.'

Serena focussed on Stevie's phone. She struggled to take

in the glut of likes, hearts and emojis that were accompanied by hundreds of comments pouring into her Instagram feed. #SaucySerena was trending on Twitter too. Guests at the party had uploaded scores of photos of Serena wearing the hat and used hashtags in their posts. As the posts were retweeted, the number of followers increased.

'You're giving me a hat attack!' @FreddyFedora

'A hat is what it's all about,' @thesexysombrero

'You can pass the hat to me any time,' @PanamaPete

'I feel as mad as a hatter for you,' @Hattrick13

But the images that had caught social media by storm were those that had gone out on @DailyMailCelebrity on Twitter and Daily Mail Celeb on Facebook. The Mail Online also ran a story under the headline:

TODAY'S FASHION FINDER – HATS OFF TO HAINES HATS!

There's a new head on the millinery block as Robin and Stevie Haines launch Chef Serena. The sexy chef, wearing their latest novelty creation, Le Chapeau Gâteau, looks like the hat - good enough to eat!

Serena scanned the article, which praised the ingenious liaison of the chef with the famous milliners.

'How on earth has this gone online so soon?' she asked, her expression incredulous as she stared at Robin and Stevie.

'It's not what you know, darling – it's who you know.

Robin's magazine mentor has pulled one or two media strings in our favour.'

'All the nationals will pick this up,' Robin said. 'Lady G's people have already messaged me on Instagram. Lots of pop stars love new and creative items to wear on their heads at their concerts and we have prepared bespoke versions of Le Chapeau Gâteau ready for interested parties.'

'Nigella has retweeted your post on Twitter.' Stevie stared at his phone.

'B... but she has nearly three million followers,' Serena stuttered.

'You've done an amazing job of promoting our product,' Robin said.

'And in turn the product will promote you.' Stevie turned to his laptop and studied a Haines Hats YouTube video of Serena entering the party. He nodded his head in approval. Their camera team had worked wonders to edit and upload it so quickly, and already the video was gaining hundreds of views and comments.

Serena dropped to the sofa.

Was she dreaming? Had she really gone viral as she'd hoped and prayed? How on earth had such a simple event as Bridgette's seventieth birthday party bought about this incredible media frenzy? But of course, she could only have achieved this staggering result with Robin and Stevie's help. On her own, her posts would never have achieved the whirlwind that was currently happening.

'Sparadise is getting plenty of attention too,' Stevie said as he scrolled from one platform to another. 'You're picking up comments and followers on all your posts from the weekend. The owners should be delighted.'

Serena still gripped her phone in her hand. It began to vibrate as texts poured in from friends around the country who were up and about and seeing Serena in their social media feeds. She read each one and wondered if Cornelius had picked up on her sudden success. But to her dismay, there was nothing from her partner. As usual, Cornelius was wrapped up in himself and oblivious to Serena. Bemused by it all, she shook her head and was about to place her phone on the table when it rang.

'Hello?' Serena said.

'Hello, my talented chef,' Fiona McNulty of Life in the Limelight Productions said. 'You're making quite a splash in the media today.'

Robin and Stevie were staring at Serena.

'Who is it?' Stevie whispered.

Serena placed her hand over her phone. 'It's my agent.' She could hear Fiona dragging on a forbidden cigarette. 'Good morning, Fiona. It's been a long time.'

'I've no time for small talk on a Sunday morning but I just wanted to say that your link with Haines Hats is genius. Are we hitting them up for an endorsement fee?'

'No, Fiona. Robin and Stevie Haines are personal friends of mine.'

'That's a shame. It could be lucrative.'

'Lucrative or not, it's not happening.'

'Hmm.' Fiona made a sound as she exhaled and Serena imagined the woman tapping her long, pointed nails as she stared out at the city skyline of her riverside apartment.

'Moving on, you'll be pleased to hear that Yvette the Chefette's contract isn't being renewed.'

'What?'

'Rollie Johnstone has been bollocked by the top brass for being ageist.' Fiona paused to let her words sink in. 'I've just got off the phone with him.'

'What has that got to do with me?'

'It means you're back in favour, you should get your morning slot back and he wants you to make a pilot for a new cookery game show. There's a prime time slot this autumn.'

'But that's amazing.'

'There's a proviso,' Fiona said, and Serena heard the click of a lighter. 'He wants to call the show "I'll Eat My Hat".'

'I'm sorry?'

'Rollie was having his breakfast today and saw Le Chapeau Gâteau images all over social media. They've inspired him to dream up a cooking show whereby competitors compete to make a culinary millinery version of a popular dish. The loser has to eat their edible hat.'

'That's different.' Serena was hesitant. She conjured up images of wannabe chefs who'd lost the competition gagging on a poorly constructed, inedible chocolate Fedora or a burger balaclava.

'It's got winner all over it. Are you in?'

'I'm certainly interested.'

'Excellent, I'll set up a meeting for the end of the week. I expect you're still living in the back of beyond with that artist fellow?'

'If you mean Lancashire, yes, that's where I'm based.'

'But you haven't sold the London apartment?'

'No.'

'Perfect. You'll be needing it during the week while filming. Wait for my call.'

Fiona hung up and Serena, who had been holding her breath, slowly exhaled.

'Good news?' Stevie asked, his eyebrows raised.

'I think I'm going to be back on television.'

Stevie clapped his hands.

'This wonderful update calls for a celebration. What time are your friends checking out today?'

'As soon as we've packed.'

'We're staying for another couple of nights, so might I suggest a celebratory brunch for everyone, here in the penthouse, before you leave for Lancashire?'

'I'm sure that the girls would love that.' Serena felt tears in her eyes as Robin and Stevie took her hands. 'Whatever would I have done without you both? Over the course of a weekend, you have transformed my life.'

'The transformation was all your own doing. We merely provided the tools.' Robin reached out and wiped away a tear from Serena's cheek. 'Now, go and pack, then get on your phone and round up your friends. I'll book brunch for noon.'

As she left the penthouse, Serena called Cornelius. There was no reply, and the call went to the answerphone. 'Hi there, this is Cornelius. Sorry, I'm not here to lend an ear, but if you leave a word, you can be sure that I'll hear.'

'Damn you, Cornelius, why can't you ever pick up your wretched phone?'

Then, putting all thoughts of Cornelius to one side, she walked tall. At least her friends would be delighted for her. She couldn't wait to tell them her news. She felt happier than she had in a very long time and, reaching for her phone again, began to dial.

Chapter Thirty-One

On the penthouse patio, the atmosphere was upbeat as Sparadise staff, chattering about the party the night before, set out a buffet on a table under a candy-striped awning. The day was already hot as the heat from the noon sun settled across the grounds, its rays searching every corner.

Serena sat in a comfortable chair on the balcony and looked out across the landscape. She wanted to revel in her final moments at the spa to preserve all the events from the weekend.

After calling the girls to arrange the brunch, Serena had been unable to resist the lure of the lake, and she'd changed into a swimsuit and hurried down to the water. The gentle waves welcomed her. It had been a moment of sheer bliss to lie on her back and stare upward at puffy white clouds, like sluggish ships, sailing in a sea of brilliant blue sky. Turning and snaking her arms into a crawl, she'd kicked her legs for thirty energetic minutes, loving the wild water swim as birds flew overhead and ducks waddled alongside.

Now, Serena thanked Robin and Stevie for all that they had done to help her.

'Nothing to thank us for,' Stevie said as Robin went to answer a knock at the door. 'No big goodbyes because we'll meet again in London in a few days. You won't get rid of us easily. As our new millinery model, you're going to be busy.'

'If I'm lucky enough to get the television show too, my life is going to be frenetic, but I really can't wait. It will be wonderful to get back to work again and cook for people who want to learn and enjoy all the fabulous new dishes I'm going to create.'

'The work will pour in now, mark my words.'

Stevie handed Serena a drink, and they both turned to see Bridgette make an entrance.

'Hello, everyone. What a glorious morning.' Partially dressed, Bridgette wore an outfit that was comprised of layers of lei. 'It seemed a shame to waste these,' she said and ran her free hand over the colourful petals. 'So natural and cheering, don't you think?'

'You're glowing.' Serena kissed Bridgette on both cheeks.

Despite her broken arm, Bridgette appeared to be pain free and radiant. Her skin, free from any makeup, was sun-kissed and her cheeks rosy red. Her ordinarily poker-straight bob curled naturally around her face, and Serena thought that her friend looked at least ten years younger.

'You're wearing your necklace. It looks lovely.'

'It is the perfect birthday gift of friendship and I love it.' Bridgette stroked each of the tiny hearts on the gold chain around her neck.

'I have something I want to discuss,' Serena said and led Bridgette to look out at the garden. 'I'm worried about Emily and think she's making a foolish decision.'

'Whatever Emily decides to do is entirely of her own resolve.' Bridgette took Serena's hand. 'Emily has been brave enough to take a leap of faith.'

'But it could go so horribly wrong.'

'She's not the only one making big changes. I've seen all the activity on your social media today. Norman and I have been studying it over coffee and I'm so happy that you are, at last, getting back on the bandwagon you were so loath to leave. You're taking your own leap of faith.'

'Thank you. Your approval means a great deal.' Serena squeezed Bridgette's free hand. 'But what have you heard about Yannis? If he's conning Emily, shouldn't she know?'

Bridgette gazed out. In the distance, she could see the housekeeper heading towards the glamping tents, where a team of cleaners were tidying the debris from the party. The bunting was no longer draped around Norman's tent, and his windbreaker had been packed away. The dear man was due to depart today too.

'I think Emily already knows.'

'What? You think she may still go ahead with her plans to go to Greece with Yannis?'

'When I arrived on Friday, if you had told me the outcome of the weekend for Emily, I too would have been horrified. I would have done all in my power to stop her.

But now I see that Emily is happier than she's been in years.' Bridgette had no intention of disclosing her sighting of Yannis and Monika locked in a passionate clinch.

'But will it last?'

'Who knows? Emily has found something that has given her back her life. She's carried the ghost of her husband's infidelity with a younger woman around for years and now she has at last spirited him away.'

'I think I understand what you are saying.'

'My dear, if she totally fucks up, she can always come back.' Bridgette beamed. 'After all, she's got us and we will always stand by her.'

Serena began to laugh. She'd never heard Bridgette use the 'F' word.

'Flaxby Manor is cavernous. She could move in tomorrow.'

'We could always go out to Bessaloniki to see how she's getting on?'

'Exactly. A trip to Greece would be wonderful.'

'But what about you?' Serena asked.

'What about me?'

'Hugo isn't going to stand for your naturism. Are you going to start wearing your clothes when you get home?'

Bridgette shook her head and smiled. 'Not a chance. I shall have heaters installed in the garden and make it a tropical paradise, even in the winter.'

'You plan to carry on with naturism?'

'Of course I do. I've woken up like Emily. Why should I go back to a life I no longer want to lead?' Bridgette turned to stare at the garden again. 'Do you know that naturism is on the increase and there are more than three million people practicing it in this country?'

'No, I didn't know that.'

'Imagine opening the garden at Flaxby Manor to naturists – it would be a naturist nirvana. I've made up my mind. In fact, I've already recruited my new head gardener to lead up the team.'

'You have?'

'Certainly. Norman, as we speak, is about to head back to Hamilton to hand in his notice at the garden centre.'

'Good grief.' Serena began to chuckle and thought of *Life in Lancashire's* future headline.

To the Manor Born, Naked!

Local resident Bridgette Haworth and head gardener,
naturist Norman, open Flaxby Manor Naturism Days.

Serena conjured an image of the naked pair, smiling at a camera, with strategically placed plants covering their modesty. 'But what about Hugo?'

'Ah, Hugo,' Bridgette said and sighed. 'He must take his own leap of faith…'

'Who's taking a leap of faith?' Marjory appeared, plodding purposefully towards them. 'Are you still on the whacky baccy vitamin drinks? You're not going to leap off that balcony, are you?'

'Marjory, my dear, how well you look.' Bridgette held out her free arm to embrace her friend.

'I've never been better. This spa break has been the best weekend of my life.'

'I'll second that,' Bridgette said. 'Have you heard the wonderful news about our clever Serena?'

'Aye, the boys have been filling me in while you two were yakking. I've already planned my chapeau for the new TV show. A knitted bob hat, iced entirely with blue-tinted buttercream, so make sure you pull some strings to have us all as contestants.'

'Wouldn't that be fun! I could wear an edible flower hat,' Bridgette said.

'And I could wear a bowl of olives.' They all stood back, jaws dropped, as Emily swept towards them. 'Or a dish of moussaka.'

'Emily! Where have you been?'

'I've been having a chat with Danka, but I'm here and we're together now.'

Laughing and smiling, they all embraced.

'So, you're actually going to up and leave Flaxby behind and set forth on a Greek adventure?' Bridgette asked.

Looking pretty in a pale pink cashmere wrap cardigan tied to one side of her waist, Emily smoothed fingers over her rainbow-coloured skirt. 'Our flight leaves this evening and Edmond, the driver, is taking us to Manchester airport.'

'Oh my goodness.' Marjory's eyes were wide.

'You can always come to us if things don't work out,' Serena said. 'Our doors will always be open.'

'I'll be back to check on the house – if one of you could stop Joe and Jacob from barricading themselves in. As keyholder, Serena, could you arrange to take it in turns to keep an eye on them?'

'We will be your first visitors, my dear,' Bridgette said. Her eyes were teary, and she reached out to take Emily's hand. 'I think yoga on a Greek beach will be invigorating, but could you ensure that the beach is for naturists?'

They giggled as they imagined a naked Bridgette attempting the eight-angled pose.

'I'm not sure how Willie's ancient wheels will travel all that distance, and Fred will need a pet passport, but come hell or high water, we'll get there.'

Everyone turned to stare at Marjory.

'You're moving out of your house in Flaxby?' Serena did a double-take and Emily was wide-eyed, but Bridgette had a serene smile on her face as they heard Marjory's plans.

'Aye, I can't ask Reg to pack up his pigeons and all their paraphernalia. He can keep the house and we'll have to reach a settlement. Whatever happens, I'll manage and Willie has a nice little bungalow just off the Flaxby Lane estate. But the pair of us are going to hit the highroad and see where it takes us. I'm sure Greece will be on the trip list.'

'But what about your job at the Co-op?' Serena asked.

'What about it? It's time I hung up my crappy uniform.'

'I think it's a wonderful decision,' Emily exclaimed.

'Bravo, Marjory,' Bridgette said.

'Bubbles for the Sparettes!' Stevie held a tray of champagne and Robin carried four beautiful bouquets.

'Flowers and champagne! How kind,' Bridgette said and raised a glass with her free hand.

'I think a toast is in order.' Robin stood back and turned to face them all. 'Stevie and I have stayed at Sparadise many times, but never experienced a weekend quite like this one.' He smiled as the friends looked at each other. 'We're honoured to have met four such amazing women, who it seems have all changed their lives over just a few short hours.'

'Hear, hear. Truly inspirational,' Stevie added.

'To the Sparettes! Good luck, lovely ladies. Be happy and live long and fruitful lives.'

'Good luck everyone,' the four friends chorused and gave each other hugs.

Serena's phone rang and she moved to one side of the patio.

'Tuck in, the food is ready. Fill your tums before you travel,' Stevie said.

Marjory had a mouthful and Emily was nibbling a king prawn when Serena came back to the group.

'Everything alright? You look like you're about to burst,' Bridgette said.

Serena held her phone and clutched it to her chest. 'I am... well, surprised. Shocked even.'

'Come on, spit it out.' Marjory licked pastry from her lips.

'That was Danka. She put me through to the owner of Sparadise.'

'And?' They were poised as they waited for Serena to answer.

'He wants me to be the face of Sparadise, a brand ambassador for the whole group.'

'Oh, *wow!*'

'But that's amazing!

'Congratulations!'

'I can't believe it. The money he mentioned is crazy.'

Stevie nodded his head. 'I think there's been a touch of magic sprinkled over everyone this weekend and your lives are all about to change for the better.'

The four friends looked at each other and smiled. 'It must be the magic of Sparadise.'

Chapter Thirty-Two

A porter stood in the doorway of Serena's room and waited as she took one last look around to check that she'd packed all of her possessions.

'Please take my bags to reception,' she said and tucked a tip into the porter's hand. Dressed in the white shirt and faded jeans she'd arrived in, Serena's braids were loose and lay thickly on her shoulders. She glanced at her reflection in a mirror and was pleased with the relaxed and happy face that smiled back.

Serena felt as beautiful as she looked.

Never again would she criticise her age as she got older. Years of experience had put her in the position she would relish as her celebrity chef status resurfaced. The more mature Serena was back with a bang and in demand, and she was going to enjoy every single moment.

Slipping her feet into Sparadise's complementary slippers, she wished that Cornelius was waiting in the car park to take her home. If only her partner had taken the trouble to keep in touch and share in Serena's delight. It would be an empty feeling, going back to a lonely cottage with no one to celebrate her news. Cornelius and Dodger were bound to be out, wandering across the fells as the artist searched high and low for his wretched muse.

'Come on, Lady Muck,' Marjory said as Serena reached reception. 'Get your celebrity body in the group for a selfie with the girls.'

Bridgette was dressed in a layer of leis and her suitcases bulged with redundant clothing.

'Let's stand on the steps,' Emily said and picked up her walking boots. 'I don't think I'll be needing these on the beach.'

'I'll have them. We're the same size,' Marjory reminded Emily, 'and they may come in handy.'

Serena slipped into her gold trainers, and Bridgette pulled on her leather pumps. The four women posed on the steps of the main house. Robin, Stevie and Danka shuffled phones between them to ensure that everyone had a memorable photograph of the group.

A minibus tooted its horn. The signage along the gleaming paintwork read 'Lancashire Automotives' and in moments, the sales team appeared.

'Goodbye and good luck, Sparettes!' they cried and all piled in. They waved as the driver started the engine.

'Wait for me!' a voice called out, and Monika appeared, dressed in jeans and a T-shirt. Her expression was self-assured as she hauled a suitcase onto the bus and sat down. The youngest member of the team gave a thumbs-up.

'Monika's buggered off,' Marjory whispered, out of earshot of Emily.

'What's Monika going to do?' Serena stared as the bus drove off.

'She's joined the Lancashire Automotives. Apparently she's their new showroom hostess.'

'Her pretty face will help sales,' Bridgette said.

'Aye, and that young lad should stay pimple-free if Monika has a good supply of green gunk tucked in her suitcase,' Marjory said and chuckled.

Several taxis appeared, and with Barry in charge, the runners split into groups and loaded up their luggage.

'See you next year, Sparettes,' Barry called out and waved goodbye.

Next came the yoga students who'd hired a coach to take them home, and as sports bags were placed in a side compartment, they too said their goodbyes.

'Keep working on your downward dogs!' Marjory hollered as the coach pulled away.

'It's going to feel very strange without you all,' Stevie said as he kissed the four women, a tear glistening at the corner of his eye.

'Stevie hates saying goodbye. We won't linger or he'll flood the drive. Until we meet again, you wonderful women.' Robin waved and they disappeared into the house.

'Goodbye, ladies,' Danka said, 'or should I call you Sparettes? I can't stay to wave you off as we are very short-staffed.'

They said goodbye to Danka and thanked her for

everything as they watched the manager, still immaculate in her white tunic, head into the house.

Serena turned to Bridgette. 'Where's Norman? Are we giving him a lift home?'

'No, he took a taxi earlier. He said he had much to do to prepare for his new job.'

A loud hooting rang out, and smoke billowed down the driveway as a vehicle slowly approached.

'Here's my ride!' Marjory shouted and grabbed the handle of her suitcase. Emily's walking boots, the laces knotted, were strung around Marjory's neck. She tucked her handbag and flowers under her free arm.

'Aren't you coming back with us?' Serena asked.

'Like hell I am. You lasses are going to have to keep yourselves amused until we meet again.'

'You're setting off with Willie already?' Serena asked.

'Aye, I am.'

'We thought you had things to sort out in Flaxby before you left?' Emily said.

'Everything will get sorted in the fullness of time.'

'May the open road embrace you both.' Bridgette hugged Marjory.

A cloud of blue and grey exhaust cleared, and the vehicle appeared with Willie at the wheel and Fred, a jaunty bandana around his neck and paws, on the dashboard. Willie tooted again as he pulled up and leapt out to scoop Marjory up.

'Put me down, you old fool. You're crushing my carnations.' She thrust the flowers into Willie's waiting hands and threw her bags into the back of the motorhome.

'See you all soon. Next stop, Bessaloniki!' Marjory yelled through an open window, her blue hair bouncing in the breeze, as she pulled Fred onto her knee. Together with Willie, they sped away.

Suddenly, the driveway at Sparadise felt very quiet.

Emily took a deep breath and checked her phone. Her fingers tapped out a text to Yannis. *'Edmond, our driver for the airport, will be here in a moment.'*

'Where's Yannis?' Serena asked.

'He's on his way.'

'Are you *sure* you know what you are doing?' Serena's dark eyes searched Emily's face.

'No,' Emily replied and shrugged her shoulders, 'but what have I got to lose?'

'You could lose everything!' Serena suddenly grabbed Emily's arm. 'I'm sorry, Emily, but I can't let you go without saying that I think you need to be very careful. Especially with money and legalities. Are you *absolutely* sure about leaving everything and going away with Yannis?'

Emily took hold of Serena and Bridgette's hands, then glanced over her shoulder to ensure that Yannis hadn't appeared.

'You're right, and you have every reason to be worried.' She lowered her voice. 'But I'm not as stupid as you might think. I know all about Monika and that Yannis has been seeing her, and I'm fully aware that he's only with me for my money.'

'You are?'

'Yes, it's probably all a pretence and he will try to use me to his advantage, but I've made sure that my money is secure and he'll never get his hands on it.'

'But how did you find out about him?'

'I had a chat with Danka. It seems that his thwarted ex has a habit of checking on Yannis and updating potential employers with details of the deceitful way he has carried on.'

'A woman scorned.' Bridgette nodded.

'So why on earth are you going ahead with this trip to Bessaloniki?' Serena asked.

'To teach my sons a lesson and get them to appreciate me. This is also an opportunity to prove to myself that my husband isn't the only person who can find a younger partner. I'm settling a personal score.'

'Goodness, Emily, you *have* surprised me,' Serena said.

'I will enjoy my holiday and exploit Yannis, as he is exploiting me. He has a massive knowledge of the island which could prove very useful. I have no intention of giving him any money and I will just stay with him until I tire of him and move on.'

'Wow.'

'And then?' Bridgette asked.

'I may buy a place in Greece for myself, if I like the lifestyle, or I may come home. Whatever I decide to do, I know that my life will never be the same again. Boring old Emily Avondale is buried, never to resurface, God willing.'

Bridgette pulled Emily into an embrace. 'Go forth and have your adventure, my dear, and remember that you have our friendship forever and we will always have your back.'

'Always,' Serena added. 'We're only a phone call away.'

A Sparadise vehicle came to a stop, and from the side of the house, Yannis appeared. He was sheepish as he looked around, wishing to avoid Danka. Assured that the manager was nowhere in sight, he carried two large suitcases and a heavy rucksack strapped to his back. He hurried over to the waiting vehicle where Edmond opened the trunk and assisted the young man in putting their luggage into the vehicle.

'Goodbye, my wonderful friends.' Emily, suddenly emotional, began to cry. She hugged Serena and Bridgette. 'Thank you for supporting and loving me.' Dabbing at her tears, she moved towards Yannis, who held out his hand and helped her into the car.

'Don't worry about a thing, we'll check on Joe and Jacob,' Bridgette called out.

They watched Emily peer through the rear window, waving her hand until the vehicle turned off the drive and onto the road.

'Whew, Bridgette, this all feels very strange. It's just you and me now.'

'Don't be sad. Just think of all the exciting things ahead and our ultimate reunion.' Bridgette looked up as a porter from valet parking materialised with her Range Rover. 'Ah, here's our car. You must drive, my dear, my arm will cause me problems.' Bridgette began to instruct the porter on the correct placement of her Louis Vuitton luggage.

Serena jangled the key and stood to one side. Bossy Bridgette is still alive and well, she mused as she watched Bridgette ask the man to reload and pack for the third time. She thought of the journey home. It was unlikely that there would be any food in the house, and Serena wondered if Bridgette would mind if they stopped at the Co-op in Flaxby. Deep in thought, Serena didn't hear a sleek and shiny car cruise elegantly down the drive.

But a familiar barking got louder and caused her to look up.

'Dodger?' Serena whispered as she gazed into the sunshine. The light was bright, and without her sunglasses, she held a hand to shield her eyes. Peering through the glow, she saw the shiny outline of the bonnet of a vehicle that bore a silver winged logo emblazed with the words 'Austin Healey, 3000 Mk111.' The top was off the sports car, and as it came to a stop, the door opened.

A dog bounded towards her.

'*Dodger!*' Serena cried out. The old Labrador excitedly leapt up and placed his big soft paws on her thighs, his tongue lolling as his tail thumped with excitement. 'Hello, my lovely boy.' Serena crouched down and rubbed her face in the animal's thick dark fur. His smell was like a familiar hug, and overwhelmed with happiness, she closed her eyes. When she opened them again, she looked around. 'Where's your dad?'

'Taxi for Alleyne!'

Serena straightened up. To her complete surprise, Hugo stood in front of her. He wore a psychedelic patterned kaftan in vivid orange and red. As he stepped forward, Serena saw that open-toed sandals had replaced his polished leather brogues.

'Taxi? But this is Cornelius's car.'

'My work here is done.' Hugo gave a salute and moved to one side, taking the key fob from Serena's hand.

'Hello, Serena.'

Serena stared incredulously as Cornelius unfolded his body from the back seat. He reached into the Austin Healey and pulled out a sizeable square object wrapped in thick brown paper.

'Cornelius! *Where have you been?*'

'I've been working, my love.' Cornelius held out the package and began to remove the wrapping. 'Night has fallen into day – such was my passion.'

A canvas appeared and Cornelius slowly turned it to face Serena.

Her hands flew to her face as the painting came into view and she studied the image before her. Serena heard Bridgette and Hugo gasp as they stared at the painting.

It was magnificent in detail. An actual work of art, and as Serena gazed, she felt as though she was staring deep into the depths of her own soul.

'You're painting again,' she whispered.

'The moment you'd gone, I knew how much I'd miss you.'

'But you never told me you missed me.'

'I'm telling you now.'

The painting was a portrait of Serena. It was as though a photograph had come to life. Cornelius had captured every aspect of his partner's character and her great beauty.

'It's stunning,' Serena breathed.

'Just like you,' Cornelius said. 'I never tell you how much I love you, but I hope this painting will.'

He gently placed the artwork on the bonnet of the car and took Serena in his arms. As she looked lovingly into his eyes, Serena began to melt, and her heart was full of Cornelius.

'I've so much to tell you,' she said.

He put a finger on her lips. 'Tell me on the way home, after this…'

Hugo and Bridgette stood to one side as Cornelius kissed Serena with a passion that looked likely to continue for some time. Dodger, with a sigh, flopped down on the gravel beside them.

'Sharp exit, I think, dear?' Hugo took Bridgette's free arm and guided her to the Range Rover.

'What on earth are you wearing?' Bridgette stopped and stared at Hugo. She'd never seen him in such an outrageous outfit. Gone was the staid tweed and leather-clad Hugo who'd dominated her life for the last fifty years. 'You look most unlike yourself and I'm not used to it.'

Hugo, having retrieved Serena's suitcase and placed it by Cornelius's car, stood by the passenger door of the Range Rover and opened it for Bridgette. Suddenly, he reached down and grabbed the hem of his kaftan.

'Well, my darling old girl, love of my life, you'd better get used to this!'

With several tugs, Hugo lost his balance and almost fell over. He whipped the kaftan over his head and flung it into the Range Rover. Hugo now stood on the driveway, hands on his creaking hips, knobbly knees and legs akimbo, wearing nothing more than his sandals and a wicked smile.

'If you can't beat 'em, damn well join 'em! I'm taking a

leap of faith to step out naked too.' Hugo reached for Bridgette's hand. 'Bridgette, I would do anything for you. I don't want to lose you and can't live without you.'

'But you hate being naked!'

'On the contrary, I can't imagine why we've never done it before.' Hugo stood proud and then guided Bridgette into the car.

'Good God, Hugo,' Bridgette gasped as her layers of lei rode up and her bare bottom inched across warm leather. 'I can't quite believe what I'm seeing.'

'You'll be seeing plenty more.' Hugo laughed as the engine started and the vehicle roared into life.

'Are you quite serious?' Bridgette grabbed her safety strap as wheels spun and gravel flew.

'Never been more serious in my life. I've been thinking, going forward, that our open days in the garden should only be open to naturists.'

Bridgette's face was flushed as she felt a renewed love for her husband. 'I'm in complete agreement. It will be the first stage of our new life.'

'But not the last, my darling.'

The Range Rover was picking up speed and, as it flew down the driveway, dawdling ducks and wildlife fluttered their wings and took flight. The bull, swishing his tail in the distant field, looked on.

'But what about your friends at the golf club?' Bridgette asked.

'Bollocks to 'em.'

'Yes, dear, quite literally...' Bridgette smiled and glanced sideways at Hugo's balls bouncing on the driver's seat.

The Range Rover approached the end of the drive, and Bridgette lowered the windows. A procession of eager new arrivals to Sparadise had turned into the gates and she threw off her layers of colourful lei to flutter petals and blossom over their vehicles in welcome.

Bridgette, now as naked as Hugo, watched the tropical blooms and remembered that Danka had said they were a powerful symbol of love, friendship and celebration.

'Then we're a team?' Hugo asked.

Bridgette reached out and took her husband's warm and familiar hand, his fingers strong and comforting beneath her own.

'Dearest Hugo, of course we are a team and, in our new life together, we always will be.'

As she turned to watch the arrival of the Sparadise guests, Bridgette touched the gold hearts on her necklace and hoped that the newbies would enjoy their stay.

'May you be blessed with friendships as solid and cherished as my own,' she whispered. 'What happens at Sparadise really *will* take you to paradise...'

Acknowledgments

On a rainy day in May, I received a Twitter message asking if I would be interested in a potential project, writing a novel for One More Chapter. The idea was for a later in life romantic comedy – a subject I had explored in my previous novels. Charlotte Ledger, Publishing Director for One More Chapter, was the mastermind behind the project and, over the coming months, gave me the encouragement to write *The Spa Break*. Charlotte, I thank you for the opportunity and your patience, kindness and superb editing throughout the process. Thanks too to all the fantastic team at One More Chapter.

I have always brainstormed my writing ideas with Cathy, my best friend and beloved sister. Cathy lost her bravely fought battle with cancer just a few days before Charlotte contacted me. When I thought I would never recover from Cathy's death, this project helped me focus on something that my sister championed. My writing. Like me, Cathy believed that life should be lived well for every precious moment we have, and age is no barrier. Like the characters in this novel, she valued friendship and kindness, most notably being kind to ourselves. Cathy, I miss you more than any words can say, but we shared many fabulous spa breaks together, and I know that you would have loved this fictional version.

A special thank you to Eric. My hero. Ever patient, your love and support are immeasurable. Each day together is a joy. You take me on many extraordinary journeys that contribute to and inspire my literary life.

To my family and friends who always encourage me. Thank you. Finally, to my wonderful readers, I leave you with Bridgette's words, 'May you be blessed with friendships as solid and cherished as my own.'

YOUR NUMBER ONE STOP

ONE MORE CHAPTER

FOR PAGETURNING BOOKS

One More Chapter is an
award-winning global
division of HarperCollins.

Sign up to our newsletter to get our
latest eBook deals and stay up to date
with our weekly Book Club!
<u>Subscribe here.</u>

Meet the team at
<u>www.onemorechapter.com</u>

Follow us!

 @OneMoreChapter_
 @OneMoreChapter
 @onemorechapterhc

Do you write unputdownable fiction?
We love to hear from new voices.
Find out how to submit your novel at
<u>www.onemorechapter.com/submissions</u>

Printed in the USA
CPSIA information can be obtained
at www.ICGtesting.com
CBHW011002061224
18561CB00024B/203